About the Author

Beth Kynnersley, born 7th November 1998, grew up in the West Midlands, where she still lives. Since a young age she has always enjoyed writing, especially fiction stories and poems. With watching thrillers and horror films being another hobby of hers, she often tries to include both hobbies together, which helped her to establish her first book, "*Closed Doors*". She finds it pleasurable to be driven by an interest or hobby when writing as this allows plentiful ideas to fill up the page and produce the best written work she can think of.

To Mark,
Congratulations on winning this
in the raffle! And thank you for supporting
Camp Beagle.
Hope you enjoy this read! ☺
With love and best wishes,
Bethany Kynnersley.
x   x

Closed Doors

Kynnersley.

Bethany Kynnersley

Closed Doors

Olympia Publishers
London

www.olympiapublishers.com
OLYMPIA PAPERBACK EDITION

A CIP catalogue record for this title is
available from the British Library.

ISBN: 978-1-78830-847-2

This is a work of fiction.
Names, characters, places and incidents originate from the writer's
imagination. Any resemblance to actual persons, living or dead, is
purely coincidental.

First Published in 2021

Olympia Publishers
Tallis House
2 Tallis Street
London
EC4Y 0AB

Printed in Great Britain

Dedication

To my parents, grandparents, aunties, uncles and cousins for supporting and believing in me.

To my friends and best friend, Michelle, for supporting and believing in me too.

Thank you all.

"Here we are, girls, our new home," Susan happily expressed to her daughters, Lilly and Leila. The car jolted forward as Susan harshly pressed the brakes, leaving enough distance for them all to take in and admire the whole of their new home through the front windscreen. "Isn't it just beautiful?" Susan finally said, interrupting the minute-long silence as the three of them looked at the house in awe.

The house stood tall, a picturesque scene fit for a postcard, standing bold in the autumn sunset. The trees from behind formed a pattern of shadows on the tiled roof, created by the slowly disappearing ball of fire in the oncoming dusk.

Susan turned off the car engine, unlocked the car door, and stepped out onto the sea of stones forming the driveway. Lilly opened the passenger car door and began dragging her biggest suitcase out of the car and across the driveway to the front door.

The noise of the suitcase running over the army of stones silenced the "Wow!" of amazement coming from eight-year-old Leila, as she left the car and looked up at the many upstairs bedroom windows. She attempted to carry three bags at once to the front door, desperately wanting to make the least trips as possible to and from the car so she could get inside her new home and be first to choose her bedroom.

It was dusky darkness when the family of three had unloaded the car and placed all bags and belongings in the hallway. Lilly was far more interested in taking pictures of their new home on her phone, whereas Leila was adamant she was going to have the biggest bedroom, after her mom's. She raced up the stairs and checked every room, deciding within seconds which bedroom she'd claim.

The family unpacked as much as they could, or at least

what they individually considered the essentials, leaving any boxes of non-essential items in the garage to be dealt with in the coming days. Freeing the hallway and de-cluttering the overall spillage of plentiful boxes wore Leila and Lilly out whilst Susan made their tea.

It must have been strange for the new neighbours of the Archfield family; the house which had been empty for a length of time up until now was to be inhabited again. Now it was occupied it would take some getting used to for both the Archfield family and their neighbours.

"Let's shut out the darkness of autumn and enjoy our first night in our new home," Susan announced, before standing up from the black fabric three-seater sofa and heading towards the cream-coloured curtains of the lounge. The lamppost just to the right side at the end of their driveway glared, highlighting an area of the pavement which unveiled a gentleman walking his Staffordshire bull terrier, as Susan pulled the curtains shut.

Lilly, still overwhelmed with the whole house, continued to appreciate the pictures she'd taken of her new residence, both internal and external. Following the prolonged inspection of the photos she'd captured of their new home, commenting repeatedly that she'd never seen a house so lovely before, and due to an exciting yet exhausting day, she decided to head off to bed, later followed by Susan and Leila.

Morning came around fast. Leila was the last to wake, at eight o'clock, however, the dull autumn morning led her to believe it was still the middle of the night. Minimal light seeped through the edges of the purple blind covering her window. She checked the clock and could hear slight mumblings from her mother and sister downstairs; this disproved her belief of the time by the limited daylight enhancing the outline of the blind. She ventured downstairs and into the kitchen, where she was greeted by her mom.

"Sleep well, Lei? How's about our first night in our new house, eh? I wasn't quite sure if I had dreamt it when I woke up this morning! It seems so surreal," Susan yawned, preparing Leila's breakfast.

Leila responded, "Yeah, Mom, I was so excited to wake up to unpack and arrange my new room! I wish I had woken up sooner, though," as she wandered off into the lounge, carrying a big bowl of cornflakes.

Lilly sat on the sofa listening to the news, turning her head every so often and peering out of the window as a member of the public passed their house, going about their daily lives.

"Are you excited, Lil?" Leila repeatedly asked her sister until she replied, eagerly cramming spoonfuls of her much-loved soggy cornflakes into her mouth so she could race back upstairs and arrange her new bedroom.

"Yeah, I can't wait to unpack my bags and put my favourite duvet cover on my bed... and then... oh, go back to bed!" giggled fourteen-year-old Lilly before slipping into a yawn.

Both Lilly and Susan hadn't slept well, which was why they were both awake rather early. Susan had been up since four after fighting a losing battle of stress-related tossing and turning. Worries surrounding unpacking played on her mind as well as being disturbed and stressed out by Lilly, who kept banging down her alarm clock every time she saw that the time had hardly moved on.

As the day progressed, the Archfield family household began to look like, and resemble, a home rather than a house. Each room within the abode was filling with the family's property and each of their bedrooms resembled the mental image of the room they had wanted. Their first full day, despite Lilly and Susan's lack of sleep, proved positive as each of their independent bedrooms was to their individual satisfaction and liking.

Leila worked immensely hard to perfect her new room. When she was contented with her bedroom arrangements, she intended to invite both Susan and Lilly up to see her new and tidy grown up bedroom that she'd longed for ever since she knew they were moving house. She kept glancing around her room whilst lying on her bed, amazed by the self-defined masterpiece she had produced.

Lilly hadn't progressed very far with her unpacking and bedroom arrangements as she went back to bed mid-morning exhausted from being awake half the night. She'd managed to put her favourite duvet cover, hot pink, on her bed, which was her most immediate desire. She'd hung up her clothes in the built-in wardrobe, her shoes neatly placed in pairs on the wardrobe floor. Her bedside cabinet slid nicely between her bed and the windowsill, where she'd placed her table lamp, alarm clock, and a coaster for her glass of water throughout the night. She'd completed the basics, mainly ensuring her phone charger was able to fit behind and plug into the wall at the back of the bedside table, and that the television was on top of her white chest of drawers where it was in perfect view. With more boxes of belongings lingering in the garage, she'd at least managed to empty three before falling asleep.

Susan had worked her magic in numerous rooms,

placing things where she wanted and making sure everywhere was tidy and items were in the right place.

The bathroom was the easiest of all. Shampoo and conditioner and shower gel bottles and soap stood along the rim of the bath, varying in size and colour. All the towels and other bathroom accessories were packed away in the airing cupboard, apart from their toothpaste and toothbrushes which poked out from a blue plastic cup on the windowsill.

She'd carefully unpacked the majority of the bags and boxes they'd stuffed and carted over in the car journey last night, though the remainder were still in the garage. Each room looked plentiful and homely, relaying a warm loving feeling.

Susan gently unpacked the last of all the boxes they'd brought to the house on the car trip, which had been stored in the garage overnight, feeling a sense of achievement and proud of herself. Remembering the number of boxes and bags the removal company had put into their outdoor garage, she sighed, yawning and shaking her head in realisation. She sat on the edge of her bed and placed the last item of the final box she'd brought in; her battery-powered clock with hearts at the end of the two fingers. A Mother's Day present from the girls three years ago. She smiled and placed it on her bedside table, right at the front where she could admire it each time that she wanted to know the time.

"Mommmm!" Leila bellowed from her bedroom across the landing.

Susan winced as she'd just laid back on her comfy bed after hours of unpacking. Bending down and reaching up and pottering around on a full night's sleep would be tiring, but sleep deprived and stressed, made her unwillingly sit up and traipse over to Leila's room after more beckoning calls. "What?"

"LOOK! My new room! Isn't it amazing and tidy! And so much purple! Please can I paint all my room purple to match my duvet cover and blind? Please, please, please," Leila begged, bursting with pride and excitement, in total admiration at how lovely she'd presented all her possessions and furniture all by herself. She also had purple curtains, but disapproved of using them very often, preferring her blind.

"Lovely!" Susan smiled, sleepily wandering around the room, glad she didn't have to help Leila unpack and set up her bedroom too. "Yes, if you like. We will go shopping soon for food and maybe paint and furniture. We can see if there is any paint when we go. I expect we will be nearing the end of our food supply sometime in the coming week as I packed a lot of the food we already had at home. I knew we wouldn't have time for going out and gallivanting especially within the first week with many more things to unpack and rooms to arrange. I'm going to go and make us some tea and have a look in the cupboards to see how much we have left until we must do a food shop. There's a lot to do without having to go out and find the nearest shops."

Evening soon rolled around and Susan, Lilly, after waking up at long last, and Leila gathered in the lounge again to watch the television and eat their tea, hoping for a better night's sleep that night. They muttered between themselves, all giggling and laughing, yawning too, huddled up together on the black three-seater sofa.

After five busy days of unpacking, getting the house to resemble a home, and settling in to 10 Wikkington Way, their time had been extremely limited leaving no time for much else. They decided it was now time to venture out of their abode and see the different places and surroundings in their new neighbourhood. Sue managed to concoct a breakfast using the final grocery items in the cupboard, before they all got ready to go out and see their new local area.

"Everywhere looks so... posh," Lilly expressed surprisingly, the shock causing her to pause in disbelief and find a suitable word, "It's like somewhere you think of in your imagination, it's like... fantasy!" she continued, withholding her statement for a short moment as her phone vibrated in her coat pocket.

Leila had skipped ahead, almost tripping up as she picked up her pace, skipping even faster so she'd be first to spot any attractions. The mid-morning sun poked above the cluster of clouds, eliminating the remaining streaks and glistening droplets of frost on the surrounding landscape.

Susan called Leila back when she saw "The Co-operative" that her younger daughter had purposely not pointed out because they'd have to go there for provisions, meaning they couldn't continue exploring laden with bags full of shopping. The sly, yet typical Leila plan backfired.

"Mom! There's a café!" Leila pulled at her mom's coat excitedly after running back to Susan when she'd beckoned.

"Oh! We can all have a delightful drink and then we'll get some shopping," Susan assertively responded in annoyance at the repeated tug of her coat as they walked along the fresh tarmac of the footpath, past the window displaying an almost empty café area.

Leila huffed and sighed as Susan led the way to the entrance, knowing that any chance of exploring further that day was off the cards.

"Can I have two teas and a hot chocolate, please?" Susan ordered at the counter, whilst Lilly and Leila got a table.

"By the window! This one!" Leila shouted and beckoned her sister, waving her finger in the air pointing at her chosen table which seated four.

Susan carried their drinks over, on a flower-patterned tray, weaving in and out of the islands of tables and chairs en route.

Leila impatiently grabbed her hot chocolate before her mom even had chance to put the tray onto the table. "Can we come here every week, Mom, like a routine? This is the best hot chocolate ever!" Leila suggested, surprised by the wonderful taste.

"Not every week, Lei, it's expensive and we have just moved. I go back to work tomorrow, so let's see if we can find somewhere or something else. There may be another café somewhere that you'd like to go to regularly. We need all the money we can save at the moment having moved house. Anyway, we are only ten minutes away from the house. You're a funny kid you are, Lei, it's not like it's a thrilling trip out, is it?"

"Come on then, let's go and explore some more now to see if we can find somewhere," Leila said, eagerly springing up from her chair after rushing her hot chocolate, thinking it would quicken things up.

"Just sit still and wait. Stop rushing all the time!" Lilly snapped at her little sister in complete annoyance. Much to Leila's disappointment, after both Lilly and Susan had finished their drinks, they then had to do the shopping.

Silence; soon interrupted by the stomping of Leila's feet

on the ground and the rustling of the carrier bag she swung from side to side, as it bounced off numerous garden walls on their walk back home. Her excitement and happiness had completely drained. What she thought was going to be a great day of exploring the new neighbourhood, in her view, had been a "boring rubbish boring day", she repeatedly reminded Susan and Lilly. "Why couldn't we have explored for ages and then gone shopping?" she asked herself, sighing as she stopped swinging the carrier bag due to her arm now beginning to ache.

"Lei, we can go exploring later, or tomorrow, you and I, and we'll explore for hours and we can stay out as long as you like as long as we are home for tea. It's not the end of the world, is it? Food is the priority and we can go exploring tomorrow just as long as you don't go in a strop for the rest of today because then I won't take you," Lilly certified, losing her patience quicker than she liked.

"No, I'll go on my laptop and search the area online," Leila argued back, immediately rejecting her sister's offer, showing her frustration hadn't yet ceased.

Lilly and Susan sighed, continuing to converse with each other while Leila lagged behind, humming a tune to herself in replacement of swinging the bag and stomping her size three feet. When they arrived back home, they all took the carrier bags of shopping into the kitchen and unpacked them, just in time to start preparing the dinner.

The rain fell from the pale white and slate-grey, depressing looking sky; droplets slid down the freshly cleaned windows, racing each other to the window ledge. Lilly and Leila couldn't go exploring after all. The heavens had opened, forming numerous puddles at the end of the driveway. The aggressive downpour dampened the outdoors, muddying the fields and flooding the pavements. Susan's happy mood was soon washed away by the rain as her freshly washed uniform was utterly sodden after being pegged on the washing line in the warm sun earlier that morning.

"You know, I am actually okay with us not going out exploring this afternoon, Lil. This way we get to stay in all afternoon, and it means I'm now even more excited to go exploring tomorrow!" Leila said.

Lilly paused, putting down the book she was now halfway through reading. "Tomorrow?" she questioned Leila, having no recollection of saying anything about exploring tomorrow, in her unpromising, yet highly convincing, negotiation with Leila.

Her eyes widened and her hand involuntarily let go of her book, her eyes closed in realisation… they couldn't go exploring today, so they'd have to go tomorrow, as she had mentioned earlier to stop Leila going on about it. "Blooming great!" she murmured to herself, regretting ever saying anything about the exploring scenario now, more annoyed at herself than she was at Leila.

"We can go tomorrow, Lil, if it's not raining. And we can stay out for as long as I like—you said, remember? I say we stay out allllll day long."

"Oh, er, yeah! That'll be nice, exploring and spending time with my little sister." Lilly was hopeful that it would rain tomorrow, therefore being able to keep her promise of taking Leila out if it weren't raining, but not having to actually do so.

"Let's keep our fingers crossed that it doesn't rain. We have to go exploring, and," Leila whispered, leaning in towards her sister's ear and cupping her hands round her mouth, "we can go to the café again." She beamed. Her radiant smile showed her innocence and utmost gratitude towards her older sister, thankful that she would take her out. She joyously waved her crossed fingers in front of Lilly.

"Yeah, let's hope. Fingers crossed." Lilly unwillingly went along with the idea, without mirroring her sister's action of crossing her fingers. She covered the left side of her face with her hand in dread and rolled her piercing blue eyes in despair.

Leila merrily sprinted out of Lilly's room back to her own room with an immense level of uncontrollable joy.

"Blooming great," Lilly grunted to herself again, knowing there was no way she'd get out of going exploring now. "How am I supposed to make friends when I'm hanging around with my eight-year-old sister? Or find a boyfriend? No one will take me seriously," she asked herself in fear and uncertainty.

When Leila finds somewhere she enjoys going, she wants to go there regularly, and she knew with her mom being at work full time, she'd have to take Leila out a lot and look after her, due to Susan only having the weekends off. She threw her hardback book off the freshly made bed, causing it to land with a great smack on the floor. She wasn't really a going out person, much preferred to be indoors and in her own company but was hopeful to eventually make a new friend or friends in her new neighbourhood.

She rolled over onto her left side, staring out at the darkness; it seemed much later yet it was only five thirty. The breeze outside blew the droplets of rain harshly against the window, like a rough sea overriding and thrashing against the rocks.

She was beyond grateful for the rain as it had stopped her having to go out exploring that afternoon, meaning she was able to read more of her book which she'd thoroughly enjoyed until Leila had come bounding into her bedroom muttering about tomorrow. She felt an emptiness within her stomach, nervous and dreading exploring tomorrow in case they got lost or Leila refused to leave a place and they'd be out all day long.

Six-thirty came, it had stopped raining, but the damp and cold of the present evening reflected Lilly's mood as she walked into the kitchen filled with the aroma of pizza.

"I've been waiting for our pizza and chips night since we moved in. My favourite meal," Susan announced, sitting down at the wooden table for four, with her daughters.

Lilly wasn't a huge pizza fan, after that one time she'd eaten some and was going to her friend's birthday party and she had thrown up in the car, all down her brand-new dress she'd desperately been waiting to buy for months and months.

The short but taunting reminiscence turned her stomach more. Feeling queasy, she sat at the table glugging her way through three glasses of lemonade, only eating one slice of pizza which she forced down so as not to be rude.

Later in the evening it had dropped colder, the road and pavements glistening in the light radiating from the lampposts and the mystic brightness illuminating from the moon; frost. Susan shut the bathroom and landing windows to keep the heat in as the cold began to overrun the warm. She also shut her window, as well as Lilly and Leila's before going back downstairs, by the fire, in the lounge.

Lilly lay across the black three-seater sofa, covered by her pink fluffy blanket and was lost in her book.

Leila lay on her stomach by the fire, colouring in pictures in her colouring book, ensuring not to colour outside of the lines on the pictures.

It was the quietest it had been at the Archfield family address, apart from when they were all asleep during the night. There were a few minor disturbances of the blissful not-complete-silence that accompanied Leila's pencil crayons sliding across the paper.

Quick rustlings were heard every so often when Lilly turned a page in her book, Susan likewise with the newspaper. Leila made a few rustles too as she finished colouring in a full picture and turned over the page. She could colour for ages, colouring four or more pictures in a night, she enjoyed it so much. Susan lay across the matching black fabric two-seater sofa, reading the paper with her feet hanging over the right-hand side arm.

The sound of the occasional odd car passing by, and short bouts of barking from the neighbours' dogs who lived a few doors up interrupted the quietness every so often, but they took no notice.

The curtains blocked out the coal-black night. Only the crescent moon lit the starry sky, accompanied by the light emitted from several street-lights. As the night progressed the wall clock seemed to be ticking at an increasing speed. It felt as if one minute had seemed to be ten minutes. It heightened Susan's nerves as if she were a contestant on "Countdown". She felt uncertain, a little queasy at the thought of returning to work tomorrow.

Soon ten o'clock came around fast, and Susan decided it

was time to go to bed, being unable to stand much more of the nervous fluttering in her stomach. She had the same job as when she lived in their old house but had to get up earlier as she had further to travel now. This worried her the most; extremely unsure of the correct time to set out to arrive on time, especially with having to travel further amongst more of the morning rush hour traffic.

Lilly hoped and pleaded for rain tomorrow, whilst Leila for the total opposite.

The bright, bold, beaming sun lit up the border of Susan's black-out blind. Birds chirped happily outside, far happier than Susan was to have to get out of her warm, cosy bed for work, and do a longer journey than she used to. She pondered on how light it was. It seemed extremely unusual for her that morning; it seemed to be lighter than it normally was when she actually got up at a later time.

"Weird," she whispered to herself in confusion, unwillingly pushing the duvet covers away from her, as she climbed out of bed. "Shit!" She immediately jumped up and threw her clothes on, caring more about getting to work than her appearance and appetite for her breakfast. She was late! Overslept!

She'd not altered her alarm. It was still set at the time she'd set it when she didn't have to go to work, like last week which she'd booked off to settle into and sort out her new home. It was 7:50 am; she'd got to be at work for 8:30 am. It gave her forty minutes to do a forty-minute drive alone, get dressed, eat, and wade her way through the morning rush hour traffic. This was already turning out to be a bad day and she hadn't even left the house yet.

Susan finally left for work at 8 a.m., deciding to eat a cereal bar at her office desk, and wait until her break time to get a morning coffee. She eventually arrived at work at 8:55 am and took another five minutes to park the car and get to her office on the fourth floor of the building. She explained to her boss in a fluster the reason for her lateness, but it didn't do her any favours nevertheless, and meant she would have to stay over for half an hour to make up her hours.

Lilly awoke suddenly to the high-pitched ringing of her mobile phone. The piercing, headache-inducing melody repeated over and over until it eventually ceased. Her hearing returned to normal within a number of seconds. She rolled over in annoyance and picked up her phone. "Missed call from Mom," she read on the dark screen, perfectly suiting her ability to see it in her dimly lit curtain-drawn room.

It dinged loudly in her hand as she received a text message from Susan.

"Overslept. Was half an hour late for work. Got to stay over an extra half an hour to make up my hours. See you about 17:50. Love you both xx."

Lilly looked at the time on her phone. It was 10 am. She got out of bed and wrapped her pink fluffy blanket around her, and slowly walked over to her window to open her matching pink curtains. She tugged on them squeezing her eyes together tightly as the bright sun took her vision, a sharp pain in her head.

She opened her big blue eyes slowly, embracing the warmth on her face and neck. "Great, exploring day today it is then," she disappointingly mumbled to herself. She headed downstairs to prepare herself and Leila some breakfast.

Leila met Lilly on the landing as she was leaving her bedroom. "What was that noise? Was it somebody's car alarm?" Leila curiously questioned. "It frightened me to death!"

Lilly laughed and explained. "No, it was my ring tone on my phone because Mom called, and then it dinged whilst I was holding it as I received a text message from Mom." She giggled, "I had no idea what it was as my phone is always on silent! It's enough to wake the dead. I don't know how it had been set to loud because I certainly didn't do it." She continued laughing, finding it much more amusing now than she did at the time it happened. "Come on, Lei, I'll make us some beans on toast and a cup of tea for me, orange juice for you."

The house seemed odd to the girls; the absence of Susan made the place seem lonely, rather empty. Due to the girls being home-schooled, they would find this a regular thing after having Susan off for a week with them; now it was back to being alone during the morning and afternoon of the weekdays as Susan had returned to work.

"We can go exploring this afternoon, Lei. We'll take a brolly, but if it gets cold or pours with rain, we come back, okay?" Lilly said with great authority, living up to the protective yet stern standard her mother would expect in her absence.

Leila nodded, grinning in total admiration and gratitude towards her older sister.

After a short discussion, they decided upon going to the café in the Co-op for dinner. "I'll pay out of my money. Don't tell Mom we've been in here again, though." Lilly held her little finger out to Leila to pinkie promise.

"I promise," Leila strictly agreed, looking her sister right in the eyes to show she was serious.

Arriving at the café, the smell of pasta greeted their noses as they entered through the continually opening and shutting automatic doors. The place was busy today. "I want pasta, Lil, please," Leila notified Lilly.

Lilly agreed that she also wanted pasta and told Leila to go and get a table and she would be over as soon as she had ordered their food and drinks.

Leila chose a table for two and admired the view through the window. A whole new neighbourhood and area that she knew nothing about, was awaiting her in this new chapter of her life. She stared out in a short-lasting trance, growing more and more curious, yet ecstatically rejoicing as she was finally able to get out and explore, and to see what different attractions and shops were now considered her new locality.

Lilly sat looking on her phone, interrupting Leila's daydream by telling her to smile as she prepared to take a photograph of the two of them. Her contagious smile brought out her emerald green eyes; she was the spit of her older sister, apart from the eye colour; Lilly had blue eyes.

The pasta was delivered to their table by a young waiter, about ten minutes after she'd placed their order. Lilly thanked the waiter, tossing her blonde hair back over her shoulder with her right hand.

Leila watched. "You fancy him."

"No, I don't," Lilly quickly denied, getting more defensive.

"You so do!" Leila tormented before eating her dinner.

After they'd finished eating and allowed a substantial amount of time to pass to enable the food to digest, Leila started getting restless, aggravating Lilly until she gave in and agreed they could now go exploring.

After an hour and a half of exploring in the bright yet warmth-deceiving sun, they'd discovered their new neighbourhood had many different attractions.

First, an extraordinarily great looking park which took their breath away, a far more exciting one than they had ever seen or expected. An astoundingly huge play area, consisting of some straight and curly slides, two roundabouts, four different pairs of swings and climbing frames for both younger and older children. Monkey bars and a see-saw, a swinging tyre from one of the trees which hung over the edge of the play area, and a brilliant set of zip wires and treetop obstacle courses, from one side of the park to the other. The latter area was used weekly by the owners of the park and open to the public, as mentioned by a signpost on the park gate entrance.

There was an extensive pond; more of a lake, for fishing and radio-controlled boating races. Families of different kinds of ducks glided across the smooth water, dipping their heads beneath the surface for food and huddling close to their parents and other siblings. They swam across the pond in great numbers, ridding the location of the pond where folk were fishing.

A wonderful outdoor paddling pool for use in the summertime was covered up by a tarpaulin as it was now October and too miserable for paddling. The gates around the paddling pool and sand-covered area surrounding the jumbo sized pool were locked and several feet high to prevent anyone climbing over and getting in. A lovely bright yellow sign announced the seasonal openings and queries regarding the pool. All water is drained when not in use and the pool emptied, however covered by tarpaulin to prevent water from getting in and filling it up and someone possibly getting in there and drowning. It was actually rather deep, at five feet, but one end of it was only shallow and perfect for all the family.

Lilly admired the stunning scene, taking pictures of the play area and the busy fishing pond where there were crowds of people with fishing rods and bags and little dinky camping stools, sitting around the edge. She took a snapshot of the huge tarpaulin-covered pool, and the army of gates around it.

"I can't believe this is really just down the road from us, Lei. Isn't it incredible?" She enthusiastically jumped up and down, excitedly. "I love it! Think how much fun we will have in the summer! Oh, we will have to tell Mom and get her to bring us down and we can go on the zip wires and in the pool and maybe even fishing or we could buy a remote-control boat." Lilly rambled on, getting Leila so excited she couldn't quite possibly believe her luck that Lilly was actually having fun too!

Soon after, they found a doctors' surgery. This was located not far from their new home, and would be their new surgery. Lilly told Leila that they and their mother would need to register themselves online and she would do this when they got back home. "Wikkington Medical Practice," Lilly repeated, taking a picture of it on her phone to remember the name and exact location.

The best thing, to Leila, apart from the park, that they'd found was an arcade. "Please can we come here regularly? I love the 2p machines!" Leila asked Lilly a few times whilst they were there, showing no further interest in wanting to regularly visit the Co-op in future.

When twenty minutes had passed in the arcade, the girls decided to move on with their exploring as they'd spent enough time in there looking around at the different amusements and spent enough of Lilly's money too.

As well as the previously mentioned discoveries, they'd spotted numerous bus stops on their wanderings around their neighbourhood. They were definitely the least appealing, and as there were so many, after the first six they'd seen Lilly told Leila to stop counting every bus stop that they saw because it was getting on her nerves.

"I think it's time we should head back now, Lei, it'll be getting dark soon," Lilly mentioned to her sister, who still had as much energy as she did when they had first left the house.

The pair of them frantically relied on each other's memory in an attempt to remember their way back home. "Well, it's ten past four now, so we'll be home in about ten minutes," Lilly informed Leila, who was still, but only in her head, counting every bus stop she encountered.

"Thank God we are nearly home!" Lilly thought to herself, wanting to go back to bed.

"Errr, I don't remember th…"

"Wow!" Leila interrupted Lilly, as she realised, they'd clearly taken the wrong path. After going through a kissing gate, before them lay a path which divided into two smaller paths, one filtering off into the right direction, and the other into the left. As there were no signs, and they'd been all over the estate and the whole area was so new to them, it made it easy to get lost, take the wrong paths, and end up practically anywhere.

"Isn't it awesome?" Leila gasped, clapping her hands to her cheeks; her face alight and beaming a contagious smile.

Lilly sighed loudly, knowing that with Leila's fascination with graveyards, it would be a long while before they'd actually make it home, despite being almost there anyway. "It's a graveyard, Lei."

"A very, very, very old graveyard. Look, look, this one is from 1720!" Leila excitedly pointed out, standing far back enough to be able to read the gravestones nearest the wall where they were standing. Of course, this new discovery meant they could explore it, and as they were nearly home, there was no need to rush. Leila was utterly overjoyed at the prospect.

Lilly stood back, whilst Leila ran up to the old, rusty, iron gate, just about held shut with a piece of fraying rope, which was tied to the wooden stump next to it creating part of a surrounding fence. Leila saluted the lonesome magpie that sat before her, almost immediately flying off as she startled it, approaching the gate.

"You still do that? You still believe in that superstition?" Lilly asked, thinking Leila had "grown out" of the saluting idea now.

"Yeah, so what?" Leila shouted back, her response faint as the distance between them grew.

Lilly kicked the dust path with the front of her shoes, slowly walking towards the graveyard, blowing out and vibrating her lips. "Nothing, nothing," Lilly responded quickly and without any further question, trying to avoid an argument.

"Come on, Lil, climb over. We can quickly look around. I want to see how old some of these gravestones are to tell

Mom."

"No, I'll open the gate, I'm not climbing over it when I can walk through it, and fine, we can look around but not for too long. It's not exactly an ideal place to hang around, is it? You might thrive off all things ghosts and paranormal but it's not a place where I'm particularly desperate to spend my time," Lilly muttered, untying and unhooking the rope from the stump to enable her to push the gate open. "I'll spend enough time in a place like this when I'm dead."

"Shut the gate behind you, Lil," Leila whispered.

"No, I'll leave it open, we won't be long. The rope's fraying and struggling to hold it shut as it is; give the rope a little rest until we leave," Lilly said, pushing the gate to, but not tying it with the rope.

They ventured around the graveyard, each calling out different death dates of the individuals buried beneath the grave stones. Each step they took was accompanied by the rustle of the freshly fallen, crispy autumn leaves lying on the damp ground, as they were stepped upon. The crunching continued as they persisted with their walk, in search of the oldest grave they could seek.

"Shhhhh! Stop going so fast!" Lilly called ahead to Leila, in a rather loud, but sharp whisper. You're making enough noise to wake the dead!" Lilly, not realising at first, how literal this statement was, but not fully true, as those beneath them were deceased and there was no way of waking them.

"1874, 1856, 1710, 1759, 1896, 1832, 1909, 1902," Leila read out as she wandered down the continuous aisles of ageing, eroding, gravestones.

Leila had wandered out of Lilly's sight, religiously

devoted to finding graves as old as she possibly could, and rather enjoying herself too.

Lilly sat on an old bench, looking around at the surrounding memorials to the late individuals, covered in a sea of leaves in shades of oranges, reds, yellows, and muddy browns. The repetitive rhyme of Leila reading out death dates grew fainter and fainter as the distance between them increased massively now. Lilly sat peacefully, enjoying the sudden silence and grateful for a much-needed sit down.

She bunched up many leaves with her feet and scraped them to the left and right, building small mounds at either ends of the bench. The crispy crunching of the leaves, one of her favourite sounds, helped her settle and rejoice over the relaxing sit down, the gentle breeze blowing her lovely blonde hair, gleaming brightly in the sun.

"Lilly! Lil!" Leila yelled after a peaceful five minutes where Lilly sat looking at her phone waiting for her sister to come back. "Lilly, come quick!" she called out, causing Lilly to jump up alarmingly in great concern. She followed the unceasing calling out of Leila shouting her name, her heart beating faster than the rhythm at which her sister was reading out the dates.

"What's wrong?" she managed to say in between catching her breath, having reached her sister.

"Look, I found this building. It's so far down here we would never have seen it! The trees just about show it, look, it sticks out a little bit above the bushes. And… see…" Leila pointed out, and then diverted her and her sister's attention to a lonesome gravestone not far away. "This gravestone is all alone, it's just here with nothing around it, and it's not even that old compared to others we have seen."

31

The concrete gravestone had clearly been affected by the weather it had encountered, and was in a rather shocking state, which wasn't surprising due to it being surrounded by trees and dirt; no one could see it or even know it was there, so it hadn't been attended to for years. The writing was just about possible to make out, yet the stone, due to the weather and no attention paid to it for a long time, looked like some of the oldest ones there, yet it was the one with the most recent death date compared to all of the others they'd seen. "Norris Ericson. 1856–1924. Aged 68 years old. Maybe they're starting a new field and that's why it is all on its own," Leila read aloud, and questioned the reasoning behind it.

"I don't know, could be," Lilly agreed in hope it'd satisfy Leila, and mean they could leave then. Her heart had now quit playing a melody in her chest and returned to normal pace.

"What's the building, Lil?"

"I don't know, maybe where they keep tools, or care-taking facilities, a crematorium, I'm not sure. Let's go now. Mom will be back soon." Lilly tried her best to hurry Leila up, giving her sharp-toned ideas and theories as quick as possible as she started making her way to the gate.

Leila ran ahead, as she had done all day. "Lil! You said you weren't going to shut the gate!"

"I didn't shut the gate. I pushed it to. I didn't tie it shut." Lilly argued.

"Liar! It is shut now and no one else was in there with us!" Leila shouted back.

"I swear I didn't, I'm not ly…" She paused as the closed, rope-tied, gate came into sight. "Someone must have come in and shut it behind us, or maybe someone saw it was open like I'd left it, just shut to, and they tied it shut. I didn't tie it." Lilly tried to convince herself as Leila climbed over the gate and made her way back up the path to the kissing gate.

Lilly climbed over the gate almost as quickly as Leila had. She picked up her pace, almost walking as quick as her sister, who was repeating 1710 over and over, the oldest death date they'd found on the gravestones during their search.

Lilly was unsure as to what happened, and began second guessing herself, even though she knew she hadn't tied it shut. They were both glad to be heading home, no more guessing which path to take now they knew that the one they'd just taken was the wrong one.

Dusk fell fast. The delightful sunset of merged oranges, reds and yellows was like a reflection of the leaves on the burial ground floor, yet it soon turned to a coal grey, then to jet black as the October night drew in at a quick pace. The Archfield household soon livened up when Susan got home from work, with fish and chips for the three of them to have for tea.

Afterwards Lilly took herself to bed to watch the television and relax, following such a tiring day.

Leila went into the lounge to watch her programme whilst her mom washed up and then went for a shower.

As the evening progressed, Susan came into the lounge and accompanied Leila with watching the television and changed the channel at the correct time, ready for the soaps to begin.

Once Susan and Leila had watched the episodes of the soaps for that night, and began to feel tired, they decided to go up to bed, despite it being rather early.

"It's only nine o'clock but I am so tired. I don't know what's come over me. The unpacking and unloading and new routine and then not sleeping all too well and then going back to work and getting into trouble for being late, I just can't seem to regain any energy at the moment," Susan spilled out to Leila, who nodded and "hmmed" when appropriate.

"I'm not tired as such," Leila conversed, "more like, I don't really know, I'm not tired tired, but I'm just like, I don't know, lacking energy."

"It's all the excitement and exploring and new room and everything else going on. It soon catches up with you, but it'll pass. Lilly is always asleep anyway, so for her it's normal. But for myself and you to be tired, Lei, it's got to be exhaustion, eh?" Susan laughed and ruffled Leila's blonde hair, before kissing her goodnight.

"For goodness' sake, Lei, it's 1 am, go back to bed," Susan sleepily moaned, having just been disturbed by the whining and creaking of her bedroom door slowly opening, only a touch, then forced wide open, hitting off her bedside cabinet with a thrash. She waited to see if Leila, or maybe even Lilly if she wasn't feeling well, as that was the only time Lilly usually came to her mom's room at night, appeared. But neither did.

Five minutes dragged and passed during which neither of the girls appeared. Leila used to go and sleep in her mom's bed in their old house if she got scared in the night, but as neither Leila nor Lilly had appeared, Susan turned over and patiently waited, expecting one of the girls to creep in as she heard the wailing of the door again and banged right off her bedside cabinet second time around. Half an hour, to be exact, dragged on by, before Susan was finally able to go back to sleep.

Much to Susan's disappointment, she was again disturbed by her alarm. Last night she'd set it to the correct time to get up, following her disastrous first day back at work yesterday, but now she was again disturbed by her alarm. It was 7 am, and she felt as if she hadn't even been back to sleep since the 1am situation. She unwillingly got out of bed and did what she had to do in order to be able to leave the house at a reasonable time and actually, arrive at work on time.

Lilly woke up at just gone 8:50 am, feeling a cold breeze blowing from the bedroom window to the left of her. The billowing of the curtains let the dull daylight in as the continuous breeze caused the curtains to sway from one way to another and also slightly separate, until she could be bothered to get up and close the window. She climbed out of bed to do so and reaching the window suddenly stared out at the back garden. She heard her sister coming across the landing and making her way to her bedroom.

"Boo!" Leila screamed as she joyfully burst into Lilly's room.

"Nice try, but you didn't scare me. I heard heavy footsteps, well more like stomps, as you got closer...and closer..." Lilly laughed, slowly walking over to Leila, "and closer..." she got nearer and nearer "and... BOO!" Lilly shouted and hugged her little sister, as if she'd captured her. Leila screamed, then laughed so much as Lilly finally let her go. "Come on, Lei, let's go and eat before the tutor gets here," Lilly beckoned to her sister as they made their way out of the room.

"Oh yeah, I forgot she was coming today." Leila's tone suddenly dampened as she'd forgotten about Mrs Berkshire coming.

"Come on, she will be here in an hour. We must be ready when she comes. We can't have her thinking that we doss around in our pyjamas all day," Lilly laughed quite worried in saying that to Leila, who seemed as if she wasn't at all in any rush.

"She might think that we are ill if we stay in our pyjamas and she might cancel or not stop as long as usual." Leila tried to convince Lilly it was a good idea. It didn't happen; Lilly made Leila get dressed and be ready for when the tutor came at 10:30 am.

The doorbell rang; the first time anyone had rung it since their move and the tune quickly filled them with shock. The new melodic noise was far different to the doorbell at their other house. This one was louder and went on for a lot longer. They were not yet used to it.

Mrs Berkshire was welcomed by Lilly who invited her in and showed her to the kitchen area where they could sit at the table for the tutoring session. She admired their new house and complementarily pointed out all the different elements of the house and arrangements she liked.

The tutor had been at their house now for what felt like an hour to Leila, but it was only half of that. Her routine with the girls stayed the same though, despite the move. She always had an hour with Leila, and then an hour with Lilly.

As the morning passed by the girls changed over with the tutor. "Lilly, now we have finished what I'd planned for today's session, is there anything you want to go over in the last fifteen minutes?" Mrs Berkshire asked, before setting her some homework.

"Erm, I th…" She was interrupted by an excruciating, nerve-inducing bang from upstairs in the bathroom. "Lei, what are you doing?" Lilly immediately yelled upstairs, suddenly filled with dread and fear at what the heck the almighty bang was.

"I don't know, do I? I'm down here!" Leila shouted from the lounge, completely frightening Lilly as she thought Leila had gone upstairs after her hour of tutoring. She sat and waited for Lilly to respond, before finally giving up and moodily stomping her feet across the cream carpet, then onto the tiles of the kitchen floor. "I said it wasn't me!"

"It's a good job you didn't have shoes on or with all that stamping you would have muddied the carpet." Mrs Berkshire laughed, diverting the attention from the great bang they'd just heard.

"Go and have a look then. I'm still in my lesson," Lilly ordered, thankful she was in her tutor session as the thought of going up there herself made her stomach churn with uncertainty.

Leila ventured up the stairs, completely unfazed by whatever could possibly be waiting ahead, but thankful that she was downstairs when the loud noise happened, so she could not be blamed. She paused for a little moment.

"Leila?" Lilly shouted up the stairs having just shown out the tutor, ready for her to attend to her next student. The silence continued. "Leila!" she waited.

"It's just… weird?" Leila responded, full of confusion.

"What's weird?" Lilly nervously asked, as she began to

make her way, slowly, up the stairs. "What's weird, Lei? What made that noise?"

"Well, that's just it, nothing."

They both stood in the bathroom entrance and looked around the room. Everything was in place just as it was before the bang.

"BOO!" Leila yelled after a long pause of silence. Lilly shrieked and pushed Leila further into the bathroom for making her jump, and then went back to her bedroom.

The long, boring, but unusual day continued. The weather outside was dull, wet, and gloomy. A hefty feel of oppression accompanied the full, dark, grey clouds that had just began to release thousands of little raindrops, before a heavy downpour followed mid-afternoon.

Lilly was doing her favourite thing—sleeping, so Leila decided to do some drawing in her bedroom, a picture for her mom. She closed the door behind her in case Lilly came in to see what she was doing. Lilly would only tell her mom before Leila had the chance to surprise her with a picture. The closed door was also in case her mom got back and came to see her before she'd finished her picture. She gathered her pens, pencils, paper, and a rubber.

"This will be the best picture ever," she said to herself using her freshly sharpened pencil to colour in the overcast sky. She lay on her stomach on her bed, leaning on a hardback book, putting her full effort into her drawing.

Half an hour or so flew by and the continuous sound of the pencils across her drawing had become such a familiar sound she'd not noticed that she'd been drowning it out for so long, until she could hear voices.

She paused, and slowly got off her bed, and very lightly

made her way over to her bedroom door, to listen to the voices. She gave a sigh of relief and was filled with reassurance that it wasn't her mom on the way up the stairs, or Lilly about to come into her room. It was the TV.

However, this close call made her find something to cover her drawing so that if anyone came into her room, she could quickly disguise the picture and they wouldn't see it. She wanted to surprise her mom with a picture and didn't want anyone to see it until it was finished. Grabbing her colouring book and opening it so it had two A4 pages of some other drawings, would hide her picture and she could pretend to be colouring, if anyone were to come in.

As she was getting towards the end of her picture, she held it up in front of her and admired it with pride, giving a jubilant smile. She was particularly pleased with the oranges, reds, and yellows which were used to colour in the leaves. They added brightness to a picture of something that's not really very thrilling or isn't something you'd expect to be full of colour; something duller, depending upon someone's mood. The leaves brought it to life, which seemed so odd considering the picture was of something representing the total opposite of living; a memorial ground, a graveyard of individuals who had once dwelt here in Wikkington, or wherever they had spent their time whilst alive. It was strange as you'd at least expect a few of the gravestones to have flowers by them due to friends and relatives visiting on memorial dates, perhaps, but this graveyard had none, just the autumn leaves and their many colours, and damp, cold, and black soggy soil from all the rain.

"LEILA!" Lilly moaned forcefully, shoving open Leila's bedroom door, cutting Leila's admiration of her picture short.

Leila urgently grabbed her colouring book and covered her picture, and pretended to be colouring in. "Can't you turn the TV off after you've finished watching it?"

"What? I haven't been watching the telly. I've been in here all the time colouring. I thought it was you or Mom watching the TV downstairs," Leila confusingly questioned and explained, amazed that she'd been given the blame for it when she'd not the foggiest.

"Lei, just because I know you didn't have anything to do with that unexplained bang in the bathroom earlier doesn't mean you can't, or haven't done anything now," Lilly argued in disbelief.

Leila sighed in fury, "Lilly, I *haven't!* I have been here, in my room, all this time. Look," she said, taking the colouring book away and revealing the picture underneath the book she had hidden, "I've drawn a picture for Mom."

"And *you* expect me to believe that? You could have drawn that downstairs whilst watching the television. So, *what*, the TV came on all on its own?"

"Well, if it wasn't you, and it wasn't me," she mumbled.

"Don't be ridiculous! It's getting boring now, just admit it."

"Well, how do *I know* that it wasn't *you*?" Leila snapped, "You're so quick to blame me, as if you're incapable of doing anything wrong or by mistake. I HAVE NOT touched the television. I have a TV right there!" She pointed to her own television, on the chest of drawers, "If I wanted to watch the TV, I would watch it up here rather than carry all my pens and books and paper down there. I only do that on evenings."

"I have been asleep, Lei. I have been asleep. I have literally just woken up because it was so loud. My room is right above the lounge, you know, so it is loud when the TV is on, it practically makes my room vibrate!" hissed Lilly, who was getting really fed up now, and being overtired didn't help her mood, nor did it help how sharp she was being with her sister, and how it made Leila feel too.

"It has *only* just woken you up? It's been on about twenty minutes. I thought it was you or Mom down there watching the TV. I didn't come and look because I want to finish my picture to give to Mom when she's back from work." Leila adamantly, and truthfully, refused to back down.

She placed the picture to the left-hand side of her, as Lilly sat down to her right. The pencils she'd used to draw and colour with all rolled down into the little ditch made as she sat on Leila's spotted quilt, followed by the rectangular rubber awkwardly rolling behind, lagging as each straight side of it helped keep it still for a second before rolling again.

"Look, just forget it now. Carry on drawing and lying."

"Have you turned it off? I can't hear it now." Leila asked, now unable to hear it.

"Yes. I'm surprised the neighbours didn't come round at how loud it was."

"That's why I thought it was you or Mom because it was so loud. I thought it was you and Mom talking at first but then I heard a man's voice, a dog bark, oh, and a theme tune so I knew it was the TV." Leila again tried to make her older sister believe her.

"Whatever. I'm going back to bed for a bit," Lilly said rising, which lead to a pink pencil and a red pencil falling off the bed and rolling across the floor. She picked them up and placed them back where they had been, before walking out across the landing, back to her own bedroom, but not without complimenting Leila on how good her picture was, regardless of if she had anything to do with the TV or not.

Thankfully, after just over a quarter of an hour, which had seemingly dragged and felt more like another hour to Leila, Susan had finally arrived back home.

"Helloooo!" she cheerfully harmonised, shutting the cold, dark, wet night out, as the front door closed behind her.

"MOOOOMMM!" Leila ran down the stairs and hugged her, absolutely delighted now that her mom was home.

Susan made a cup of tea for both Leila and herself. "Where's Lilly?" she asked in a state of concern rather than displaying signs of panic.

"Asleep. Has been nearly all afternoon," Leila explained in a way which made it seem as though her answer was obvious.

"Oh yeah," Susan laughed, as if she was expecting it, but also unsure as to whether Lilly actually was asleep, too. "So what have you been doing then whilst she's been sleeping?"

"I've been drawing you a picture. I'll show it to you after tea." She went silent for a few moments, moving her eyebrows whilst she thought, and then curiously queried, "Wait, what is for tea?"

Susan smiled, mentioning numerous different meals that they could be having. She stared at Leila, her facial expressions denying approval of all the meal options she'd mentioned. "McDonalds?" she sneakily mentioned, in the same tone of voice as the other options she'd listed. Leila's face lit up, she got up from her chair and hugged her mom.

"Yessssssss! I'll go and tell Lilly!" she ecstatically repeated as she climbed up one stair to the other, before quietly making her way across Lilly's room and tapping her to let her know they were having McDonalds for tea.

Susan followed Leila up the stairs a couple of minutes later, and joined them both in Lilly's room to tell them the plan of leaving in half an hour once she had had a shower, and they could then settle down when they came back home to eat their meal.

Leila added the finishing touch to her mom's picture whilst waiting for Susan to finish showering. She wrote a lovely message on the back of the picture, announcing her gratification and contentment.

"Dear Mom,

I love you so much. I am glad we moved, and I love our new house. I really enjoyed exploring with Lilly and we found this old graveyard and it had lots of really, really, really old graves. I hope I can show you it one day. It's amazing. I also really like the kissing gate! Love you Mom!

Love from

Leila xxxx"

Susan left the bathroom and asked both girls if they were ready to go. Before she could even draw in breath after asking, she was ultimately set back by the fastest response ever, "YEAH!"

Sue sighed and groaned. "Well, that's strange," Susan muttered, searching around in a fluster of panicked confusion. She emptied her handbag out onto the floor of the hallway, kneeling down beside it and catching her lipstick and mascara as they began to roll away. "What the? Tut." She fumbled around in the pockets and smaller compartments of her bag, before checking around the back of the radiator and the hook she always hung her keys on.

"What, Mom?" Lilly asked, filling herself with panic

and concern as to what had happened now, as if today hadn't already been odd enough.

"My car keys, I can't find them, but I know I left them here, on the hooks. Now they've gone. I left them right here. I thought maybe they'd fallen into my handbag or down the side of the radiator. How will we lock the door tonight if I can't find them? How will we go and fetch our tea? How will I get to work tomorrow if I can't find my keys? Oh no, no no no," Susan exclaimed, hurtling around the house, scraping her hair back as if it were going to help her think better.

"Leila, give Mom the keys!" Lilly sighed. "Stop this now. All day you've been playing tricks," Lilly falsely accused her innocent sister, blaming her for the disappearance of the keys.

"Shut up, I haven't had them. Stop blaming me, why don't you give Mom the keys?" Leila vented, now fed up of being under suspicion for everything that had gone missing or any unexplained happenings.

Susan looked over at Lilly, who had been quick to believe Leila had something to do with it.

"I haven't had them. I can't drive. Why would I take them?" Lilly quarrelled.

"Leila has been with me ever since I got home apart from when I had a shower and she went colouring in her bedroom. Let's just forget who has done what and search for the keys so that we can get our tea. I'm so hungry. I won't be happy if I find out it was either of you and you have lied and blamed one another. I thought I'd take you to get a McDonalds as a treat and now this happens. Come on, let's find the keys before I decide not to take you." Susan sternly raised her voice to prevent any more bickering, as it was only wasting more time, time that they could be using to find the keys.

They'd practically turned the house upside down, looking everywhere until Susan shouted loudly enough for half the street to hear, "Found them!"

"Where?" Both girls asked in happy relief. They could go to get their McDonalds now, but were also nervous as to how the keys were moved in the first place, if neither of them was responsible.

"In the washing up bowl. How on earth did they get there?" Susan reported, attempting to question the logic of placing car keys in a washing up bowl as both objects are completely irrelevant to the purpose of one another. "Come on then, let's go to the drive-through and get our tea."

The night was drawing to a close, and all three of the Archfields were feeling out of sorts following the key incident.

Susan had only just remembered that the girls had had their tutoring today for the first time in the new house and was keen to hear how it had gone. Both girls shared their experiences of that morning, and then Lilly went on to explain to Susan about the suspicious bang that had happened towards the end of her tutoring session, and about the TV coming on in the afternoon, but she still believed Leila was responsible for the television part.

"What, so nothing in the bathroom had fallen over? And you are both being one hundred percent honest that you had nothing to do with the television coming on?"

Leila and Lilly denied anything to do with the TV, and agreed that nothing had fallen, nor was there any reason as to what it was that made the noise or had caused something to even fall or cause such a noise in the first place.

"Maybe the wind blew the blind and it bounced off the wall as it came back towards the window? Or maybe it hit the window causing the bang? Or even the wind blowing the bathroom door shut. It blows a gale in that bathroom; maybe it closed one of the doors on the landing, one of our bedroom doors. I'm completely lost about the TV and the keys. At least I know about last night," Susan explained, and tried to suggest reasons for the happenings that had occurred throughout the day.

"Last night? What about last night?" Leila questioned intrigued.

"Last night, just after 1 am, I woke up to hear my bedroom door slowly creaking open. I thought it was you, Leila, at first, but then thought maybe it was Lilly coming in if you weren't feeling well, like you used to at the old house when you didn't feel well, but then I thought it must have been Leila when you didn't come in. Anyway, so I waited, and as neither of you came in, I thought maybe it was one of you opening my door by accident instead of the bathroom door. It could have been you, Lil, feeling ill, and coming into my room but then maybe you felt sick and went to the bathroom? I didn't know what was happening or who it was, so I waited, and when no one came, I decided to go back to sleep. It took me long enough because the door blew all the way open with such force it banged right off my bedside cabinet."

Both girls looked at their mom unsettled. "We didn't get out of bed all night, Mom. We both said how well we had slept, this morning when we got up," Lilly added.

"Probably the wind then that made that bang earlier

today and blew my bedroom door last night. It was awfully windy during the night," Susan, who thought nothing more of it, led herself and the girls to believe. "Before we head off to bed, show me the picture you did for me," she reminded Leila, also changing the subject for now.

Leila fetched the picture from her bedroom and brought it to her mom in the lounge. "It's a graveyard. The stone on the left is the oldest stone there from 1710, and the one on the right is the newest stone, but it's all on its own, Mom, not with all the other headstones. Oh, and this is the building by the grave and that's all on its own too. And here's the kissing gate. I went through it loads of times, it was so much fun!" Leila enthusiastically, and very proudly, showed her mom the picture.

"Oh! It's really good but a weird thing to draw. Didn't it scare you?"

"No, Mom. It's really old and historical. 1710 was a long time ago. There's a message on the back for you to read. " Leila instructed, adding "Goodnight" before heading up to bed.

"Night, Lei, Night, Lil," Susan shouted up the stairs, and was soon afterwards heading up to bed herself.

A sudden voluminous, unnerving crash of thunder awoke Lilly, accompanied by a howl of wind which blew the pouring rain against her bedroom window. She lay there, for a moment, silent and still, but was quickly interrupted by another roar of thunder. She rolled onto her right, grabbing for her phone to check the time: 2 am. Her room lit for a few seconds; lightning. "Great," she whispered to herself, having been woken from a pretty good, well-needed sleep.

Getting out of bed she crossed the landing, trying not to wake her mom, as if somehow her small, slow footsteps stood more of a chance of waking Susan than the rumbles of thunder did. She walked up to Leila's bed, climbing onto it and lifting up the duvet which was all stuffed up in the middle, as if Leila was lying underneath. "Lei, whe…?"

"Shhhh!" Leila interrupted her.

"Wait, where are you?"

"Under the bed, the thunder can't see me here," Leila nervously whispered back.

"Well, why is your duvet all stuffed up in the middle of your bed as if you are under it?" Lilly questioned her sister's actions.

"To make the thunder think that I am in it and that I am not scared of it so if I show it that I'm not scared, it'll go away."

Lilly laughed, kneeling down to see Leila lying on her back under the bed, holding her favouring cuddly toy, Hooter the Owl, very close to her body. "The thunder won't go until it is ready, Lei. Shall we do something to keep ourselves busy? It might help you get used to the thunder and see that it's nothing to be afraid of. If we stand at the window and look out, and when we see the next flash of lightening, we start to count until we hear the next crash of thunder. The higher the number, the longer the time between each rumble or flash," Lilly explained. "That means the storm is moving away from us."

Leila crawled out from under the bed once Lilly had managed to coax her out.

Lilly grabbed her nervous shaking hand, and lead her to the window.

The raindrops ran down the drowned window, the lightning highlighting their tracks as they slid down the glass. They stood with the curtains behind them, touching the back of their heads and shoulders. Leila stood on her tiptoes, one hand on the windowsill, the other clutching hard at Hooter, keeping him close to her chest for reassurance. "Together, okay, Lei?" "One…"

The thunder interrupted them before they could make it to two. Leila jumped, clutching at Hooter even more, and quickly clenching Lilly's hand.

"And together again, Lei, okay?" Lilly began, "One… two… three… four." They both counted as soon as lightning lit up their garden, as well as all the surrounding neighbours' gardens too. It was followed by a powerful, abrupt rumble of thunder.

"And again." Lilly urged Leila to stay at the window and count, even though she could tell that she was frightened. "One… two… three… four… five… six." They counted, when another strike of lightning and another bout of thunder sounded Leila knew the drill, count again. The storm continued for a long stretch of time, finally vanishing. They'd only stopped counting when they'd reached thirty-seven. The sound of the rain pattering on the window calmed, the stormy weather ceasing at 4 am.

"See, Lei, the thunder and lightning are nothing to be scared of. It'll come and go. I don't know how you can be fearful of thunder and lightning but not of the old graveyard." Lilly laughed, yet still trying to reassure her little sister. "Now it's finished, let's go back to bed. If I wake up before you in the morning, I'll let you lie in. I could sleep all day, well most of the day anyway, you know me."

Leila smiled at Lilly, tears in her eyes due to fear of the storm, and being tired, but finding Lilly funny as, of course, she knew Lilly was always sleeping.

"I love you," Leila hugged her big sister tightly.

"I love you too. Don't worry, the storm has gone now. I believe you when you said none of the happenings were you, Lei. But there's something going on. I think a neighbour might be trying to trick us or something. But nothing more than a prank. Maybe the wind blew something or slammed the bathroom door and it hit something but whatever it hit didn't fall over and that's why we can't explain what it was that made the bang. Or maybe the TV coming on yesterday was something to do with the storm we have had tonight as a storm can cause power cuts and affect the electrics. I don't know. Anyway, night, Lei," Lilly explained, before heading off to her bedroom to go back to bed. Leila climbed into bed, still holding tightly onto Hooter.

Susan awoke at six-thirty. "Strange," she muttered to herself as she was wide awake and there was still half an hour before her alarm was meant to go off. She allowed a quarter of an hour to stay in her warm and comfy bed before she dragged herself out, and opened the curtains to the damp, dull morning outside of their warm, cosy home. She sighed.

After getting dressed to be ready to head out to work, there was just about time to prepare herself some breakfast, and a hot cup of tea, and turn the television on. Her eyebrows raised and forehead crinkled into temporary lines as she watched the television in confusion. The storm, which she had slept through and didn't even know had taken place, was said to be one of the worst thunder and lightning storms they'd experienced in years. "At least I won't have to scrape the car this morning." She smiled, picking up her car keys, which were still on the hook where she'd left them last night, to head out of the front door and set off for work.

Lilly and Leila were both shattered after their early morning disruption. The house was peacefully quiet, just as it should be during the night when everyone in the house is fast asleep.

The sunny bright morning seemed to have rolled around so quickly, just like it can some nights, when it's time to get up and you feel as though it's only been five minutes since you got into bed the night before.

"Twelve-thirty?" Leila questioned, looking at the purple, sparkly clock on the wall directly in front of her bed, and checked her clock on her bedside table suspiciously, thinking the wall clock must have stopped last night without her knowing.

She glared at both of the clocks, her eyes flitting between the two before remembering why she'd woken up; a dreadfully stern knock upon the front door. She listened intently, holding her breath, hoping whoever was knocking would go away soon when after waiting several moments more no one bothered to answer the door.

But the knocking continued, seemingly getting louder and louder, increasing in power and assertiveness. She climbed out of bed, and gently stepped across the landing and into her mom's bedroom, where she could get a better look out of the bedroom window to see who it was. Climbing over Susan's bed, she then perched herself on the very edge, so that if it was someone she didn't know, they wouldn't be able to see her, and she wouldn't have to open the door.

Leila sighed in annoyance; no one was there despite the knock being so demanding and determined as if to gain one of the householders' attention. She wandered back into her own bedroom and climbed back into bed.

Much to Leila's surprise, an hour later there was another knock at the door. The sun shone brightly and warmed up each room as it shone through the lounge and Susan's room, heating them to a comfortable temperature and suitable for wearing just a t-shirt, with no need for a jumper.

"Arghhh!" Lilly grunted loud enough for half the street to hear, after hearing the latest alarming bash at the door. "Lei, who the hell is that knocking? They're gonna take the door down!"

Leila raced across the landing and back into Susan's room, hoping to get a sighting of whoever was causing such a disturbance and making such a terrible row on their front door.

"No one again!! This is the second time now and no one is there. It frightened me the first time it woke me up it was so sudden. I thought it was thunder, the way the knock seemed to come fiercer and fiercer," Leila reported, strolling into her sister's bedroom. "I think you're right, Lil, it must be someone playing a trick on us. I mean, it's a lovely day outside and broad daylight so it's not like we won't be able to see who it is. They're vicious knocks, and they don't allow for someone to actually get to the door!" Leila rolled her eyes, shaking her head.

"I won't be happy if it is someone knocking for no reason and then dashing off. Go and do us a bowl of cereal and a cuppa for me and some orange juice for you. I'll text Mrs Berkshire and see if it's her who's been knocking at the door. I'll explain we were up all night due to the storm, so we've slept in until late. Maybe she was knocking hard to show it was someone who we knew, or she thought we had maybe overslept and was knocking extra hard to wake us up," Lilly ordered and explained.

"Well, she certainly did that. Whoever it was woke me up in a flash." Leila laughed. "Say we are ill and then she won't come for the rest of the week," she hinted, and then headed downstairs to sort out their breakfast.

"Hi, Mrs Berkshire, I am very sorry to bother you. Was it you who was knocking at our door this morning? Sorry we didn't answer, we have been up in the night until 4 am with the storm, so both woke up late. On the two occasions you knocked Leila did go to see who it was, but you must have left as no one was there. We weren't aware you were coming, or I'd have made sure we were up and ready. Once again, we're very sorry," Lilly read aloud, composing a text to Mrs Berkshire.

"Ohhh, damn." Lilly heard Leila complain from the kitchen.

"What's the matter, Lei?" Lilly questioned, sitting up in bed, dreading something else had happened without their knowledge or a legitimate explanation.

Leila shuffled around in the cupboards, slamming the cupboard doors and rearranging the fridge, looking for more supplies. "I've just used the last tea bag for your cuppa, so I can't have one later. Oh, and there's only a tiny bit of milk left," Leila shouted up the stairs as she carried up the tray with their breakfast.

"Don't worry, we will go and get some from the shop after breakfast. I tell you what, we can even have a drink there. I'll have a cuppa and you can have a milkshake. I'll write a list of all the shopping we need to get too." Lilly took her breakfast and cup of tea from the tray Leila had placed on her bedside table.

"Yesss!" Leila exclaimed, climbing up beside Lilly sitting with her legs crossed in the middle of the bed, resting her dish of shreddies on her lap.

It was 2:30 p.m. by the time the girls were dressed and had reached the shop. Their list was rather short. "Let's have a drink first before we get the shopping," Lilly proposed, walking into the café area to find a table.

"Everyone's looking at us. We're the only kids here," Leila nervously whispered, walking behind Lilly, trying to hide, as she led the way to a table she had chosen.

"We are home-schooled Lei, overslept and missed our lesson. You should have bought that copy of your award you got when you were at school, for your outstanding vocabulary, writing and spelling. You could have showed it to everyone. Then they'd think you are too clever to go to school." Lilly laughed, teasing Leila. "Now, what milkshake do you want?"

Leila sat proudly, as Lilly raised her voice so several other Wikkington residents heard and turned their heads. "Chocolate, please."

Lilly went up to the till to order Leila's milkshake and a cup of tea for herself. The cashier took their order. "Shouldn't you be at school?" She laughed.

Lilly bit her tongue in case she hissed something about it being none of her business. She composed a smile. "Teacher training," she replied through gritted teeth, before weaving in and out of the chairs and tables, heading towards her sister.

"Shouldn't you mind your own business?" she laughed and muttered to herself as she sat down at the table with Leila, waiting for their order to be delivered.

The girls finished their drinks in their own time and worked together to get the shopping: two bottles of milk, two boxes of tea bags, a tin of spaghetti and a tin of baked beans, one bag of frozen chips, two loaves of bread, one pack of eight yogurts.

They carefully placed their items into carrier bags, apart from the two bottles of milk. Upon discussion, Leila decided she would carry the two bottles of milk as Lilly had reminded her of the time they'd previously been shopping and she swung the bag around carelessly, hitting off people's driveway walls and hedges. Lilly sensibly carried the bags containing the other items.

As Lilly made her way up the driveway, Leila placed the shopping bag containing the two milk bottles on the sea of pebbles on the drive, as her arm was aching having carried them all the way back from the shop. She turned around at the sound of footsteps fast approaching.

Lilly tried desperately to open the front door, not liking the sound of how fast, and loud the footsteps got due to heaviness; the person was running. Lilly paused, failing to get the front door open whilst Leila crouched down on the floor grabbing hold of the two milk bottles. The person stood at the end of their drive, staring right at them.

"Hello." He stood tall, with his hands in his pockets. His black hair was an unknown length beneath his black cap. His mud brown shoes co-ordinated with his hazel brown eyes, and a black waistcoat didn't particularly complement his blue jeans and green shirt underneath it. "I was wondering, have you heard any knocking in your house?" he curiously asked, looking around as if he was frightened to be seen.

The girls looked at him, before turning to each other in confusion, dipping their eyebrows and narrowing their eyes.

"We've had someone knock at the door, but we know who it was. Why?" Lilly replied, desperate to get inside the house, still fiddling with the key. Shaking with nerves made it a lot harder to complete the task.

"Oh." The man gulped, showing a nervous look, and backing away from the house. His hair dropped from the cap, as he tried to re-adjust it after scratching his sweaty head, and capturing the sweaty droplets sliding down his forehead.

"I said why?" Lilly repeated.

"Never mind. Forget I asked. Good luck." He wavered but he seemed unable to remove himself from the situation.

"Good luck for what? What do you mean 'good luck' and why did you specifically ask about knocking? You followed us all this way to ask us? How did you know where we live? Is someone playing a trick or something by knocking on doors?"

"Errr, yeah, something like that," he mumbled, shuffling from one foot to the other. "Just, you know, just don't answer the door unless you know who is there. How long have you been here now?"

Lilly stumbled, growing wary of why this stranger was showing such great concern without disclosing any genuine or logical information. "Wait, about three weeks. Why? What's this all about?" she further questioned.

"Lil, the milk will go off soon, and the yogurts," Leila interrupted, sitting on the doorstep, throwing the little stones on the driveway as if skimming them on water.

Lilly bought her finger to her mouth, gesturing for Leila to be quiet.

He was stumped. "Nice to have you in the area. I followed just to tell you in case you didn't know. Think nothing of it," he responded before running off after warily making eye contact with the bathroom window.

Lilly looked up at the bathroom window to see if something had attracted his attention to provide her with any suggestions as to why the stranger was so put off. She glared for several moments but failed to see anything at all other than the bathroom blind swinging in the gentle warm breeze.

"What the...?" Leila managed to say before being interrupted by Lilly.

"Come on, Lei, inside quick. We'll lock this door now. Whoever is playing this joke is ridiculous. He is probably part of it. Telling us not to open the door or anything. He might break in or do anything. He was weird. I don't like the sound of this knocking business especially having just been followed home by some total stranger as if we'd invited him round for tea," Lilly verbalised and harshly added, "If only you'd have hurried up and not dropped the bag, we'd have been in the house and he wouldn't have seen us to have spoken to us." Lilly finished, locking and bolting the door behind her.

"The only thing he could be doing out of all the happenings we have experienced could be the knocking at the door. He can't bang upstairs or turn the TV on without being in the house," Leila argued, placing the milk she'd carried home into the fridge in the kitchen. "But you said it was Mrs Berkshire knocking on the door today."

The girls continued unpacking before both of them spent the afternoon doing what they liked to do, any hobbies they enjoyed.

Leila was torn between many things; draw, colour in, go on the computer, watch the television, play with her teddies, she was spoilt for choice.

Lilly, who didn't go to sleep for a change, decided to bake a cake for them to have after their tea. She began looking at various recipes on her phone, and decided to make her own cake, exactly how she wanted it.

After rummaging through the cupboards and fridge for ingredients, she was able to come to a decision with regard to what cake she would like to make. Once she'd sorted out all the ingredients and washed her hands, she made a start on the cake. It was 4:20 and their mom would be home soon, so she wanted to have it at least in the oven before her mother arrived home.

While she was stirring the combined ingredients in the mixing bowl, she heard the familiar sound of the stairs creaking. She ceased stirring to listen, the ingredients getting thicker with every passing second and smiled. "Leila," she thought to herself.

She ignored the squeaky stairs and continued mixing until the ingredients were all as one and it was suitable to be poured into the cake baking tin. As she dropped the whisk and spoon into the sink and weighing scales into the cupboard, she was startled by another longer, louder squeaking from the stairs, causing her to turn her head sharply towards the kitchen door.

She put down the now empty cake mixing bowl leaving it on the side for Leila to lick after putting the cake into the oven. "I know it's you, Lei, waiting on the stairs, ready to lick the cake mix out of the bowl. Come on." Lilly heartily laughed, talking in a loud voice for Leila to hear her from the stairs, as the kitchen door was shut tight "Lei?" Lilly called out, about to open the kitchen door. "Leila!"

Leila appeared at the top of the stairs, after racing across the landing, fearful as Lilly's voice had sounded urgent and rather cross. "What's the matter?"

"Have you been on the stairs waiting here? I know it was you. Rocking on the stair to make it do that annoying squeaking wailing sound. Stupid floorboards."

"No, I've been in my room drawing a vehicle I want to make for my teddies to go in. I need some cardboard boxes."

Lilly looked at her sister, speechless for a moment. "I heard an annoying creak on the stairs twice. I thought it was you waiting to lick the bowl. I called you and you didn't answer. That's when I came out here and called you," explained Lilly, still managing to hear Leila above the sound of her hurried heartbeat like a boom box in her ears. "Come down and lick the bowl. I've just found an almost empty cereal box. If I tip the remaining cornflakes into a bowl for Mom to have for breakfast tomorrow, you can have the box."

"I didn't even know you were baking! What cake is it?" Leila asked, hovering and licking her lips as she scraped around the mixing bowl with her finger.

"Ah, wait and see. You'll love it."

"Oh my! Oh, my life!" Lilly widened her eyes and brought her hand to her O shaped mouth, staring at her phone.

Leila looked across at her from the other sofa. "What? What now?"

"Mrs Berkshire. It wasn't her because she's written, 'Hi Lilly, it wasn't me at the door. I've had to cancel all lessons for today as I'm not well. But I shall see you tomorrow as I'm feeling a lot better this evening. I think it was the atmosphere from the storm. See you tomorrow.' Oh, my God, who was it? They're playing some kind of horrid joke." Lilly read aloud, now feeling even more unsettled.

"Woof Woof, Woof Woof!" the dog timer on the shelf that they'd bought a few years ago, barked, as it was time to take the cake out of the oven. They both jumped when the loud barking interrupted their nervous, prolonged silence. Lilly went back to the kitchen whilst Leila stayed in the lounge, watching out of the window for their mom to get home from work.

Susan arrived home just as Lilly had finished the cake and left it to cool on the cooling rack. "Hi, Mom!" they both called out as Leila unbolted and opened the front door, letting Susan in.

"Mom, Mom, there was this man, he ran to catch up with us and asked if we'd had any experiences of knocking on the door, and…"

"Wow, wow, wow, slow down. Let me get into the house and put my stuff away." She interrupted Leila from carrying on talking.

"Mom, I made a cake for pudding tonight."

"Oh lovely, Lil. Speaking of food, what do you want for tea? Something on toast? I don't feel like cooking after today's shift, it's been so busy my head is pounding," Susan explained, accompanied by a yawn.

"Beans on toast, please, and plenty of brown sauce, yummy," Leila answered very quickly, eyeing up the cake

Lilly had made.

"Cheese on toast for me, please," Lilly ordered.

"Okay, Lil, I'll have spaghetti on toast, I think. What about this man anyway?" Susan queried, flopping down onto the sofa and slipping off her work shoes. She rubbed at her black socks, massaging her sore feet.

"We'll tell you at the dinner table at teatime," both girls agreed, both hungry and eager to have a piece of cake.

Later, once they'd finished their tea, and eaten a piece of Lilly's delicious chocolate cake, with chocolate cream on top, caramel in the middle and white chocolate drops sinking into the chocolate cream on top, the girls began to tell the story of the man they'd had an encounter with today. "Well," they began with the story of going shopping, "anyway, as we'd reached our driveway, this man came running to the end of the drive."

"I," Leila continued, "put the bottles of milk on the drive as they were sooo heavy and made my arm hurt and he caught up with us."

"He asked us if we'd had any knocking in our house. I replied yes but we know who it was, well at the time we thought we knew who it was anyway," Lilly followed on from Leila's shopping bag explanation, "I said, is someone playing a trick by knocking on doors? He said yes, well, 'something like that' were his words and to not answer the door unless we know who it is. He wished us good luck as if he couldn't bear to stand outside the house much longer and then asked how long we've lived here for. I said about three weeks, to which he answered that it was nice having us in the area and then he ran off rather sharpish after looking up at our bathroom window."

As both girls contributed and spoke, providing Susan with more and more information until they'd reached the full story, the uneasy look on Susan's face increased.

"What on Earth? How odd. Who was at the door?" Susan shuffled nervously, staring around the kitchen.

The girls explained that at the time they'd thought it was Mrs Berkshire who'd been knocking, but then received a text from her stating it wasn't her at all, and each time Leila had looked, she was unable to see anyone at the door, and therefore couldn't identify the person causing it all.

"If I see anyone tomorrow such as one of the neighbours before I get in the car to go to work, or when I get back and I'm getting out of the car, I'll ask them about it. Just keep the door shut and locked, and don't answer it unless you know who is there. Understand?" Susan instructed.

The girls nodded, both feeling a little uneasy.

Not long after Susan had washed up, the three of them ensured they could all lock the doors, even Leila. Susan took them into her bedroom, overlooking the front garden and drive, and told the girls to always look out of the window in there, very secretly, so that they would be able to see who is there, and praised Leila for doing this earlier. The family of three then headed down into the lounge, once they'd all washed, and changed into their pyjamas, ready to spend the rest of the evening watching the television, before going up to bed.

During the night, Lilly, Leila and Susan all managed to sleep well considering the dreadful and unnerving episodes they had previously found themselves in during their short stay in their new home.

Susan especially was up early and ready for work the earliest she had ever been, and managed to eat breakfast and have a cup of coffee, and was planning on leaving the house slightly earlier, to see if it would help her to combat the rush hour traffic.

"I'm not even joking now. There is something in, or about this house that isn't right!" Susan yelled frantically searching through her handbag. "Not again, oh yes, just when you are about to leave, you can't. Not a-flaming-gain!" She ran to the kitchen sink, where her keys had disappeared to last time, with no explanation. She would have to let her boss know she would be late again now.

"Hello, no I'm not okay, I am going to be late as I can't find my car keys, I will be in as soon as I can," she explained stressfully entering and leaving each room, rearranging and turning the rooms upside down to see what silly place they'd gone to this time. "Have I looked where I left them? Oh of course I haven't, why would I do that? How silly am I, of course I have looked there. I know where I left them, but they aren't there now… where I always leave them… no, the kids are in bed, I had them ten minutes ago if that!" The conversation continued between Susan and her boss. "Bye, I will be there as soon as I find them," she hastily snapped, cutting the phone off abruptly.

A sudden clink overtook the whisper of Susan furiously muttering to herself. "What in the world?" She jumped. "Lilly? Leila?"

"What was that?" Lilly asked, appearing on the landing as Susan sprinted up the stairs in a hurry.

"Stay there, I'll go and have a look. I'm sick of looking.

I've been searching round the house like Sherlock Holmes trying to find my car keys… again."

"What, again?" Lilly queried, frightened of the ridiculous location they'd be in this time.

"Oh my… Good Lord. I can't deal with this house!" Susan called out in shock, overwhelmed, and desperate to get to work.

"What, Mom, what?" Leila asked, slowly making her way to the bathroom, afraid of what was behind the door and causing Susan to become so distressed.

"My car keys, they're here, in… the bath." She winced in confusion, rubbing her forehead, tracing the forming wrinkles.

Lilly ventured into the bathroom to join her mom and sister, witnessing the car keys at the bottom of the empty bathtub.

"Listen, I have to get to work. Stick together and don't go out of the house. Mrs Berkshire is coming today, isn't she? Check who's at the door through my bedroom window before you open it. I'll be home as soon as possible. I'll have to stay over to make my time up but will be back as soon as I can." Susan flounced off down the stairs and headed off to work.

Later, a knock at the door interrupted Leila's colouring session and Lilly from reading her book which she had just that morning got into again. Leila scurried across the landing, tiptoeing into Lilly's room so they would both be together to check outside Susan's bedroom window. An elderly woman with a grey perm, white blouse, black cardigan, and a black skirt was present at the door. "Mrs Berkshire," the girls confirmed before they headed down to their tutoring session.

When the girls' lessons had finished, and Mrs Berkshire had left, the girls enjoyed their afternoon, despite Lilly feeling a little on edge about what had happened first thing that morning.

"Lil, what do you think happened with mom's keys this morning?" Leila asked, not fazed by the whole thing yet intrigued for answers.

"I don't know, but it's weird. There's something not right in this house, Lei. How do keys get upstairs and dropped in an empty bath?" Lilly curiously questioned, feeling nervous but trying not to show it in case it frightened Leila.

Leila laughed.

"What's so funny? I swear if this was you, Lei."

"It wasn't. You saw me leave my room at the same time as you. It's funny because who puts keys in an empty bath? What if it's a…"

"Don't you dare start that again!" Lilly sharply interrupted, disallowing Leila to continue her sentence. "Don't you dare start this whole ghost thing again." She lay down and stared at the ceiling, preparing for a lecture from her sister. She pulled her pink fluffy blanket over her, and fingered the front cover of her book, desperate to start reading it to help distract her mind.

"Whaaat? It could be. What's so 'don't start that again' bad about it? You haven't even heard me out." Leila climbed onto the bed and lay next to her.

"One, its creepy; two, we are home alone and I don't want to feel like there is someone else here with us; three, why would a ghost be interested in some keys? and four, I've told you, ghosts are bad, not good," Lilly elaborated, getting more uptight with Leila. She flicked through the pages until she found where she'd read up to.

"No, that is your opinion, not a fact. Ghosts aren't all bad; they can be spirits of our family or friends or just be around us and mean us no harm. You think good ghosts don't exist because the person's at peace and that only bad people come back as ghosts," Leila strongly argued, objecting to her sister's belief.

"Why would someone at peace decide to come back and torment us? All this banging, knocking, random happenings all the time, its creepy, it's discomforting, it's distressing."

"They could be at peace and coming to tell us they are okay, or to pass a message on, or show us that they are around us by doing all this stuff that is happening. If you judge this could-be ghost and say it's bad when, really, it's good, it could get a lot worse," Leila added.

"Who do you think you are? A paranormal investigator? You're always on about ghosts and graveyards and weirdness like that. It's not normal," Lilly continued, sitting up and looking at her sister for an explanation.

"I'M INTERESTED!" Leila bellowed, sitting up and climbing off the edge of the bed.

"You're eight! You should be interested in the park or playing dolls, not about ghosts and graveyards. It's strange, bizarre, and erratic." She wound Leila up even more and watched her approach the bedroom door.

"I don't want to play dolls, I'm not a baby! Believe what you want, don't come to me when you're worried or something's happened. It'll be your fault for saying they're bad. Leave me alone." Leila slammed Lilly's bedroom door behind her at full force and stomped her way across the landing back into her own room, pushing the door shut behind her. She picked up her television remote and turned the volume up loud to drown out Lilly's voice if she shouted her. "I'm eight, so what?" she whispered to herself, flicking through the channels to find something to watch.

She managed two minutes of channel hopping before she gave in, complaining of nothing of interest to watch. Taking out her laptop from inside one of the drawers in her unit she turned it on and opened the internet tab.

"Wikkington," she typed in once the laptop had loaded. "Wikkington Library, Wikkington Dental Practice, The Wikkington Public House, Wikkington Medical Practice," she read aloud, her eyes lowering down the list of suggestions following "Wikkington".

She found their house online, an image taken via a satellite. Below this was an article which she was unable to open due to parental consent needed. Susan had put the parent setting on Leila's laptop. She sighed and turned off the laptop, then lay back on her bed, before another episode of knocking began.

"What?" she mumbled, awaiting a response from Lilly, thinking it was her. "Urgh." She sighed as no response was received. She laughed to herself. "A paranormal investigator," she recalled what Lilly had said. "If anyone is out there wishing to make contact, please give us a sign." She tittered, pretending to be a paranormal investigator. She stopped and looked at her bedroom door as another knock was heard.

"HELLO!" she wearily said, thinking again it must be Lilly. Another knock followed, making Leila more annoyed at why Lilly didn't just come into her room. "Come in if you're going to keep knocking, Lil, it's getting annoying now." She waited for Lilly to enter when the door opened just ajar, immediately followed by another knock. Leila got up off her bed and went over to her bedroom door.

"Look, I said come in if you're going to keep knocking. Don't you underst…" She paused after hastily yanking her bedroom door open in annoyance, to find there was no one there. She ventured out onto the landing, sneakily making her way to Lilly's room to see if it was her playing around. Leila peered in through the crack between the door and the wall where the hinges are attached, to find Lilly fast asleep on her bed, with the hardback book she was reading rising and falling on her chest as she breathed. "Weird," she said to herself perplexed, wandering back to her own bedroom, for another lie down.

It went dark within the next half an hour or so, which made it hard to see who was waiting outside the front door, when another unexpected knock had occurred. Leila tiptoed along the landing creeping into Lilly's room to wake her. "Lil!" she whispered, trying not to make too loud a sound so whoever was outside wouldn't be able to tell if anyone was in. "Another knock, Lil, we need to go and see." Leila woke Lilly at last and they both carefully made their way to Susan's bedroom to glimpse out of the window.

"If this is another knock without anyone there, I will be so annoyed. I was enjoying that sleep," Lilly whispered, as they poked their heads over the windowsill.

Leila laughed.

"It's not funny," Lilly grunted in frustration. "You go to your room, Lei, I'm going to sit on the bed and wait and see if there's another knock. If they do knock, I'll be able to see them, and call you right away," she explained.

Leila reluctantly agreed and headed back to her bedroom whilst Lilly waited.

Lilly lay down on Susan's bed and rested her eyes whilst waiting to see if there would be yet another knock at the door. She tossed and turned, finding herself getting far too comfy and with the risk of falling asleep again and being unable to catch a glimpse of the much-hated knocker.

"Lilly! Lilly!" Leila bellowed from her own bedroom window, overlooking the back garden.

"What's the matter?" Lilly questioned, as she ran to answer Leila's unnerving, frantic call.

"There's a light, look!" She pointed to a small, distant light briefly showing through the crowded trees of their back garden and to the rear of the trees in the distance.

"Why did you call me for that?" Lilly asked, her heart still racing, Leila's hand clutching hers.

"Because it has never been there before. I know because I check every night to make sure my window is shut tight because I hate when the wind blows the blind and when they blow, the morning light gets in and I can't go back to sleep once I've woken up.."

"I still don't get what is so strange about the light?" Lilly grew more puzzled at what Leila was trying to get at. She sighed and went to turn around and back towards Leila's bedroom door.

"The light! It's the graveyard... It's that building, remember?" Leila clarified, feeling a touch of nerves.

"The... No, it can't be! Not the bui...? Not that old building?" Lilly's eyes widened and she shuddered, immediately turning back to look through Leila's bedroom window. The realisation had sunk in.

Leila nodded, shutting the blind behind her, climbing onto her bed and grabbing Hooter. Lilly came and sat down next to her. A sudden silence became apparent; Lilly's deep breathing adding suspense to the atmosphere, and Leila cuddling Hooter into her neck.

Lilly interrupted when a sudden thought came to her during the intense period of silence, "It can't be, can it? I mean, there's no record of any further deaths since the date on that man's gravestone. His gravestone was the one with the latest date, 1924. I don't get how the building looks so old and untidy and overgrown as if it's been totally cast aside and forgotten about, because if someone goes there now, then surely it is still used. Surely someone must be there and attending to it at night, maybe it's a caretaker? Or a volunteer? Or someone is protecting it from burglars. Or what if it IS burglars! It did look a dump, though, didn't it? And all the flowers looked dead; the only colour was from the fallen autumn leaves. And what exactly could you steal from a graveyard? I don't understand how the light can just suddenly come on. Surely when we went looking, whoever was occupying the place would have noticed us, introduced themselves. It's not like we were quiet, chanting out death dates as loud as we could. Tomorrow we will have a look online and see if there's any information we can find," Lilly suggested.

"I looked at Wikkington online today and found our house. There was an article underneath it, but I couldn't access it because of the parent setting on my computer that Mom put on there. Nothing on the graveyard came up either. I kept hearing knocks, and I thought it was you, but I checked, and you were fast asleep," Leila told her sister, noticing the surprise and confusion on her sister's face.

Lilly gulped, and looked at Leila, "Oh God, no."

"What, what?" Leila asked, "What, Lil, what?"

"The gate. Remember I left it open, and then, when we came back, it was shut with the rope tied around it? I said I was going to leave it open. And the whole time we were there we didn't see anyone, or hear anyone, and I was sitting in view of the gate for a long time while you looked at the dates on the stones. I would have seen or at least heard a big iron gate close whilst I was in sight range of it. I feel sick. What if someone saw us and has followed us back, and is playing these tricks on us? It could have been a passer-by shutting the gate, but I would have heard it; we would have seen someone because the fallen leaves were making a right crunching row when we were there, but not enough to hide the sound of a heavy iron gate closing," Lilly reminisced.

"But, Lilly, for it to explain all the happenings here, the person would have to have been IN the house, not just outside it. Someone would have to have access to our house, but we have no proof of someone breaking in or climbing through the windows. It could be someone that has followed us or anything like that, but we would know if another person was in the house." Leila moved closer to her sister, feeling panicky by the point she had just made.

"Leila." Lilly stared at her sister; her voice quite shaky. "Not some*one*."

"Some*thing*," Leila said, knowing Lilly now considered what she had said all along was correct.

A sudden tap, knock, and a jingle came from down the stairs at the front door. They quickly hugged each other, standing as still as a statue in Leila's bedroom.

"God, I feel sick," Lilly whispered, her stomach churning with nerves, and rapid breathing increasing with every passing second. A louder jingle was heard before the front door slowly opened.

"I'm back!" Susan called up the stairs as she closed the door behind her, putting her car keys in her bag so she knew where she'd put them and would be very cross if they went missing again. "It's absolutely freezing outside. My fingers are so numb I dropped the keys trying to unlock the front door." Susan laughed.

The girls exhaled in relief before running down the soft carpeted stairs as fast as possible, almost slipping on the laminate floor as they hugged Susan, feeling a lot safer and a lot more comfortable now their mom was home.

"Goodnight, girls," Susan wished them both as they headed off to bed later that evening. "Luckily it's Saturday tomorrow, so I'm not at work. We will see if anything happens tomorrow, while I'm at home."

The next morning Susan awoke naturally, rather than by the continuous loud, pulsing sound of her alarm. The once loved early morning get-ups now a chore; Getting up early was great when she had time to get to work, but now with further to travel during rush hour times it sucked the joy out of any early get up when work was involved. The extra time added to her journey to and from work, Monday to Friday, limited the amount of time she spent at home, often resulting in staying up later to complete the tasks she wished to do, as well as those needed, before going to bed. This shortened the amount of time spent sleeping, before having to get up again the following morning.

The birds outside and to the right of her window, in a great, tall oak tree sang a pretty little song. She decided not to open the curtains, not get up, taking full advantage of the Saturday morning. "This is the life," she whispered to herself, pulling the blankets up closer to her chin so she could snuggle back down.

Leila crept up the stairs, taking each step slowly and quietly, trying not to disturb her mom or sister as she lightly stepped across the landing to the bathroom. She brushed her teeth after demolishing an oversized bowl of cornflakes she'd prepared and a glass of orange juice.

After falling asleep again to the luscious lullaby that the little birds sang outside, Susan woke up for the second time. "Blimey, 10 am. Half the day has gone, I must get up," she muttered to herself as she climbed out of bed and headed over to draw back the curtains.

Suddenly, it was as if all the cheerfulness had been sucked out of her, as she stood at the bedroom window looking down to the damp ground outside, and the murky grey clouds which hung above, covering any chance of sun. She sighed. As soon as she put on her dressing gown to cover her most comfortable pyjamas, she ventured downstairs to prepare herself some breakfast, and see what the girls were doing.

"Leila, Lilly! Is there any particular reason the television is on, and why it is turned up so loud that those who live three streets away can hear it too?" she called out, awaiting an explanation, and turning the volume down lower so she could just about hear her daughters answering.

Lilly, frustrated, left her bedroom having just dressed, and stomped down every step until she reached the hall at the bottom of the stairs. "No, no, I don't know anything about it. I thought you were down here watching it, when I woke up. I've just got dressed and was about to come down for breakfast. This is the first time I've left my room."

"Leila, Leila!" Susan bawled, "Where is she? Why isn't she answering?" she questioned, feeling panicked.

"I don't know. LEILA, LEILA!" Lilly bellowed full blast sounding a lot louder than the television.

"What?" Leila asked as she entered the house via the back door, having just been out into the garden.

"Where have you been? And why is the television on and why was it on such a high volume? I wouldn't be surprised if those in the library at the end of the road heard it. They'd be listening to the words on our telly rather than reading their books in silence."

"I went to put some bird-food on the bird table. When I came down for breakfast, loads of little birds flew down into the garden and there wasn't any food out for them. I don't know about the telly—I had it on this morning when I came down for breakfast but turned it back off when I went to get dressed. When I came back down, I thought you or Lil were in there, but I came downstairs and went straight into the kitchen to get some bird food from the cupboard," Leila disclosed.

"No, it wasn't your sister or I. Never mind, I'll prepare mine and Lilly's breakfast and then we can all have a cup of tea."

The morning passed rather quickly; dinner time felt as though it had fallen right on top of breakfast. Well, it wasn't too far behind anyway; they did only eat two hours ago. Susan told the girls that she was only making something on toast or a sandwich for dinner, as she needed to do some shopping. With Lilly using the ingredients for the cake, and Leila using more milk than normal on her humungous bowl of cornflakes, and each one of them having multiple cups of tea, plus Leila improvising and using some of the bread because she'd finished off the bag of birdseed and thought the birds hadn't got enough, made the contents of their cupboards look rather diminished.

"If we stay here, we can look at the article about our house, and look on the internet about the graveyard," Leila excitably mentioned to Lilly.

Lilly enthusiastically agreed, remembering the conversation they'd had last night, following the discovery of a new light in the near distance that they hadn't seen before, and in the same direction as the churchyard.

Once they'd eaten their dinner, Susan told the girls to get ready to leave to go shopping.

"What? We are coming too?" Lilly widened her eyes, turning to Leila, who frowned with disappointment.

"Yes, it'll do you good to get out of the house a bit, and you can choose what shopping you want, too."

"Pretend to be ill, Lil. Please, go on," Leila begged and pleaded when they were on their own, whispering encouragingly for her to pretend.

"No, don't be silly, that won't work. If I'm ill, Mom doesn't have to stay and look after me; I'm old enough to stop on my own. You need to pretend to be ill, and then I will have to stay here to 'look after you'," Lilly explained, hurriedly.

Leila agreed and nodded, ready to put the plan into practice.

Leila walked down the stairs taking her time, scrunching up her face and holding her head in her left hand, whilst holding the banister with her right.

"What's the matter?" Susan asked suspiciously, lowering her eyebrows in confusion.

"I don't feel very well, Mom." She dragged out each word in a low tone, frowning.

"Awww, Lei, what's wrong, sweetie?"

"Headache and I feel sick," Leila continued, "like really sick."

"Oh no. Come on, we won't be long. The fresh air will help and do you good. You've been indoors a lot recently, that's probably caused your headache."

Lilly stood watching, her eyes flickering to and from her sister to her mom, as the chat continued.

"I feel really sick, Mom. I don't think I can walk all that way and then all around the shop and then all the way home. I feel like I need to lie down." Leila remained in her role playing out their plan.

"It's okay, we can use the car, that way we only have to walk around the shop. I think being out in the damp for longer than necessary when you're already ill will make you feel even worse." Susan, also, showed no backing down.

"Hmm, I think using the car will make me feel really sick."

"Come on, the sooner we get there the sooner we get back and you can have a lie down then. Let's get in the car," Susan snapped, reading more into the act than she was meant to.

"Don't worry, Lei, I've got this covered," Lilly assured her, whispering in her ear, and they left through the front door, showing she was ready to put her part of the plan into action.

They pulled up on the car park and found a space close to the shop entrance. Whilst Susan went to the machine to purchase a parking ticket, Lilly developed a strategic plan.

"Right, come on then, let's go, let's get it over an..." began Susan, having returned and opened the car door.

"Mom, Leila's been heaving, I don't think she should come. She's hot too. Let me take her home, we will walk it, and the fresh air might help her and at least if she is sick, it's not in the shop or in the car. I'll look after her," Lilly rudely interrupted her mom considering it necessary to do so.

"Oh dear, okay. Take it easy and don't eat anything, Lei, drink plenty of water. Lilly, when you have seen to Leila, the boxes out in the garage need sorting. Even if you only manage to clear a couple of boxes that's another two down. I won't be long anyway." Susan headed to the shop, and the girls started their walk home.

Ten minutes of walking and their home was finally in sight. It seemed as though they'd been walking for hours, they were so eager to arrive and read about their house and the graveyard on the internet.

"Excuse me," a tall, blonde male called out to them from the opposite side of the road, "Do you know who lives at number 10, Wikkington Way?"

"Er, yes, we do. Why?" Lilly answered sharply, yet in deep confusion, hoping to end this involuntary chat as soon as possible.

"Just wondered if anything had happened since you have moved there. Anything weird, unusual, unexplainable."

The girls turned to each other, both rather on edge as this

wasn't the first person to ask them the same sort of questions.

"Sometimes… We have to go, sorry," Lilly harshly ended the chat before walking off speedily. "Come on, Lei, keep up or you will actually be ill after being out in all this drizzle and dampness."

The fine yet depressing drizzle soaked their hair, and faces, the wind blowing in the opposite direction to the way they were walking. Their house seemed so near, yet so far away at the same time.

Approaching their home, Leila was sharp to identify a middle-aged female who at present was standing on their front doorstep. The sound of the scrunching pebbles as they walked up the driveway disturbed the lady, causing her to turn around, rather startled.

"Can I… we help you?" Lilly nervously challenged her.

"Hi erm, hi, I'm from further up the road, number 30. Sorry, is your mom or dad around?" she asked bemused.

"No, not right now. Can we go into our house, please? My sister is ill."

"Yeah, sorry, erm, this might sound weird but erm, have you noticed any abnormal or outlandish things happening within your home?" Quickly, she stepped back from their doorstep allowing them access.

"Yes, but I'd rather not talk about it right now, and why does everyone keep asking us that?" Lilly commented.

"Oh haha, everyone around here knows things about the house. It's 10 Wikkington Way. It's…"

Leila interrupted, pretending to sneeze, emphasising the fact to the woman that she was indeed ill, and wanted to get into her own house.

"Oh, bless you. Hope you feel better soon, sweetheart,"

the mysterious woman said in a comforting way, before walking off down their drive and back up the street in the direction of her own house.

"Oh my gosh, Lei, that was great!" Lilly laughed loudly, high fiving her sister proudly.

"Well, she was driving me mad. It's drizzling, she's on our drive. I fake sneezed so she would go and let us get indoors." Leila laughed.

Lilly fumbled about in her pockets to find the front door key, whilst Leila went to the end of their drive, making sure the lady had gone.

"Oh hey, do you guys liv…?"

"Yes, we live here, yes, we have strange happenings, no, we don't want to talk about it, nor do we know why it's so important for you all to know." Leila shut down the conversation before one of a group of three boys, who ranged in height and hair colour, had even finished their sentence.

"Woooooow, that's creepy! That's insane. How'd you even know we were going to ask you that? Told you guys there's something not normal about that house." They reacted to Leila's quick, final, non-negotiable message, before continuing their way past their house and walking into an alleyway.

The girls finally got inside. Leila took off her coat in a great rush, throwing her shoes across the hall floor, and dashing up the stairs.

"Hang on, where are you going?" Lilly stood and watched as Leila paused halfway up the stairs. Her blonde ponytail swung into her face as she vigorously turned.

"Upstairs… your laptop, remember?" She stood balancing on the middle stair slumped as if Lilly had completely forgotten what this was all about in the first place.

"Well, Mom said that we, okay, 'I' need to sort out one of the boxes in the garage. If we do that first, when she comes home it will look like we've done it. Whereas if we go on the internet first, she'll wonder what we've been up to," Lilly speculated, holding out her hand to Leila as she disappointedly but quickly came down the stairs, and jumped off the bottom stair.

"There's a lot of 'we' mentioned, to say that Mom specifically asked *you*," Leila hinted, desperate for Lilly to have a change of plan and let her start looking for the article on the internet.

"Yeah, because she thinks that you're not very well."

"Exactly, so I don't have to," Leila continued to argue, forgetting that she actually wasn't ill.

"But you aren't actually ill! Come on, stop moaning, it'll get done quicker if we both do it."

The girls sifted through a box each, both containing plenty of papers, objects, and old toys that could only be described as junk.

"Look, Lil." Leila laughed, putting on an old witch's hat she'd worn for Halloween a few years ago. The long green hair attached to the back of the hat, now tangled into plenty of knots, hung over her shoulders, disguising her long, blonde ponytail that was held in place by a red ribbon.

Lilly laughed, amused at Leila and the hat. "Why is there an old lampshade, enough old mobile phones to suit everyone in the street, and four empty dustbin bags all in this box? Why wasn't everything taken to the tip? These are all old mobile phones, and wait, an old house telephone too. Look!" Lilly listed all her findings, "Oh, and there's a pair of old gardening gloves right here at the bottom of the box," she added.

They put all the rubbish that they'd found into one of the empty dustbin bags that Lilly had just come across.. The garage looked a fraction tidier after they'd cleared two boxes. They had a great struggle to get out of the garage, climbing over full boxes, plus the empty boxes they'd thrown closer to the door to take out with them for recycling.

Lilly clambered over them all, dragging the dustbin bag of rubbish behind her. "AAArghhh, that bloody hurt," Lilly angrily shouted in frustration, landing on her stomach after sliding on a damaged cardboard box.

"OMG, are you okay, Lil?" Leila immediately manoeuvred around the boxes, rushing to her sister's aid.

"Yeah thanks, I'm okay. Stupid box," she assured Leila, getting onto her knees and then stand. "Be careful you don't slip, look at this here, what's this, let's move that before one of us slips again and gets properly badly hurt. It's stuck, under one of these boxes, and it's sliding about. There must be something really heavy in this box and it is holding it down. Let me pull it out because we might slip on it when we come in next time." Lilly pulled and tugged until the piece of cardboard was free and able to be picked up. "Wait, what is this?" Lilly grasped at the large rectangular board poking out from under the pile of boxes that had caused her fall.

"Wooow, is it a board game?" Leila snatched it from Lilly, thrilled. "And a magnifying glass, look! It's got numbers and letters on it, maybe the magnifying glass is for people with glasses or find it hard to see small writing, but these letters and numbers are huge, even old people could see these."

"I don't know. Come on quick, Mom will be back soon," Lilly prompted Leila to get a move on.

"I'm bringing this. We can see if we can find out what game it is," Leila chuntered, shutting the garage door behind her and racing through the kitchen, into the hall, and straight up the stairs to Lilly's room, where she grabbed her sister's laptop, and waited patiently on Lilly's bed,

"Lei, do you want a drink while I'm down here?"

"Yes please, bring it up, though."

"Okay, fetch my charger too. It's in the bottom drawer of my bedside cabinet. I'll have to find a new hiding place now I've told you," Lilly instructed, and joked.

"Wikkington," Leila read aloud, typing it into the search bar. "It's under 'Wikkington'. Keep looking down the pages and a picture of a house comes up, our house," Leila explained, refusing to take her eyes off the screen. "THERE!" She thrust her finger forward, poking at the screen as the picture of their house popped up.

Lilly clicked on the picture, which took them to the article about their house. She read aloud, "'10 Wikkington Way—what would the caretaker say?' What's that supposed to mean?" She questioned, before continuing reading.

"Scroll down! Scroll down!" Leila chirped in.

Lilly's eyes widened. Her mouth dropped. Her reflection in the laptop screen displayed fear, as if she'd seen something menacing.

"What, what?" Leila grabbed the laptop from Lilly. "What does it mean?"

"Don't you get it? We need to turn this off and just forget it. Leila, promise me you will not look at this again, not even mention it," Lilly warned, slamming the laptop screen shut, and hiding it from Leila.

"I didn't even get to read it." Leila whined, watching Lilly put the laptop away.

"You don't want to read it and you don't need to read it. Forget all about it. All this paranormal business, I know you like all of it but just… just… it's okay."

Leila ran off to her bedroom, taking the suspected game with her.

"I'm home!" Susan called, carrying in the bags of shopping she'd taken from the car into the house. Leila ran downstairs, and threw her arms around her Mom, hugging her tightly. "How are you feeling, angel?" she asked with concern, dropping the carrier bags to pick her up.

"She's still not well… Are you, Lei?" Lilly urgently interrupted, appearing at the top of the stairs, only giving Leila the chance to open her mouth to breathe.

"Erm, well, I feel a tiny bit better." She eyed Lilly up, filled with guilt.

"Awww, go and lie down, I'll come and check on you. If you're still ill tomorrow, I'll make an appointment at the doctor's on Monday morning, that's if we can register there anyway. Lilly, come here."

"Why, Mom?"

"Just come here."

"Why? What have I done?"

"Nothing, just come here," Susan assured her, slightly bewildered as to why Lilly was being so uptight and edgy. "Your elbow is bleeding, why is it bleeding?"

"Oh, I fell while I was cleaning the garage, slipped on a damaged cardboard box," Lilly responded. It was only the truth after all.

Leila helped Susan put the shopping away before heading to her bedroom. Lilly returned to her room, this time looking up the article on her phone rather than her laptop.

"Come on, Hooter, let's play a game." Leila grabbed Hooter off her bed and sat him opposite her, with the board between them. "I don't know how to play, and Lilly wasn't interested in it. Let's make up our own game. I'll use the magnifying glass to go over each letter. I'll spell a word and you guess," Leila explained to her little teddy, as if he was able to respond.

She moved the magnifying glass piece over the word "hello" which was already spelt at the top of the board. "Hello, Hooter." She giggled. She placed her finger on the wooden piece of the magnifying glass and wrote her first word. "… i… l… a… I am Leila. Now your go, Hooter." She put his little wing on the wooden part of the magnifying glass again and moved it around the board.

It pushed back. "Hooterrrrr, why won't it move? Is your wing caught underneath it?" She pushed. "N… O… R…"

Lilly read more of the article than she had done previously, but now began to feel really shaken up. She threw her phone down on the bed. "Oh… no." She felt a shiver run down her back, her heart sank yet rose to beat faster and faster. She closed her bedroom curtains before instantly making her way to her bedroom door.

"BOOOO!" Leila burst the door open before Lilly had even got there. "Lil, the game is weird."

"No, you haven't messed with it? Leila, why did you have to bring that stupid board out of the garage?"

"What's so bad? It's just a game. It's a very weird game. Me and Hooter were playing and then suddenly I couldn't move the piece and it just started moving by itself. I was playing spelling with Hooter, I said, 'I'm Leila,' and was trying to move the piece to say, 'I'm Hooter,' but I couldn't get past the force going against me. I thought it had caught his wing and it was under the piece stopping it from moving but it wasn't. It pushed its way around the board, spelling out, 'N,O,R,R,I,S'."

"NOR…" Lilly was interrupted.

"I'm Norris. I don't even know a Norris," Leila elaborated in confusion.

Lilly swallowed. Her throat was so dry she found it hard to speak. "Leila, it's a Ouija board! They are so dangerous! You must never use it again, throw it away!
Don't tell Mom, don't show her it, hide it under your bed and we will get rid of it tomorrow. Ohhhhhh no, oh my life, oh my life, Lei, Lei!" Lilly fell into a state of panic beginning to shake with nerves, causing her to drop her phone. She was unable to catch it as it bounced off the bed onto the floor.

"What, Lilly?" Leila asked in concern and complete surprise, unaware of what was about to come.

Lilly passed her phone to Leila, with the article still on display, "10 Wikkington Way—with unjustified causes, noises, and mysterious acts continuing after the unexplainable death of Wikkington Graveyard's caretaker Norris Ericson," Leila read aloud. She fell silent, and then realised what Lilly was on about. "Norris! The grave alone! He lived here!" She moved to the centre of Lilly's bed, staring at her sister who was sat with her knees up against her chest.

"TEA'S DONE!" Susan broke their panic making the girls jump and sit up quickly. Lilly grabbed her dressing gown and they both went down silent for once, to have their tea.

"Leiii!" Lilly harshly, due to annoyance, whispered as she walked past her sister's bedroom at what she saw. "I told you to hide that board and now it's on the bed for Mom to see. What if Mom had come up the stairs before us and saw it!"

She turned around fast at the unexpected reply from Leila who was behind her, traipsing up the stairs.

"I did hide it!" she retaliated.

"No, you didn't, it's here on your bed."

Leila put the Ouija board back under her bed. "Stay!" She patted it as if it were a pet dog.

A tap came in reply from under the bed. "Don't start." Leila laughed. "I know who you are now. Did you see me and Lilly in the graveyard? I wondered why your stone was all alone. Why is it? You aren't bad, are you? If you were, you'd have hurt us by now. We aren't here to hurt you; we didn't even know you were associated with this house. Everyone has been asking if we've had any noises or happenings going on, they knew, but we didn't. You aren't bad, are you? Lilly is the one who believes all ghosts are bad—she believes that if you're at peace when you've died, you don't need to come back. I believe you can be good or bad. If a good one comes back, it could be to tell someone something like that they are okay and no longer in pain, or are happier now that they've passed, but are always with them and they don't need to worry," Leila spoke to the board, assuming that the tap was a sign from Norris to leave the board be.

"Leila, who are you talking to?"

She paused quickly, turning her head in shock as there was no sound to indicate that anyone was behind her.

"No one, Mom, just muttering to myself. I'm going to bed now, I'm tired. Goodnight, love you, Mom." She hugged her mom, tightly squeezing her as she had realised how much she loved her, and hated lying to her today. This made her love her mom a whole lot more.

"Love you, Lil!" she shouted, hoping Lilly would hear her from her room.

"Night, Lei, love you too," Susan replied, shutting the door at the same time as Lilly had shouted, "Love you, Lei."

Before Lilly went to bed, she soundlessly made her way across the landing to check on her sister, ensuring she was okay, and the board was hidden.

"Goodness gracious!" Susan fearfully snapped, sitting up in her bed right away, hearing an almighty bang coming from outside of her bedroom door. "What the bloody hell was that?" she muttered, leaving a long, silent pause allowing her to listen out for it again. She heard Lilly's bedroom door open, and her attempt at stepping lightly across the landing, which was almost as creepy as the dreadful bang.

"Lilly?" she called, a look of sheer confusion upon her face when Lilly didn't enter or respond to her. "Lilly?" Susan called again, slowly filling with apprehensiveness. No reply.

"Oh, for goodness' sake," she sighed, throwing her duvet off and climbing out of bed with annoyance. "What in the world caused such a bang?" she queried, opening her bedroom door and stepping onto the landing.

Susan screamed. What was before her sent her into a terror-stricken frenzy, her head suddenly becoming a minefield of several panicked questions. "LEILA! WHAT

THE BLOODY HELL IS HAPPENING!" Bellowing, she stood at the top of the stairs, helpless and tired, staring at Leila lying at the bottom of the stairs, on her back.

Lilly distracted her attention from Leila. Appalled yet bewildered, Susan watched as Lilly repeatedly hit the banister at the top of the stairs, accompanied by an awful screeching sound she was making in rhythm with the hitting of the banister.

Lilly stood at the top of the staircase and was the cause of the terrible banging and row which was still continuing. Leila had woken up to the noise, and when she couldn't find a reason for the harrowing thrashes she'd heard went downstairs for a drink, and came back onto the landing to find Lilly there sleepwalking, traipsing around whilst hammering the banister.

"I'm okay, Mom, really, I'm okay. I could hear the hitting, and when I came out of my room, I couldn't see anything, so I went to get a drink and came back up. She frightened me. I was almost at the top of the stairs and then she appeared from around the corner, and I fell back. I am okay," Leila explained, now providing Susan with the information, and allowing her to see that it was Lilly making the row and walking around that she'd heard.

"Lilly, Lil, wake u…"

"No!" Leila immediately intervened as her mom had gone to gently shake her sister, trying to wake her up. "You must never wake a sleepwalker, Mom. She's sleepwalking, she's okay, Mom, I promise, just asleep. I'm fine too. I hurt my arm a little bit as I put it out to try and break my fall, but I'm fine. Let's just wait for her to wake up."

"Lei, it's 3 a.m. We could be up all night. I'm calling an

ambulance."

"MOM NO! She is only sleepwalking!" Leila sharply hissed, getting frustrated that Susan wasn't listening.

"Leila, her eyes are wide open! She isn't blinking or moving her eyes. She's smacking her hands on the banister and screeching like she's possessed. She isn't right!" she argued.

"Mom, stop it, and just listen to me. She's sleepwalking! Look her right in the face, at her eyes, at what she is doing. She has no idea; she's vacant, completely unaware of anything around her or what she is doing. It's all involuntary. She can't help that she's doing it. The best thing to do is ensure she gets back into her bed safely. Not pull at her, not shake her, and just watch to make sure she's alright. If you try to restrain her, she could lash out, hurting herself, us, or all three of us. Sleepwalkers usually go back to bed on their own anyway. Maybe she's having a nightmare or is doing something in her dream. She's not possessed, Mom, just asleep," Leila assured Susan, informing her of Lilly's situation.

"She pushed you down the stairs! She could have killed you!"

Lilly paused, and turned to face Susan, who was standing just outside of her own bedroom door, unwilling to get any closer after Leila's instructions.

"Oh, my life. She's, she's staring right at me. She's looking right at me right now and not blinking." Susan panicked, her stomach rolling and churning, causing her to feel jittery and sick.

"She didn't push me at all. I fell backwards because she startled me by appearing as I was nearly at the top of the stairs. She's coming out of it now, look, she's walking back to her room."

"I've never seen anyone sleepwalk in my life," Susan revealed, indicating to Leila why she was so distressed and tormented by what she had just reluctantly witnessed.

"I haven't in real life but have heard stories about it. Look, she's in bed now. We can go back to bed ourselves now too. She's safe, and it's unlikely she will do it again." Leila watched as her sister faultlessly clambered into bed, then gave assistance to cover Lilly with the lovely duvet and blanket she'd had over her previously that night.

The chiming of Wikkington Graveyard bells interrupted the deep sleep Susan had managed to slip into after the unexpected awakening in the night. Watching Lilly's sleepwalking episode had played on her mind, filling her with fretfulness. An uncomfortable feeling of both dread and the chance of it happening again had delayed her from falling asleep.

The sound the bells created, playing loudly, embraced the joy of the sunny, warm, late morning, outside of her bedroom window. Opening the curtains, she smiled. The wonderful tunefulness almost took her breath away, and for a few seconds, her mind was totally empty. For those few short moments it allowed her to focus on nothing but the heavenly melody which greeted her ears. The eleven chimes brought the short, sweet, happy tune to a much too sooner end than she would have liked.

"What a beautiful morning." Susan opened the lounge curtains and tied them back, letting the sunlight shine in.

"And you're sure you don't remember anything from last night, Lil?"

Lilly laid her knife and fork down, side by side on her empty plate; a small blob of brown sauce remained from her beans on toast brunch. "No, Mom, I don't remember anything, and from the information that you are supplying me with, I don't think I would like to remember anything, to be honest."

"Okay, it's okay. I'm going to ask if anyone at work has family members who sleepwalk. It was creepy. I don't know how Leila stayed so calm. She seemed to know everything about it. Well, apart from when you were slapping the banister on the landing. Anyway, what a lovely harmony it was coming from the graveyard this mor…"

Lilly coughed, hammering her cup down on the dining room table, as if it was too hot for her to drink. "Graveyard?"

"Yes, you know, the graveyard, the graveyard place behind the trees in the near distance."

"Yes, Mom, I do. Bells you heard? A tune from the bells?" Lilly inquired, under the impression that Susan was joking.

"Yes, bells. They ring, make a lovely chime," Susan teased, uncertain as to why Lilly's knowledge seemed so vague.

Lilly raced upstairs, thumping each step as she carelessly bounded into Leila's bedroom. "Lei, w…"

Leila paused, slowly lifting her head to look up at Lilly who stood above her.

Lilly's eyes flickered from Leila, then in front of Leila, then back to Leila. "I told you NOT to mess with that thing! What if I was Mom coming up the stairs and walking in here to find you playing with that, not giving you enough time to hide it. Are you stupid? Put it aw…"

"Wait." Leila sucked in her bottom lip after interrupting her sister's message before she'd finished, avoiding eye contact with her. "I know what you're going to say."

"No, you really don't." Abruptly, Lilly spoke over her. Shaking her head, she climbed over Leila and the board to sit on Leila's bed.

"I do, I…"

"LISTEN!!" She lashed out, a nasty growl in her tone as she lost her patience and jumped down Leila's throat. She quickly shouted, "Yes, we're okay" to Susan as her bitter snarl more than likely heard downstairs. "Mom woke up to the bells ringing, to which I didn't take much notice. Then it dawned on me…"

"Someone has to be playing the bells, but no one goes there," they synchronised, staring at each other.

"See," Leila concluded.

"How?" amazed, Lilly asked, taken aback.

Leila looked down at the board, and the notes she'd taken written on a piece of A4 lined paper to the side of her right knee. "It was me," she read aloud.

Lilly's hair on her arms stood up as an unnerving, cold shiver swept over her. She widened her eyes, raising her left hand to her mouth, biting her purple painted nails whilst giving it all a chance to sink in.

"Norris," both of them simultaneously voiced in realisation.

"That is cursed. Leave it alone. Get rid of it, or I'll tell Mom, Leila. I mean it. It is not a toy, it's not a game, and people are DEAD. This is some demonic lunatic. Get it out of the house now," Lilly assertively, hastily whispered, just so Susan couldn't hear. "It's evil, pure evil."

"No, Lilly. No. He's not evil. If he wanted to hurt us, he'd have done it by now. Don't you think so? None of the happenings have hurt any of us. This is where he lived! We know nothing about this house, him, the street, and nothing apart from what we read in that article. Not one person has told us anything, and we don't know anything, so how can you make that assumption? All the time we have been here not one happening has directly hurt any of us. You just believe bad people end up as ghosts. You have no reasoning for that, so to me if all this ends up now with us getting hurt, it's on YOU, Lilly, YOU."

Leila sat on her bed, completely ignoring her sister's belief that it's a demonic lunatic. She frowned the entire time, trying her hardest not to cry, in fear that things would get worse, a lot worse. She truly believed that spirits come back both good and bad; some are out to get people, whereas some just want to be noticed, or pass a message on from where they now reside, to loved ones, or friends, only to let them know they are okay, safe, and happy.

"What the hell was that great, awful, enormous clash?" Susan frantically yelled, racing into the house and calling up the stairs from where she stood at the bottom.

Leila threw down the planchette and raced to the top of the stairs to see her mom. Lilly dashed out of her room, woozily, in a daze as to what was happening.

"It was so loud, like a great big clash; an almighty, monumental, gigantic clash. My heart is in my mouth, girls, it really is. I was potting some plants and there was no sound at all to suggest something was responsible for such a row—only the sound of the birds chirping and our next-door neighbours' waterfall flowing into their pond." Her hand was permanently placed on her chest as she frantically explained. "I've never heard such a sound in all my life."

"It's okay, Mom, it's gone now. It could have been a lorry delivering something heavy and they needed help getting it out of the lorry and moved it onto a trolley or something. It's okay, don't worry now, it's gone." Leila tried her hardest to assure and comfort her mother.

She followed her mom into the lounge, where Susan sat on the black fabric three-seater sofa, her hand on her chin signifying she was in deep thought about the horrific clashing sound. "There's not a lot round here, like anywhere for a lorry to be dropping off something so big that it would cause such a tremendous racket. Park—no need for a lorry to be there to create that noise, doctors—no, I don't think so, the library—no, I don't think so, the graveyard—wouldn't have thought so."

Both girls' eyes widened at this when their mom included their new obsession in her explanation. "No one's been there since the 1920s," she continued.

"What? How do you know? Why?" Lilly quickly jumped in, prying to find out how her mother knew this information, as the girls definitely didn't.

"Someone told me at work," she replied, oblivious as to why it was of such importance and fascination to them.

"Why? What did they say about it?" Leila blurted.

"Just about it not being used or visited since the 1920s. I don't know; they weren't around in 1920, so how would they know? I can't ask and spread something I know nothing about. Maybe their parents or grandparents were around at the time and told them the reason and it has been passed down the generations. I don't know anything more about it, so I'm not going to spread around information I know nothing about," Susan retaliated, beginning to get annoyed with their, what seemed to her, useless questions.

"Mom, what information?" Leila asked again, totally blanking what she had just said.

"It hasn't been used since the 1920s. I don't know why. Why is it of such importance for the both of you? It doesn't matter. Let's just forget about it now." She crossed her legs and turned the television on, deciding to catch up on her favourite programmes and then try to get a bit of a sleep as she hadn't slept well the previous night.

"Leila," Lilly whispered, following Leila up the stairs, "if no one has been there since that date, how did the light come on the other night? It hadn't done that before, and how did Mom hear the bells this morning? Someone has to ring them, don't they?"

"Heaven knows. I think someone must have gone inside. The bells must be in there, so obviously someone has to get in to ring them."

"Norris, you said, remember?"

"Yeah, I remember, wait… Mom!" Leila yelled at the top of her voice.

"What are you doing? Don't tell Mom! Shut up!" Lilly argued, trying to make Leila change her mind by putting her hand over her sister's mouth to shut her up.

"Mom, ask your friend how she knew it wasn't used, and how she could explain the bells ringing," Leila instructed, digging for more information to help them suss out what was really going on.

Susan froze, alarmed. Nausea overcame her, her head felt heavy, dizzy, as if she was unable to think or see straight. She now realised. She'd never heard them before, which made her even more stunned, searching for an answer which she could not find, nor even consider a logical answer to, as no one had been there for years.

She sat for a while, thinking, thinking, until she could no longer think, or have the thought in her head. "Girls, I'm going out for a bit. I can't take it in this house with all these keys missing business and knocking, unexplainable happenings. I feel afraid to even sleep in my own home. Lying awake, full of fear, worrying. Lilly sleepwalking for the first time ever, my bedroom door opening in the middle of the night, a chaotic bang with no obvious signs to indicate the cause, I can't take it in this house right now," Susan elaborated, her voice getting shakier with every word she struggled to get out of her mouth as her heart raced, occasionally taking her breath away as she tried to vocalise what she wanted to say, though panic stricken.

Out of nowhere, two firm taps came from behind Lilly and Leila who were stood at the top of the stairs, looking down at their struggling, tired mother who couldn't think straight nor focus on anything for a long period of time. Susan was standing at the bottom of the stairs, with her back against the front door. They both turned instantly, looking behind them to find nothing to have made the tapping noises.

Following that, the lounge door slammed shut, causing the three of them to jump in shock. It seemed as though it was all happening at once now that Susan had admitted fear, and things had somehow become more frightening, much more noticeable.

"AAAAHHHHHHHH!" Susan screamed. "WHAT DO YOU WANT?" Her shaky, pale hands came up to her clammy grey cheeks and her eyes gleamed as they filled with water; tears slid down her face, dripping from her cheeks like droplets from an icicle. The red nail varnish she wore matched perfectly with her crying-inflicted, sore, strained eyes, and her rosy red nose from wiping it with her cardigan sleeve.

"It's okay, Mom, it's okay. I promise, Mom, we will sort this," Leila vowed to her distraught mother, as she ran down to the bottom step where Susan was sitting and threw her arms around her.

Lilly stood now halfway down the stairs, her eyes wide, projecting the look of shock and dreadfulness of all that was happening before her.

"It's been over 100 years since…"

"NOOOOO!" Susan wearily bawled, as in that already unsettling moment, the harassment continued as the television, without any physical help or interference, switched on by itself.

"It's okay, Mom, remember. The door slammed shut just now, it's okay. There's no one in there. I promise. Look," Leila devotedly comforted Susan, as she made her way to the lounge door and opened it, entering the room. "See, Mom, no one there. I know it's scary, Mom, with all this going on, but we will be okay. We have to ignore it, and it'll soon settle," she assured her, turning off the television, and held her mom's hand leading her over to the black three-seater sofa.

Lilly slowly followed behind them almost as if she were slipping in and out of short periods of time in a kind of vacancy, then back to the present moment, and then vacant again.

The chattering between Susan and Leila seemed of a muffled content, just as though Lilly had her head completely underwater. She, in great difficulty, made her way to the unoccupied two-seater sofa.

"Lilly?" Susan called out, distressed at how quietly, and oddly she was again behaving, but at the same time, could understandably recognise numerous reasons why, in this moment, Lilly would find it hard to talk, just like Leila and herself.

Lilly turned to her, opening her mouth to converse, except nothing, not a sound, not a word came from her mouth.

"Lil?" she called again, only this time more assertively, through suspicion and uneasiness.

Lilly turned again, able to identify where she was being called from, but completely unable to vocalise, at this time. Then she turned to the wall, becoming fixated upon a certain spot which was directly in front of her, at eye height, and rhythmically, continually hit the arm of the sofa.

"Is she, has she been, like this, all this time?" Susan tiredly questioned, unable to think straight.

"I think so, Mom. She went back to her bedroom after she'd been in my room for a while. I hadn't seen her for about an hour, until you came and shouted to say you were going out, and then we both appeared at the top of the stairs. Even then, though, she seemed to be half out of it, sort of mumbling and looking as if she were taking things in, but she's completely out of it again now. She probably was reading her book and fell asleep. She must get that off you because I neither like reading, nor do I fall asleep halfway through my hobbies." Leila giggled, not at all fazed by her sister's outlandish actions again.

"I don't get how you knew. How is she only just starting this now? She came when I said I was going out. How did she hear, or respond, if she's asleep?" challenged Susan, finding it difficult to take her eyes off Lilly.

"I don't know, Mom, it's a weird thing to watch, and I can only imagine how weird it must be to actually be the one experiencing it. She clearly has no trouble with co-ordination, then again, I suppose most sleepwalkers don't have much trouble. Some people manage to get out of bed and drive the car without crashing. Some people walk downstairs and cook a meal, or wander the street, and then get back into bed and wake up completely oblivious to what they actually managed to do. You go out if you want to, I'll look after her."

"Lei, I can't leave you, an eight-year-old, in charge of looking after a 14-year-old. No, wait to see if she wakes up. Thank you for being here and helping me. I should be the one helping you." Susan laughed, but meaning what she said.

Early evening approached fast. It felt as if somehow the rest of the afternoon had been cancelled out and skipped entirely into evening. Lilly had made her way back to bed, with Susan ensuring she didn't trip or fall along the way. Leila had gone to her bedroom, unknown to Susan, and Lilly, as her sister still hadn't woken up, and she began playing with the board again.

"Mom is really afraid, Norris, please don't frighten her anymore. Lilly and I were scared at first too, and Mom was

99

brave, now it is the other way around. Will you tell me what you want? Tell me everything, properly," Leila pleaded, awaiting a tap of approval from Norris, as she'd previously asked for one tap for yes, and two taps for no. She got out a blue biro, ready to write down each letter that the planchette was moved to.

"T, h, a…" she repeated aloud, "o, n, g…. hmm," she read and comprehended what he has said. "That's what I wanted to do all along." She finished the sentence. A single tap followed. "Okay."

She waited patiently. There was no movement from the planchette. Everything just stopped, as if someone had pressed pause on a television programme or a film. Nothing was happening.

The dark, cold, rainy evening outside her bedroom window caught her attention, as a loud, sharp, single tap came from the window and windowsill. She went to open her mouth, but she was quickly shut down by a much more powerful tap.

"Is it hailing?" The howling wind scattered the raindrops through the air throwing them in all directions, making them smash off every surface and object they came across. "It can't be hailing, it's water droplets? Rain doesn't make that sound, though?" she pondered.

She slowly stood up, following the sound of the third, strident tap. She stared out of the window, speculating what it was she was supposed to be looking at. It all seemed normal, no different to usual. She looked down into the neighbours' garden. Their security light lit up, putting all focus upon the hundreds of raindrops falling from the heavy clouds. They raced down her soaking wet window; she watched each droplet trickle down, as if competing in an unbeknown race.

Then, in front of her, shining through the gaps in between her garden trees, and those in the near distance, she located it. The old building in Wikkington Graveyard. It was visible and, the light was on. For the second time since they'd lived there, it was on.

"The graveyard building?" she muttered, turning back to the board on her bedroom floor, then back to the building and light. Her throat felt blocked, dry, and sore. Her lips also. "So that's why you were tapping the window, to get me to see it. Why, though? I don't understand."

She climbed back over her bed and placed herself on her bedroom floor. Her lilac slippers covered her white fluffy bed socks, and her beautiful purple dressing gown hid her matching pyjama top, only exposing her matching pyjama bottoms.

"Must go there, then I can explain," she whispered to herself, reading the message she'd just been given, before replying, "We've been before. Your gravestone is all alone by the old building, there's a piece of fraying rope tied around the inside of the gate and it loops over the stump to keep the gate closed. When we were there, it shut on its own. We have been there and that's how we knew it was you contacting us, because of your name on the grave."

"A, g, a, i, n," she sighed, completing the sentence she was writing and read the latest message out loud, "for me to explain, properly."

Leila ran into Lilly's room holding the piece of paper she'd written all the messages on.

"Blimey, Lei, what the hell are you doing running in like that? You scared the living daylights out of me, you maniac!"

Lilly snapped sharply in annoyance, forcefully turning her neck to look at her bedroom door as it flew open and hit off the wall behind it.

Leila bounded in, shaking her head at Lilly's overdramatic performance. "Sorry."

"What do you want now?" she complained, closing her book that she'd been reading on and off since moving into 10 Wikkington Way. "I've been trying to read and finish this book, I've been reading it nearly every day since we moved but every time I try to settle down and read it, I either get interrupted or fall asleep. I've read this same page six times, six! And I don't even remember reading it until I get to the last sentence and think, oh yeah, I remember this bit." She ranted, putting the book back under her pillow, knowing she wouldn't be able to continue reading it any time soon now Leila was here in her room.

"Don't be so frantic. Anyone would think you're auditioning for a role on a television drama," Leila rolled her eyes, jumping onto Lilly's bed, lying next to her to show her the messages she'd had from communicating with Norris. "While you had another sleepwalking episode, I came to my room and asked Norris some questi…"

"What, ANOTHER sleepwalking episode? Why can't I remember them? I'm really scared about these episodes that keep happening, I've never sleepwalked in my life according to Mom, so why am I doing it now?"

"You don't need to be scared of it. It's like sleep-talking; only you walk instead of talk. A lot of people do both, and it can usually be something making you do it, like stress, panicking, having a bad dream, or having night terrors. A lot of people do it; sometimes only once, sometimes very frequently. It doesn't mean Mom or I won't do it, we could. You're okay, Lil, I know what to do when you're sleepwalking. I'm always there for you, both when you're awake, and asleep," Leila carefully explained, throwing her arms around her sister, who was almost in tears.

Lilly smiled, hugging Leila back. "Wait, did you say you were talking to him again? How many times have I told you NOT to mess with that bloody board?"

Leila explained about the incident when Lilly was sleepwalking that afternoon.

"So I said to him that Mom was really scared and asked what he wants from us. And he said for us to go back to the graveyard, so he can explain properly."

Tension.

"Are you MAD, LEILA?"

Leila rolled her eyes— "Here we go again."

"Don't 'here we go again' me, we have been 'here again-ing' more times than I can count, and not one of those plentiful times have you taken any bit of notice about what I have said. Not one. We've been. We've seen the graveyard, we've seen the old building, and we've seen everything!"

"Except we haven't! He wants us to go back and see, so let's do just that, and get some answers. Come into my room, we will ask him and see what else he says, then all this panic, worry, stress, it can all be eased, gone, never bothersome again. Please, Lil, let's just try."

"Norris, now we're both here, you said you wanted us to go to the graveyard again, when, and why?" Leila asked, to Lilly's agonising fury and dissatisfaction as she'd been roped into this contacting session reluctantly.

They waited. Their hands jolted around the board, as the

planchette slid from letter to letter, and came to a halt. Leila scribbled down the last letter before comprehending what had been said.

"Tonight." She looked at Lilly. "Tonight," she repeated, under the impression Lilly hadn't heard her the first time as she didn't give any response.

"Yes, I heard. Tonight, as in night-time? After midnight?"

Leila sighed.

The planchette slid across the board quickly, to "yes".

"I don't think I'm too crazy about this idea. It seems a bit, well, daft. A recipe for disaster that we then have to deal with on top of everything else that has already happened. I don't think I, we, us, can take that. No, I don't think we are going, Lei, no. It's too, you know risky, we don't even know this person, the place, anything about any of it," Lilly replied, discouraging Leila from the whole mad idea.

"You're totally overthinking it. We can take a torch, a bag of food, coats, jumpers, notebook and pen, the board."

"Leila, it is a trip out in the middle of the night, to a damn graveyard, not a sleepover in primary school! Ouija board? No. You are NEVER supposed to use one of them in a graveyard, what is wrong with you?" Lilly continued to argue, becoming more and more against the idea as the conversation progressed.

Several taps on the board suddenly caught their attention. Lilly lowered her eyebrows in puzzlement. A few more taps followed, very clear.

"Okay, okay." Leila shook her head in amusement at how impatient Norris was. "That's Norris, Lil. He does it when he wants to speak, well, communicate a message," she interpreted.

Both Lilly and Leila placed their hands on the planchette to see what he had to say in the message he was so desperate to reveal. "It's okay. You will be safe. You'll help me, and the others in Wikkington, when they discover the truth. When all is said and understood, I can leave, be relieved. This will help me, and you, and the rest of the residents of Wikkington. I am stuck; I can't rest, until the truth is revealed."

Leila watched as Lilly read out the message they'd written down. She seemed disturbed, frozen even, staring blankly at the wall, her lips and cheeks moving from side to side as she contemplated the desired actions needed from her, until she couldn't consider it any longer.

The silent suspense made Lilly feel agitated and afraid, as the list of things on her mind that could go wrong grew and grew, but the dread of the things which could go wrong were even more worrying if they didn't do it. "Hasn't enough already happened? What else could go wrong if we don't do what he wants?" Numerous questions filled her racing mind. "Okay," she eventually resolved, interrupting the seemingly mournful felt silence. "It'll have to be after Mom goes to bed. What if she wakes up in the night and comes to check on us?" she quizzed Leila.

"She won't, she's not going to. She's probably shattered after being up half the night with you sleepwalking and banging the banister at such a ridiculous hour! Not to mention then lying in bed for ages terrified you were going to do it again and it'd convince her you were possessed," Leila stated, slightly laughing as she informed her sister of Susan's thought that she was possessed and had wanted to call for an ambulance.

"Twelve. We go at twelve. Then we quickly do this outrageous plan and come back as soon as possible. I don't feel at all comfortable with this. I feel queasy."

"We'll be all right, Lil. Take our torches, see what's there, and come home."

"What do you think it is that we are meant to be finding out to provide everyone with answers? How is he going to communicate with us? How will we know when we have found what we are looking for?"

She watched as Leila searched her mind for an answer to provide her with, before fixating her lovely green eyes upon the Ouija board. "I think that's our answer. He taps but that won't help us with communicating sentences, will it? Plus, it'll make it quicker as he can just say stuff, rather than us having to guess, that would take aaaages!" Leila negotiated, with as many facts as she could think of.

"Fine," Lilly muttered, scowling at the clock in her sister's bedroom, presenting the current time of 20:10.

Leila commenced with her packing, not that she had much to pack, but was far too excited and conscious of what tonight would bring. "Rucksack, jumper, torch, batter—oh, we have none. Great. Sweets, and the board. And my pack of pens and my notebook," she whispered to herself, lastly hiding the bag under her bed out of sight in case Susan came in, and then she climbed into bed.

Susan came up to get ready for and into bed at 10 pm. Quite late to say she'd had a rough night's sleep last night. She checked in on Leila, who had fallen fast asleep, with Hooter lying at her side. Lilly was lying awake, looking on her phone, when she was checked upon.

"Mom," Lilly collared her, "how did your work friend know no one goes to the graveyard anymore?"

"Remember, I told you. I don't know, I didn't ask," she repeated her words from earlier, unsure as to why it was so much of a topic of discussion and thrill to the girls.

"But don't you think it's weird how so many people seem to know, well, ask, about happenings in our house? And that the bells rang today when no one goes there or has been there for over a century?" she continued, adamant to find out as much as she could before their trip there tonight.

"Well, I guess maybe they've experienced things in their houses and wanted to know if we, and other neighbours, have too. Or perhaps one of the neighbours has heard our television on full blast and thought someone screaming or arguing on a television programme was one of us having a fright. They might have thought we were being thrown against the walls and across the floor from the row you were making last night. That poor banister." Susan smiled, "My colleague, Mellannie Mayhews, hasn't replied yet, but when she does, I'll let you know." She kissed Lilly goodnight, then left her room.

Once Lilly had heard Susan leave the bathroom, and given her half an hour to have settled down and get off to sleep, she found out her torch, a thick coat from out of her overflowing wardrobe which couldn't properly close, and made sure her phone and portable phone charger were both fully charged ready for when they went out.

At 23:00 Lilly went to wake Leila, allowing them the chance to go to the toilet, put on their coats, and quietly leave the house.

"Shhh!" Lilly hissed at Leila, who accidentally, very

loudly, hit her bedroom door with her rucksack.

They gently tiptoed down the stairs, grabbing Susan's keys so they could lock the door behind them when they left and unlock the door to get back in when they arrived back home.

"Ready?" Lilly asked with her hand poised on the door handle, the other on the house key as she started locking the door behind them. Leila shone her torch light at the front door handle and keyhole, so Lilly was able to see what she was doing and definitely lock the door.

"Ready," assured Leila, as they strolled up their street, Wikkington Way.

The dark, deep night swallowed them up. Only their shadows were present in the brightly emitted light given off by their freshly charged torches which were brand new, creating a silhouette of the two of them. The stars hung high above, like tiny little sparkling lights scattered like confetti against a black backdrop; a huge contrast when compared to the giant spotlight above them—the moon.

They followed the highlighted pathway, made easier by the glow from the natural, illuminative shimmer of the midnight moon. The torches served a purpose in a totally different way, as the bright moonlight was more powerful than both torches together. Enabling their view of the board, when they were ready to use it, was the reason they needed the torches.

The girls went through the kissing gate, this a reminder that they were now closer to the graveyard than to their own home. They wandered on, continuing their worryingly, nauseous, unknowing what lies ahead journey, until they reached a familiar, yet somehow less favourable sight despite the fascination that had grown through their time in their new home. The frayed rope threads stuck out like whiskers, as the gate creaked open. "We're here," Lilly quietly emphasised, edging closer to the gate. It seemed bigger than before. It was intimidating, different, acting as a line between the known and the unknown. And, that was just how it felt, as it was an unknown territory to the girls, and to the rest of those who lived as residents in Wikkington.

Lilly shut the gate behind her, reattaching the woeful rope to the stump, as upon their arrival, it hadn't been properly closed, and therefore easily persuaded to open by the wind.

Leila took the board and planchette out of her ready-to-burst rucksack, laying it on the brick wall to the side of the gate, as it was a good hard surface, and wide enough, to fit and lean the board on. The girls put their hands onto the planchette, ready to receive a message and write it down, in readiness for what was to follow.

Three letters in, an overpowering screech interrupted the flow and recording of characters. The fraying rope was no longer fraying, nor a rope. The great, admirable, heavy gate forcefully opened with no explainable cause. It squeaked with every jolt, performing a quick, monotone moan as it opened wider and wider, suddenly stopping, and all fell silent.

Lilly stepped back, feeling as if under attack and froze in panic. She watched, unable to take her eyes off it and look anywhere else.

"What the hell?" Leila managed to spit each word out, between the collective number of squeaks and dull whines.

The slamming of the firm, solid gate was enough to have

been heard outside of Wikkington itself, the sound probably reaching the next village! The slam, which it created when the iron hit the wooden post, was so strong it bounced back away from the post, yanking the frayed rope so forcefully it had disintegrated and could no longer hold the gate shut.

"It… It just… opened, and then shut?" Lilly suspiciously described in alarm. They placed their hands back on the board, continuing the message they'd started earlier which they'd recorded as "H, A, R." Several moments of silence passed, with only interferences from the girls relaying each letter to one another to write down, before the message had been written for the girls to read. "Har, my gravestone, back," they both read aloud.

"Har? What's har?" Lilly shook her head, totally confused and without an inkling as to what it could represent or mean.

"I don't know. Maybe he meant like, here? 'Here, my gravestone, back', or 'has, my gravestone, back'. I don't know, but definitely gravestone and back." Leila attempted to understand, hoping for some kind of approval or an act of dissatisfaction from Norris.

The gate opened again. However, this time, no sound came to suggest any action from Norris was taking place, only the sounds of their own footsteps sounded across the cobbled path as they then trudged further into the graveyard. At that moment, a sudden feeling came over them, a feeling of uninvited company.

They timidly made their way along the path—the darkness increasing the further they stepped into the graveyard, and the more the trees were disguising the moon, taking away its glorious shine.

110

The various different gravestones seemed somehow to turn into a pair of eyes focused upon them, each stone watching their every move. The girls were on their territory, trespassing, and their unknown visit was not expected nor accepted easily by these wondering eyes. The two young girls were the ones to watch, the ones it all centred on. As they trudged deeper, and deeper into the cemetery the more atmospheric, tense, and hostile was the feel towards the girls from the crowd of suspicious eyes.

"Ahh! Bloody hell!" Lilly threw her hands onto Leila's shoulders, following the unnerving, unpredictable, and incredibly unexpected smash of the gate hitting off the wooden pole again as it somehow managed to slam shut once more.

Now, with the gate shut for the second time and no sounds to suggest otherwise, it was out of their sight, and they were following the last little turn in the path which brought them to Norris's memorial. Approaching their instructed destination, it became more apparent. A wave of terror-induced nausea came over Lilly.

"What in the world?" Susan thought to herself. A short, loud, but rather joyful sound filled her dark, cosy bedroom. She lay on her back, as still as possible, staring up at the ceiling in a complete state of uncertainty of what the noise was.

Moments passed before the same sound filled her room again. Her erratic heart pace increased further as the silence-breaking, awfully intense sound sent her into shock. She moved her eyes to the left, then turned her head to her bedside table when she realised the actual rather pleasant-sounding noise was in fact her mobile text tone. "Oh, my phone! It's on silent that often I forgot it even made a noise, and what that noise sounds like," she tutted, smiling in relief and realisation. "Strange, though, I don't remember putting it on loud," she thought to herself, calming down slowly after waking up to think she was at a concert.

She reached out for her mobile phone, noticing she had received a text message. "Who's texting me at this time?" Susan asked herself, soon finding out it was a message from Mellannie Mayhews, her work colleague.

The more she read of Mellannie's text, the more her face displayed several terror-induced characteristics before she removed the suddenly formed lump in her throat by dashing to the bathroom and vomiting.

Mellannie had delivered news; news that explained everything. News that made Susan feel and be sicker than any illness she had ever had in her life. News enough to cause nothing but sheer panic and shatter any happy memories she and the girls had created in their new home. Only now it felt far from a home, just a building.

She stood up from the toilet she was sat on whilst harshly vomiting into the sink. She'd sat afraid. Afraid to move, talk, leave the room, turn the lights on, afraid to breathe. Her worrying, fretting, distracted mind compiled many questions, only this time, thanks to Mellannie's text, she was able to answer most of them. Susan sat back down immediately, as if the questions she was formulating were like a carousel inside her head, getting faster and faster until she felt light-headed, dizzy, causing her to vomit again.

Her main question was, and yet there was no answer to, was "How will I tell the girls?" She pondered, totally oblivious to the fact that both Lilly and Leila already knew a lot more than she knew herself. Little did she know that that question wasn't in fact the main one, nor was it of any comparison with regard to her discovery soon afterwards and the more important question of, where are the girls?

"We're here, Norris," Lilly assured him, just as if he was there in human form. "So what next?"

The girls took the board and laid it on the grass next to his place of rest. They both placed one hand on the planchette, Lilly freeing the other hand to hold the torch with, and Leila freeing her other hand to write the letters down whatever the planchette was moved to.

The rustling of trees in the cold breeze and leaves dancing across the burial grounds offered an uncomfortable feeling that the girls weren't alone. Owls called and bats soared through the night sky. The snapping of twigs joined in with the nocturnal wildlife orchestra.

"B, a, c, k. Go back?

Does that mean our back? Back what?" Leila tried to suss.

"Let's just go back home now," Lilly quickly jumped to say, desperate for Leila to agree.

"No, no. We can't."

"We're out here taking instructions from a board which you're probably pushing the letters to! It's 1 am! We are in a GRAVEYARD, Lei! This place is never visited. We should be in bed! Not strolling around a graveyard. Now, let's go," Lilly sharply responded.

"Shhhh! Just shut up a minute! Back what, Norris?" Leila demanded.

"Behind," Norris spelt out.

Lilly argued, "Well that is a load of use isn't it," rolling her eyes, sighing.

"Someone is behind us?"

The planchette zoomed across the board to "No" right away, as if they had given up already. "The back, around the back."

"Around the back!! Behind the back of something!!" Leila immediately whispered across the few feet distance between herself and Lilly, having now understood what Norris meant.

"What? Around the back? Back of what? It's like some game of hide and seek, only we don't know what we are trying to seek, nor have any idea about where it is meant to be hiding other than around the back? Back of what? How can we locate whatever it is when we don't know what it is nor where it would be apart from the back of something? How are we going to locate it? It's the middle of the night and we're searching a graveyard in total darkness for something we don't even know what, or if it even exists. I mean, does Norris even exist? Does any of this exist? Because right now I'd love to wake up and for all this to be a dream, well, a nightmare. This is lunacy, foolishness, idiotic," Lilly bickered.

Leila walked further away from Lilly, full of wonderment, and hesitant as to why on the rest of the field where Norris's grave was, there were no other memorials or gravestones present. There were neither visual indicators nor physical evidence to suggest any attempts at gravestones ever being laid there.

She roamed around the deserted looking, bare, eerie field, using her torch light to locate her surroundings. She adjourned, staring up into the barely-illuminated sky. The moon had been overshadowed, and the dying battery in her torch reduced the radiant emitted glow. This left her feeling vulnerable, insecure, and also in two minds as to what to do without the full brightness of the torch light. She wouldn't be able to help or contact Norris in response to his messages if the battery ran out altogether.

"Hi, Susan, sorry for taking ages to reply, had a very busy day today! Hope you have had a nice weekend. What do you mean, you didn't/don't know about the graveyard? The old caretaker who used to work there, Norris Ericson, was murdered there in the graveyard. He used to live in your house!—10 Wikkington Way. Everyone has since felt uneasy about the place as nothing ever was found. One day Norris's grave just appeared. There were no other clues as to how it appeared or people present to ask about it. With no evidence nor person coming forward or people ever being proved guilty of murder, people stayed away. Strange occurrences first began taking place when Norris took over as caretaker. A lot of Wikkington residents at the time believed it was someone playing tricks on Norris, and that they had lured him to the building many a time and tormented him, then ended up murdering him. Because different happenings had occurred so regularly, and each time he investigated, there would be no sign at all of anyone being there or responsible, there was nothing to prove for the different things. A lot of folk believe he purely went to go and see what was responsible for the happening. He'd got used to no one and nothing being there so people just went along with that, but the murderer had probably caught him out and therefore succeeded in his murder because poor Norris hadn't expected anything at all. The residents think the murderer tricked him and no one has ever been back nor has the graveyard been occupied by another person since. I think it would be best for me to tell you the entire story in person as it would take so long to write. See you at work later, that's if I don't oversleep, haha. Mellannie, Xxxx"

Lilly approached Leila, her trainers stepping carefully around the wet, slippery, cobbled path, slightly covered in sodden moss and all size of twigs which had fallen from the leafless trees standing over them both. The chilly night breeze felt as if it was slicing into her as she reached out her icy, bitterly, numb fingers, to tap Leila on the shoulder.

Leila turned around, suddenly stepping back, as she saw her sister's face.

Lilly squinted her eyes, not once focusing on anything else, purely just on her sister.

"Lil? You're scaring me now." Leila stepped back again, her heart pulsating so much she could hear and feel her heart pumping in her cold numb ears.

Lilly looked right, left, lowered her eyebrows, and then viciously threw her head back. She straightened up her head, her teeth chattering. The sound of her teeth nervously clanking off each other accompanied her involuntary shaking and paper white complexion, all panic induced. She opened her mouth, releasing air and trying to converse; the inability to gain her breath and do so aggravated her terribly.

Her body seemed no longer to be hers, as if anything she wanted to say or do, was being prevented. "Paralysis," was her immediate thought. She was unable to move her stiff cold hands to wipe the tears gently running down her flushed cheeks as her colour began to return. Her eyes widened as much as was possible, feeling wet for a second before the freezing wind dried her tears without giving them the chance to actually fall from her cheeks. The wind blew harder. Her eyes kept open despite her trying to close them in the piercing, howling wind. She stood staring, staring, staring, but only at Leila. She opened and closed her mouth, forcefully trying with everything in her to try to talk.

Leila ran. She ran to the back of the building just opposite Norris's grave, clasping at the Ouija board and notebook. She collapsed in a heap onto her bottom, laying the board down at the side of her. For a few minutes she left the board alone, merely sitting on the floor, gazing into the infinite darkness, surrounding her from all angles. She became aware of a dim light emanating from the building.

"Norris, what's going on? Please tell me," she pleaded, clutching at the planchette, trying to keep it still as her hands shook so badly due to her shivering. She sat up straight and watched in awe at it moving. Halfway through his message, the light in the building increased in brightness, allowing her to have a clearer view of the board and her notepad so that she could scribble down the message much easier than squinting in the dim torchlight. The brightness cancelled out the tormenting dark and gloom; that masked the daylight.

A sound of thud, thud, thud becoming nearer made her feel more tense, the small but heavy steps seeming so much louder the closer they came sending her into a stressful, trying state. She closed her sore, red, tired eyes as she heard the steps come to a pause right at the side of her. Unwillingly, yet pressurised, she opened them. A full beam of light shone over her like a spotlight, expanding the amount she could see, and enhancing the full coverage of the board. She felt a light touch as a coat rubbed against her own.

"Lei, it's me," Lilly whispered down her ear.

The younger girl slowly turned her hood-covered head to the left, experiencing difficulty in choosing whether she actually wanted to see who it was, or if, in fact, it would scare her more. Her stomach nervously somersaulted, as she looked. "Lilly! Lilly!" She threw her arms around her sister, her bare wrist touching Lilly's ear.

"Gosh, your wrists are cold. Here, luckily I brought two pairs of gloves." She handed Leila a pair.

"What happened? Where have you been?" Leila interrogated, full of happiness and total relief to have her sister with her again.

"I... I... okay, I don't know how to, urgh. You know, earlier I said, 'Lei, look' and you went ahead instead of looking? I found this on the ground, right where you are sitting now. This grass patch you're sitting on. The grass is so long you never would have found it unless you had all the time in the world to wade through all this overgrown stuff and intruding weeds, and were dedicated to looking, as well as having the time and exceptional eyesight to see through grass that's several feet tall! Whilst you were looking at Norris's grave and around the empty field, I thought 'behind' and checked behind the building. Only, I can't... I don't want, I don't like what this says, or what happens when you read it. Just, please, Lei, don't say his name," Lilly explained, after finding something she wished she hadn't due to the unnerving horror she'd experienced earlier. Leila read aloud.

"'This building holds burial equipment inside, and other

garden tools to keep the grounds tidy, and certifies everything is done to an incredible, unforgettable standard. The caretaker who won best organisation and ground keeping standards every year since 1854 has now sadly passed away. He was an exceptional worker who enjoyed his job so much and wanted to keep the graveyard looking lovely, and a place for visitors to come and visit/ respect their late friends' and family members' memory. He spent the majority of his living years working here and it seems any caretaker to follow will have to have high expectations and standards to match, or better. After much time and effort and dedication to ensuring Wikkington Graveyard was a lovely, tidy, quiet, scenic place for mourners to visit their loved ones, and those resting, he has been awarded this plaque due to his dedication and determination to fulfil mourners' lives with a splendid peace of mind that their family members and friends are able to rest in peace and tranquillity. Their loved ones can be visited in a well-respected and taken-care-of area. They are truly well looked after and tended to and the gravestones are regularly cleaned and the groundwork is in the mourners' and deceased's best interests to make visiting their family members and friends graves a positive experience and will show they are cared for even if they have passed on. A well-deserved and earned award, and so sad to be awarded it only days before his passing.'"

"Oh, oh my God, that's the picture of him? It's a newspaper article from 1899! How has it not been ruined after all these years hiding in the grass, or at least never been found?"

"I don't know, Lei, but we have to ask Norris what it is he wants us to find or do and get out of here," Lilly hurriedly steered the chat, grabbing the planchette, missing Leila's half-written note which she'd interrupted.

"Let's find out what you want us to know, Norris," Lilly asserted, getting hold of Leila's hand and placing it on the planchette.

"I… t… w… a…" They both read aloud as it glided from letter to letter, giving more volume and emphasis to each consecutive letter. It all came to a standstill, providing Lilly and Leila with some time to puzzle over and try to discover their received message.

"It wasn't him. It was me. Lilly you know. I wasn't murdered. He showed you."

Leila frowned, confused, turning to look at Lilly.

Lilly held the picture out in front of her. She gulped loudly as the saliva trickled down her sore, dry throat, and into her churning stomach. She closed her eyes and then opened them as if trying to rid shampoo from them.

"His name, H… Harmond, Harmond Hordenton. Don't repeat it, Lei. I didn't feel anything, I just, the light came on. It was really bright, like I could see better, well, so I thought. Then, I trod on something, sharp, the corner of this picture. I trod on the corner of the picture and a bit of glass pierced the sole of my shoe. This picture has fallen, but not now. It's been on the ground for a while, look, you can see it has started to rot and the colour deteriorated making the water stains turn part of the image from black and white to grey. I looked up at the building as I bent down, so I could see the area where the light was covering, because it would make it easier to identify what I had trodden on. I continued looking up, and then, after picking up what I'd trodden on, this paper, without even seeing the picture, and I saw someone in the window... that window!

"I'd never seen that person before, never. I thought maybe it was someone up there who was doing a night shift and keeping guard of the place and ensuring we weren't up to any good. After all, if I was him and saw two kids in the graveyard at this time of night, I'd ask myself what they were doing here too. I looked down at the picture. Shocked. I couldn't understand or believe it. So it must have been Harmond! That was him in the window, the person I saw. I looked up again, and he was still there!

"His big hazel eyes were focused on me, no movement of them, no movement of his body at all, just him, standing there, staring, looking down right at me. His black short hair complemented the widened eyes that seemed unable to focus anywhere else. He had on a black blazer which mirrored his shade of black hair. The perfectly folded white shirt collar beneath his blazer and perfectly folded sleeves made him look ever so smart and tidy. Then I looked down at the image which featured in the article, it was the same suit worn by the man in the picture. Exactly the same!

"Then I actually read the article... and saw... he was dead! THAT MUST BE WHAT HE MEANS, LEI!! HARMOND!! HE MUST BE INVOLVED," Lilly slowly explained. Her shaky voice synchronised with her heart racing, as though she was living that moment of discovery all over again. "It was just like, well, any of us. Just like any human standing there gazing through the window."

"W-where is his grave? Lilly? Lil, what did he do? Did he say anything? Ohhhhh, my, oh I don't believe this." Leila gasped, turning back a few pages to their messages upon arrival.

"What? What, Lei? What?"

"Remember when we came in like right at the start of the night, we came through the gate, remember, and Norris said 'Har' then as the gate opened, we stopped?" Leila recalled on reflection. Lilly nodded, now sharing the same, thought, as Leila. "Harmond!" Leila concluded. "I feel so ill. But what, what does this have to do with Norris?"

"I don't have a clue. Haven't the foggiest. Wai—wooow! Pass me the notebook quick!" Lilly raced through the pages until she came to the most recent page of messages from Norris. "It wasn't him. Lilly knows how I felt." Her stomach rolled, causing her to heave. "I didn't get killed. Lilly has felt it." She swallowed, getting worked up into a state of panic. "Bloody hell's sake, Lei, why couldn't you have just left that damn board alone! Now what if I die? It has some link with me. I don't know what, I don't know what I am meant to have felt, he wasn't killed?? I don't understand any of it. Help me, Lei!" Lilly frantically cried, "I don't want to die!"

"Norris, what do I do? Please tell me what to do!" Leila aggressively demanded a response, anticipating a message as she felt more and more helpless. She tightly held onto her sister's hand as if that was the only comfort that she could provide without knowing what she had to do.

"Come into the building, into the upstairs room. I can tell you then. You will both be okay."

Lilly let out a loud sigh, feeling as though the whole time they'd been waiting, recording, and reading the reply, she'd been holding her breath. "There is no way I am stepping foot in there! You didn't see the figure, Lei." She shrugged as the idea of going in there gave her a haunting shiver.

"I'll go," Leila bravely decided, "I'll go."

"No, you won't. Not over my dead body, pardon the phrase," Lilly immediately intervened.

"Both?" Leila suggested, "We'll be safe the both of us. We'll find the stuff out quicker, go home, and tell Mom everything. Come on, we've done everything else we've been told to do. We've been fascinated and wanting to find out about this place for weeks. Do you really want to give it all up now?" Leila challenged desperately egging Lilly on to agree.

Lilly thought long and hard, every now and then glancing up at the building as if she had decided, then looking up again to make her completely disagree with wanting to go up there. She looked once more at the window, where she'd seen Harmond. She turned to Leila and nodded down at the board before using it again. "Let me ask something that will help me decide," she assured Leila, showing she was still indecisive.

Leila passed her the board and planchette, watching as her sister communicated with Norris. "Norris, if I go in there with Leila, will this end everything, all the happenings, all the worry, stress, mysteriousness and terror we've had? Will it stop it all? You're the one doing all of this, so will you stop it?" she pleaded.

"Yes. You will help me, let me rest. It will all be over, for everyone," she read aloud, feeling somewhat comforted that it would bring all of this to an end.

"Harmond, Norris, please explain about Harmond. Will he harm us if we go inside, will he do anything bad to us?" she finally asked, querying their safety before she and her little sister went inside.

"Come inside, I will explain it all. It is a little bit warmer up there and shelters you from the slicing wind and heavy rain. Harmond, no, he won't harm you," Norris assured them.

The girls made their way to the old wooden, rotten door which was hanging in a slanted position where the top hinge should be connected but had rotted away. The smell of damp and rotting, sodden old wood greeted their noses as they stood before it. The night seemed strangely quieter, as though all was relaxed in order to help the girls and Norris.

"What I don't understand is, if it's this easy to get into, this rotting, old, sodden door, why hasn't someone been already? They could have restored it and made it usable, clean, tidy, and the graveyard Harmond is meant to have made it, from the newspaper article award picture we found." Lilly elaborated, reaching for what remained of the door, which once was enough to keep people out of the building. "Yuck." she groaned, as she touched the soaking wet door, and several scraps of wood and mould fell off, wetting her hands and shoes.

"It absolutely stinks!" Leila laughed, in both disgust and humour. The damp clung to everything within the old, cold, yet intriguing building. Clumps of moss grew on the stairs, walls, the inside of the door, as if they'd been flung around aimlessly by a slingshot. Everywhere inside looked dull, the concrete stairs added an eerie feel as the staircase and surrounding walls were just as if they'd found themselves at the bottom of a well. The girls thought the place was bigger, as from outside it looked a lot more structured, taller too, as though there were rooms both up and downstairs. The walls enclosed on them, little room to move, only the stairs themselves which led to the one room upstairs. Another wooden door stood at the top of the steps, however, it wasn't in such a state as the front door.

"No wonder no one's been in, there's nothing in here. Only a staircase leading to a closed door!" Lilly grumbled.

"Shut up, Lil. You don't know anything about this place yet. Just shut up," Leila snapped in fury, aggravated by Lilly and her comments, and constant moaning.

Leila stepped on the first step, looking up at the old white door ahead of her, rather intact. Her footsteps echoed throughout the steep, enclosed layout, her wet shoe soles leaving patterns on each long, high, bewildering step.

She reached out to touch the wall, each hand on either side. "Woahhh!" she yelled in fear, a loose brick jolting as she rested her hand on it.

Lilly followed close behind, turning around every few seconds with intense paranoia in fear that someone was behind her. A chilling breeze accompanied them, as they continued to hobble up the steps. The wall surrounded them cosily, preventing the wind from being as sharp and slicing towards them as it was outside of the building. It blew the remains of the open door, causing it to rattle, creating an annoying ticking sound like that of a clock. Lilly's focus drifted, as she became far more concerned about the feeling of something behind them and refused to look in front of her, at Leila's back, for more than ten seconds at a time.

Leila struggled to climb up the forever-seeming mountain of steps; 30, feeling like 300. Her knobbly, shaky knees had carried her up the slippery, mossy, daunting stairs, to the big white door that had been in sight since they'd entered the building. She turned around before opening it to see her sister who was still only halfway up the steps, feeling fearful, tired, and extremely nauseous. "Come on, Lil, it's okay. We are safe," Leila reassured her, encouraging her to hurry.

"I don't feel safe," Lilly argued, "I feel anything but safe," she murmured, in between the many butterflies she felt fluttering around her stomach. The darkness surrounded them; only a glimmer from the dimly lit torch lights which had been necessary all this time, and which by now were running low from being in use for such a long period of time. There they were, in what felt like a brick cylinder, with only a few feet between their shoulders and the walls, just like being in a well.

The chilling draught swept up the many steps that the poor excuse for a door had failed to keep out and shield them from. Lilly shuddered. "The wind is still cold in here, and I feel like ice. Still, at least we aren't stood or sat outside in it. I guess it'll be better when we are in the room as we can shut the door behind us. It looks heaps better than the outer door, at least this one at the top of the steps actually resembles a door rather than some kind of small garden gate which had fought many battles with the weather."

Leila grabbed at the handle on the cloud-white door, with slight streaks of grey running its length, almost like a silver lining. She came to a halt, ensuring Lilly was close behind her, unwilling to enter alone, or have her sister turn back without her. Lilly gave an unwilling nod, instructing Leila to go ahead and open the door, before shaking her head in despair and utter disbelief that she had gone along with this whole trip for tonight. This was it.

The dusty moonlight dimly lit the spacious room. After a rather hard push, and an awful scraping and grinding of the door on the concrete floor of the upstairs room, the girls ventured inside. An army of tools, some standing, some leaning against the wall, and some on the floor. Shovels, spades, rakes, different sized trimmers, an extremely old looking lawn mower, and four watering cans varying in size and shades of green, and some other strange looking tools they'd never seen before! "I haven't ever seen anything like these sort of things before," Leila exclaimed in surprise, like a child at Christmas racing over to them to see what they do.

"Wow, and a wheelbarrow! How did they get that up here? Carry it up those stairs every day?" Lilly pondered, noticing the black, rather heavy wheelbarrow to the far side of the circular room, from where she stood.

A firm tap followed. Leila looked around, swiping her numb, stinging, frostbitten fingers off each of the tools, contemplating, full of curiosity as to what it all meant. "Yes," she answered Lilly, "yes, they carried it up here every day," informed by Norris's strong, singular tap.

The window had no glass, which surprised the girls, as they'd always believed that there was glass when looking up at the building. It allowed the girls to have a view of the burial grounds from above, like a bird's eye view. Leila watched, feeling more and more confused, unsure, having noticed a shadow moving in the now fading moonlight, as it slightly disappeared behind a gathering of dark, grey, angry clouds.

They sat down after having a wander around. Lilly shaking with fear, whilst Leila wandered from tool to tool having the time of her life. Lilly closed the door, for safety, and comfort, believing it would give her peace of mind. The practically leafless trees, their short, long, thick or thin branches, gave their best efforts in rustling in the early morning breeze, as the girls took out the board, pen and paper, and sat, ready to finally put an end to all of this uncertainty and the unknown.

"Do we ask something?" Leila asked, feeling a little unsure as to what happens next, as now Norris was in control.

"I think we just say we are ready, and to go ahead."

The girls nodded and murmured they were ready. They hunched up together away from the tools and away from the window, as without glass, the entering breeze had no obstruction to keep it out, but the circular room and walls helped barricade the wind far more than the awful shameful entrance door at the bottom of the steps.

"Here, at Wikkington Graveyard, it all began," Norris communicated, ready to reveal the entire truth, in hopes to allow him to rest, and bring all the stress and worry and frightening tales to an end.

"Began?" Lilly formed a sudden list of questions in her head.

"I became caretaker here in November 1899. It was due to the passing of Harmond Hordenton, who had died earlier that year in August."

"1899! Gosh, that's ages ago!" Leila piped up.

"Well, it says on his grave he was born in 1856, that was also a long time ago. Don't say you'd forgotten," Lilly sarcastically tormented her. The girls entered a horror-induced pause as they heard the graveyard gate begin to creak. They remained still, quiet, focusing purely on denying anyone the chance of thinking that the premises were occupied. Only the light inside the deserted room suggested to anyone entering the neglected burial grounds that it was being used.

"Turn off our torches quick, LEI!!" Lilly hastily whispered, feeling under threat.

Leila turned off her dimly lit torch. The battery life had drained further than previously, in the same way as all the heat had drained from her body. At this point her temperature increased in warmness and her heartbeat began to race from the distressing fear created by the creaking of the gate. Her toes, legs, middle, chest, neck, head—the heat rose, as if the panic were exactly what she needed to keep her warm, awake, alive. She wiped her sweating forehead with her coat, then unzipped and rolled up her sleeves. "Blimey, I am hot. I feel sick. We are going to die." Leila closed her eyes, taking deep breaths to try to help the awful sickly feeling to subside.

"No, no, no! You're the one who said we are gonna be fine, Lei, we'd be safe together, you said. Stop it. We are getting out of here once we know everything we need to," Lilly calmly reassured her, although the increasing fear and uncertainty she was feeling inside turned her stomach more than once. Moments of overwrought tension and silence passed by, lasting only minutes, but feeling like hours.

Susan managed to gently assist herself up by holding onto the sink next to her. Fearing movement, sound, sights, the darkness and what is lurking in it, she reached out steadily, fumbling her way to find the bathroom door handle. Each slight sound she made, or heard, made her flinch, allowing herself several seconds to pass before she moved again. In this way, the spinning, nausea, and horrific vomiting had stopped.

She opened the bathroom door, peering around it as she pushed it open centimetre by centimetre, before exiting what she thought of as her safety net. She felt across the wall for the hanging rope to switch the bathroom light on. The sudden vibrant, radiant brightness caused her to suffer a sudden pain and quick feeling of disorientation as her eyes adjusted to the surroundings within the area of light. Her vision went black and slightly blurred, just as if she was standing up too quickly like it did sometimes of a morning, her blood pressure plummeting before restoring to normal. The bathroom light offered plentiful coverage for the whole landing, enhancing what she could see, providing her with the confidence to move around, and in safety when doing so.

Susan slowly peered around the door into the darkness filling Leila's bedroom. Her curtains were drawn, the light off, and her clock wasn't hanging up on the wall. Susan knew she'd taken it down and put it in her bedside cabinet so she couldn't hear it ticking. Leila could not stand that. So from what she could see, the glow provided by the bathroom light, offering minimal, but sufficient light to this room across the other side of the landing, everything seemed normal, just how it usually is when Leila is in bed. She turned, ready to leave her daughter's room, then hesitated, checking for certain to make herself feel better, more at ease.

Turning around and back into Leila's room, she, with care, and determination to do it as quickly and as silently as possible, so as not to wake her, turned on the bedroom light, hovering her finger over the switch. She stood confused as to where Leila was and why she wasn't in her own room. After a few seconds of thought, she had an idea that Leila was in Lilly's bedroom, guessing she'd had a nightmare and went to sleep in her sister's bed. "Maybe she didn't come into my room because she knew I didn't sleep too well the night before, so went to Lilly instead," she thought to herself.

A minute or two passed by, yet she still found herself staring at the empty bed, almost in a trance as her head filled with many ideas to try to explain Leila's absence. "Ah," she second guessed herself, "I bet Lilly was sleepwalking and Leila put her back to bed and stayed with her to make sure she is safe," were her thoughts, nodding to herself afterwards, believing it was the most realistic reason she could think of. Susan turned out Leila's bedroom light and strolled across the landing, lit purely by the bathroom light, and into Lilly's room.

Again, on first entering, she was met by the fear-inducing darkness, which had only now become such a worry to her after reading that awful text message from her colleague Mellannie Mayhews, half an hour ago. She inched forward slowly, further and further into the bedroom. The bathroom light's bright glow decreased, hindering her sight as Lilly's door gradually started to close behind her. She aimed for the bedroom light switch which was situated behind the bedroom door. Without help, the door had shut to, not locked, but shut to, eliminating any light from outside of the bedroom door. She found the light switch after feeling across the wall, afraid of treading or tripping on something. "Damn door. I must either get someone to move the light switch, or the bedroom door so you don't have to keep going behind it to turn the light on." She harshly blamed herself, grumbling at her own guilt and growing more and more annoyed. Her fear had intensified, leaving her feeling panicky again after searching through the darkness, causing her to become more and more fearful from the information she'd read in the text message she wished she'd never seen

Her stomach dropped, and her heart sank. A great lump formed in her burning, sore throat from the constant vomiting; only now she felt sicker than ever. Her head throbbed, causing temporary pain, as if she'd just been hit with a hammer. Her unsettled, empty stomach prompted some bouts of violent, extreme retching, leading Susan to hurriedly make her way from Lilly's bedroom back to the toilet before vomiting once more. Her nerves were playing up badly, her body ached and felt so sore, she felt drained, exhausted, as if her life had just crumbled, at what she'd just seen. Immediately she raced to her bedroom for her mobile phone. Even with the risk of being sick again, Susan went around the house, the continuous, nerve-ridden retching in accompaniment, slamming on every light in the house, calling out, screaming their names, praying they were downstairs and she would find them.

Every room in the house was lit up but it still felt completely empty and dull. She desperately, hopelessly wished this was all just an awful, horrendous nightmare. Pinching herself, harder and harder, her face screwing involuntarily as she felt each painful pinch, tears falling from her tired, aching eyes. Sitting down on the two-seater sofa, regaining breath, she was desperately hoping they were still in the house, whilst her mind suggested other scenarios, much more sinister, unclear, and dreadful, doing all it could to provide situations based upon Mellannie's frightful text message.

Her trembling fingers made it difficult, almost impossible to use her phone. Through teary eyes, blurred vision, and uncontrollable shaking she thought hard. OUTSIDE. Grabbing the backdoor key, knocking over cups and jars with her nerve-triggered tremor, she placed her hand on the key, her other hand on top of it to keep it steady, allowing her to unlock the door.

Fearfully, frantic, and fretting, she ran out into the garden hoping for an immediate response, to prove that the girls were in the garden. She yelled their names over and over. "Oh no, no, no, no, no," Susan bawled, her throat on fire, and body ready to collapse with shock and devastation. "PLEASE ANSWER ME! LILLY, LEILA!" she bellowed repeatedly, wandering to different areas of the square garden.

Standing alone, in the dark, she called and called until all she could voice was a whisper. The garden felt a lot bigger, and Susan, a lot smaller. The Archfield abode stood behind her; every light on in the house, yet Susan's mood had never felt darker. The midnight harmony of strong, whistling winds chorused along to her sadness, and disparity. She mournfully dragged herself back indoors, only expecting a miracle that the girls were inside.

"Lil! Lil!" Leila bluntly repeated in distress, and menacing torment. Her emerald eyes were wide, hypnotic and bright. She repeatedly opened and closed them. The groaning of the downstairs front door being dragged by a forceful wind across the cobbles forming the path travelled up the lonesome, perishing cold stairway. "L… Lil," she vocalised before fiercely being tapped on her little bony shoulder. "OUCH!" she squealed, more in shock than pain.

"What? What?" Lilly asked in terror, even more frantic at the look of horror that completely altered Leila's facial expressions, showing a petrified stare.

"H-Harmond…" she revealed, staring at the picture for a split second, glancing to and from the picture at the left of her, then behind Lilly. "It's… He's… It's him," she forced out of her dry mouth.

"What is? What about him?" Lilly questioned in stunned confusion. The feel of concern increased incredibly in Lilly's stomach. She swallowed, and again, her gulps sounding so loud disturbing the intense, unwanted silence which presented as Leila was still having difficulty bringing herself to form a sentence. "LEILA!" Lilly yelled, thinking Leila was in a trance as although the younger girl was looking in Lilly's direction, she was actually looking beyond her.

"He's… right behind you," she unhurriedly whispered, each word so monotone. It was as if she was unwilling to take her eyes off the apparition standing behind her sister.

"Lilly! Come on, for heaven's sake, answer your phone!" Susan angrily whispered, ignoring the razor-sharp pain stinging with every breath she took. "Arrrrghhh!" she hastily complained to neither Leila nor Lilly answering their phones. Scouring through her dressing gown pocket, she searched for some painkillers. After attempting to call them both again, she was halfway through dialling Lilly's number for the third time, when she heard a quiet, delicate knock at the front door.

Susan, forgetting all fears other than where her daughters were, sprinted out of the lounge and to the front door, slamming down on the handle. "Shit!" she muttered, realising the door was locked. She violently pushed open the letter box, peering through. "Hello, please help me!" she called.

"Hello, dear," a sweet, gentle, soothing whisper greeted

her ears, filling her with a sense of calmness. "I heard someone calling, I guessed it was you." Her angelic voice was like a cushion to Susan's ears. "Can you let me in, dear?"

Hypnotised by the angelic voice, she grew calmer. "Yes… I… Oh, I can't find my keys. Oh damn…" Susan explained all of a fluster, "under the fourth plant pot to your right, there's a key. Use it—it's a red key," she added, forgetting it was dark, so it would be hard to even see the colour.

The sound of the key turning in the lock left Susan feeling comforted, although apprehensive as to who it was. The door slowly crept open. Susan waited to the side, allowing the unknown visitor room to enter and close the door. She stood there, allowing a stranger into her house at 2 am, something she would never do, nor tell her children to do either. There were timid little steps from the visitor as she politely stepped forward onto the mat, this followed by a longer moment whilst the lady closed the door. A little old lady!

"Hello, my dear," she softly spoke, leaning onto her walking stick.

"Hello… Hello…" Susan replied in astonishment, bewildered as to what was going on and yet in another way, thankful for the company. "I… I need to find my girls. They were here and now they're gone, and I must search, I must find them. Please, please help me!" she cried, stuttering and sniffing into the handkerchief the kind lady had passed to her.

"I heard you calling, my dear. You must have a terrible sore throat from all the shouting. I can hear in your voice that you are straining to talk. How about I talk, help, I'll be no trouble. I will help you. You must be terrified. I'll help, I can listen, and then see what I'm able to do to help," the frail, little old lady suggested. She was wearing a long black coat which was covering her floral dressing gown underneath. "Oh, by the way, I'm Mrs Bluethorn, but you can call me Mildred."

Susan led Mildred into the lounge, where they both took a seat on the three-seater sofa. "Mildred... Mil... Can you help me, please? It is my daughters I am calling for. I haven't seen them all night, not since we all went to bed I was woken up by a text message from someone and it said things. There have been things happening in the house and now the girls have gone, and I don't know what to do or where to begin or what I should be doing or where they are. I just don't know what to do." Susan sobbed, reliving it all.

"Don't worry, dear; explain further, I am listening," Mildred assured her, gently putting her hand on Susan's shoulder.

"This house. Its history. I never knew anything about that until this early morning when I received a text. My children, I don't know where they are. Happenings have been taking place since the day we arrived here: bangs, knocking, tapping, slamming; almost every time with no explanation to its cause." Susan blubbered. "It's too much and I'm worried, and my girls are only young. Oh dear, I am a silly woman. I should call the police."

Without a sound, Harmond paced around the girls, unsure whether he could be seen. Leila pushed herself backwards along the cold, concrete floor, edging away from him. His black suit, in perfect condition, greatly complemented his black shoes and chocolate brown eyes. The gas light, which had come on of its own accord and they'd had no idea of how it had done so in the first place, hung above them.

Lilly quickly thrust herself forward, reaching for the Ouija board as she thought that if she was fast enough, Harmond wouldn't notice, see, or hear her doing it. She was desperate to communicate with Norris, as now she felt more uncomfortable than ever before. "Norris, is that Harmond? I mean is it really him, or our minds?" She regretted the response, but curiously queried his presence, afraid as to what could or would happen next.

"Yes, it is him," she read aloud from her notes of conversion with Norris. She'd never felt as sick and ill as she now did. She sighed, and then breathed deeply for a minute or so to try to contain her nerves and stop herself from vomiting. She asked him another question, again, unwilling to know the answer due to being unsure what it would be, though she was pretty sure she couldn't feel any more ill and petrified than she already felt. She looked over her shoulder, seeing Harmond walk towards the window of the room, miraculously walking through the tools rather than around them. "Can…Can he see us?"

"Yes, he can see you both. He saw you when you first visited."

Leila gave a pleased smile, ecstatic to be in a situation she'd so desperately been interested in, but also a little nervous as to what Harmond could see or do.

Lilly felt a cold eerie shiver, proving to be responsible for making each hair on her arm stand, like a hedgehog with his spikes erect in alarm. She watched as Leila stared at him in fixation, looking at his face and eyes, yet getting no response from him in return.

Lilly crossed her legs; using her knees as a rest for the board as leaning over was beginning to hurt her back due to it being arched over for a long period of time. She felt baffled, as if she was no longer Lilly Archfield anymore, as if she had a completely new identity. This because before moving to Wikkington, she'd never believed in ghosts, nor had she given the thought of any kind of spirits and ghosts and anything sinister the time of day. She'd never do any of what she had done since living in Wikkington; sleepwalking, going around graveyards in the middle of the night, using a Ouija board in the house, or the graveyard itself. She felt she'd completely lost all sense of herself, and who she was. She stared at the board in reflection, realising that this was all real real real. "Can he talk to us?" she asked.

"He doesn't need to. He is free, happy, resides here. He no longer communicates with the human world, or desires human interaction. He is able to see you, hear you, and touch you, though you may or may not feel it. He doesn't communicate, and never has since he passed away, I believe," Norris explained, giving Lilly several pauses to have the chance to record all he said.

Writing each letter down was difficult for Lilly. Both girls' attention and focus was on Harmond so wasn't fully paid to Norris. They nervously, yet rather intriguingly watched Harmond move around the room just as any human would.

A sudden, abrupt crash disturbed the girls, who were thinking of their next question, alarming them and causing them to jump and shriek in fear.

"He knocked the shovel over!! Lil, look, he knocked the shovel over!!" Leila enthusiastically repeated in shock, startled and excited by an adrenaline rush, demonstrated by the ready smile upon her face following the incident. Her cheeky laugh led Harmond to come to a halt, turning around and smiling at Leila's laugh. Suddenly there felt a higher level of positive energy in the room, making it all seem calmer.

"Well, Norris did just say sometimes you may or may not feel things. He walked through tools earlier, and now he just knocked one over. It must be different pressures or force used, or perhaps it's out of Harmond's control if we feel something or not or he knocks something over or not," Lilly paraphrased in recollection.

Lilly blew out her cheeks and asked some of the eager questions rotating around her mind. "What is he doing here? Why is he here? It's all weird. What are we meant to be finding out?" Now even more inquisitive and on a high, she waited in fascination and wonder for Norris to provide an answer.

Somehow, the room seemed warmer, a lighter energy and a total distraction away from the cold weather. The girls felt they were actually getting to understand now, and found they were not so hesitant and fearful.

"He never left," Norris continued to reveal, "He stays here. All his time is spent here, just like when he was alive on earth, in human form. I was scared at first. I didn't have any knowledge of him, none at all," Leila read, turning around every so often to keep an eye on Harmond.

He soon left the room and his footsteps were heard echoing as he strolled down the stairs and out into the graveyard. Lilly stood at the open window hole, watching him vacate the old stone building through the dismantled, poor resemblance of a door. Her eyes involuntarily squinted as the brightness of the flickering light in the room was exchanged for the pitch blackness of the early hours of the morning, sparking difficulty for a few moments until she was able to see properly, her eyes adjusting from one extreme to the other.

The sound of his footsteps accompanied Harmond's apparition as he ventured further away from the building, towards the entrance of the burial grounds—to the iron gate. As the distance between him and the girls in the building expanded, the rhythmic stomping faded and he disappeared into the sea of darkness, swallowed up by trees and the limitation of light from the dusky moonlight emerging from the murky grey clouds.

When Susan had long-windedly relayed the awful experiences she and the girls had encountered in their home, and read out the terrifying yet revealing text message from her colleague Mellannie, she woefully lifted her feet onto the sofa, curling up, warming to Mildred's words of comfort. She turned to Mildred, almost giving half a smile as having her there seemed to have calmed her down greatly. Mildred watched the clock on the hearth, the second hand like a Ferris wheel, so fast, yet feeling so slow.

"Mrs Archfield, excuse me, Susan, may I ask you something?" she requested in sudden thought.

Susan gave a nod, allowing Mildred to continue.

"You said a colleague of yours told you about 'Norris' and how he passed on."

"Murdered. How he was murdered," Susan, without allowing Mrs Bluethorn to say any more, immediately corrected her upon what she had been told. "But yes, carry on."

"Well, why would he, Norris, wish to unnerve and petrify you, yet not cause harm? If he'd been murdered, I'd expected him to be a volatile and angry spirit. If he was so desperate to cause upset and dishearten you and your family, and, from what you say, many things have happened since you moved here, yet no one has been harmed. If he wanted to cause you harm, and with every opportunity he has had to do so, by the amount of times you and the girls have experienced them, then surely he would have used that opportunity to do so," Mrs Bluethorn elaborated, proving a plausible, valid point. This point being raised only echoed Leila's attempt to change Lilly's beliefs regarding Norris, and ghosts as a whole.

"I'm afraid that what Mellannie said about things happening and becoming the norm is what is happening with us now. We have all these noises and happenings that at first had confused us but we have lately not taken so much notice of. But Lilly sleepwalking, Leila talking to herself and becoming even more obsessed with graveyards, it all seems to be getting more intense. I fear that someone is playing a trick on us and causing the knocks and bangs and whatever, and now what if this time the girls heard something and went to investigate. What Mellannie believed and said others believed about what happened with Norris, well, what if they went to investigate and were expecting it to be nothing as has happened so often, but this time, they have been caught? It seems all too real and makes far too much sense to be a coincidence, in my eyes anyway," Susan explained her worries, sighing heavily when finishing and wiping her runny nose with the back of her hand.

"Norris, tell us more about him. Where is he now? What is he doing?" Leila interrogated, captivating Lilly's attention, prompting her to come and sit back down, after watching through the window for Harmond. She as well had the same questions circulating in her mind, and a hungry appetite for answers.

"Out, not far away, never far away. He walks the grounds often at night. He believes it to be busier during the early hours of the day. He passed away in 1899, natural causes as far as I am aware. I want to be at rest, be at peace, just as Harmond is, therefore this tale must end."

"Why is he at peace and you're not? What tale? He didn't harm you? We don't yet understand," Leila eagerly piped up, becoming more uptight and seeking more information, hints, and clues.

"It is not true what people believe. I must now, in his absence from the building, tell the story. After he passed, he found peace almost right away. Here," Norris revealed actively moving the planchette from letter to letter, leaving a few seconds to pause, and indicate a space between wording.

Sharply interrupting, Leila pointed and waved her finger at Lilly, recollecting something she'd mentioned to her previously, "I told you that some people find peace and still come back to visit or show they're still around us, Lil. I told you!"

"Find peace? What, really? Because all I seem to be getting from this weird, absurd situation we're in right now is that Harmond is responsible for the death of Norris. To me, coming back, in this case, is the reason Norris IS dead. What do you think the next line is? Because now we're in the place Norris looked after, once Harmond had passed. We're next!" Sceptically, Lilly trembled, frantically pacing around the room with nerves.

"What? Did you not pay *any* attention to what Norris has told us? You were all for asking him questions about Harmond and questioning our safety, *you've* asked Norris questions, and communicated with him, not just me. How can you be sceptical when it is happening here in front of your own eyes? We were in the same room as him and he did nothing bad. He isn't responsible for Norris's death. Why don't you ever listen? We have been here on a few separate occasions now and haven't once seen this Harmond fellow before, until now. If he was so determined to cause harm and was responsible for Norris's death, don't you think he'd be out to get all the people visiting here, yet we haven't ever seen or even heard of him." Scowling, Leila rolled her eyes and shook her head, at the end of her tether with Lilly.

"Well, what are we here for then? Come on. Don't you see we are next to die! Don't be so stupid. Okay, let's say he is real then. We're chatting to a spirit who has been tormenting us for weeks! He decides to persuade us to go out in the middle of the night to a building in the centre of a no longer used or visited graveyard to be told some information. Does that suggest to you that he is a safe spirit not intending to hurt us? It seems Norris did him a huge favour by stepping up to be the caretaker of here, desiring to keep this whole place as tidy and to an exceptional standard just like this Harmond did. To me, Harmond must have thought negatively of this, and wasn't happy with the way Norris was working, fulfilling his late career, and therefore killed him, and now

Norris is out to harm us as we are in his house and is targeting us in revenge. Why couldn't you just have left that stupid board alone, Leila? Why don't you EVER listen?"

"Well not once has he harmed us through the whole time the happenings have been going on. If you stop being so stupid and actually listen and let him carry on, the quicker all this will be over, and we can go home," Leila hastily reminded her, running out of patience. She insisted Norris should be allowed to continue but her sister did not entirely agree. Lilly stood to the back of the room, glancing outside as the droplets of rain hitting the ground below; some even landing inside the room, next to her, when blown in by the harsh perishing wind.

The heavens opened, dampening the ground, soaking the moss-covered paths along with the dead fallen leaves, making it much more dangerous and slippery to use and walk on if they left now. "Great," Lilly sighed to herself, looking over at Leila interacting with Norris. "Better ask him to be quick explaining as Harmond will be back soon now it's teeming down."

Leila ignored Lilly's comment, not once casting her eyes in her sister's direction the whole time she was talking. To take things further, Leila began reading Norris's responses in her head, instead of aloud for Lilly to hear and pass judgement on or other unwanted comments.

"I only found out about Harmond after he had passed away. The newspaper article, you've read it too. I used to walk past Wikkington Graveyard often despite living in Wikkington. I'd not been in the graveyard before, just strolled past it. Many a time I'd walked past, there were endless amounts of people visiting their loved one's

144

memorials then. But with every time I walked past, not once did I ever see this Harmond, never."

Leila read, smiling to herself before continuing to read some more, "I'd been walking past regularly for the two months after he had passed, and noticed the overgrowth of grass, different weeds, and more dead flowers than alive. It looked in total ruin to how I'd seen it just days after his passing, now unrecognisable."

Leila's hand ached from all the writing it took to record the message onto paper, then allowing her to take it all in. She was unable to tear her eyes away from the messages, thirsty to learn more.

"I took it upon myself, in the November, to do what I could to try and take care of the grounds again. I knew I had such exceptional standards to live up to, after all the time, effort, and painstaking work Harmond had put into it, but I couldn't stand to see what was once such a beautiful place with other people's loved ones' memory of it turned into an abandoned mess. As well, of course, tear away all the care the people had towards their loved ones who'd always ensured the graves were clean, neat and tidy, and let all of Harmond's care, attention, and time he'd put into it for all those years go to such waste and ruin. So, I took it upon myself to become the new caretaker."

Leila's jaw dropped, in awe and admiration that Norris had kindly decided to devote his time to restore the graveyard and keep it tidy and to a much better standard than it had been in for a long time since Harmond's passing. He continued…

"The keys were in the building, this building, behind the what-is-now a bedraggled, degenerated ruin of a door. It was odd to think that Harmond, in human form, had left the keys in the building, but it explained why the gate, and the building door, hadn't been locked.

"The thoughts circulated in my mind, how no one had tried to get in, or damage or steal from the property, but I thought, surely, no one could do that to such a meaningful, appreciated, well respected place."

Leila smiled, shaking her head in immense pride and appreciation of Norris.

He was now telling the story of the whole situation, and Leila was growing fonder and so far much more interested with every message he gave.

Lilly came to sit beside Leila, out of the way of the rain, and hidden as far away as possible from the open window to shelter from the ferocious wind, which was still failing to cease. She watched as Leila wrote the next message from Norris, in answer to her questions, "How did he die? What else happened?"

"Natural causes. You see, many years ago life expectancy wasn't as high as it is in the present day. My belief is that he wasn't feeling too well, so decided to go home, but he was so ill he forgot to lock up. If you're ill you aren't a hundred per cent, are you, your main thought is how unwell you are feeling and what you can do to try and help yourself feel better," he expanded the amount of information he had provided for the girls.

He believed Harmond passed from natural causes. However, this was never proven. It did, however, make sense as if he was unwell, you aren't yourself, and not giving your full attention to things and details, which supported Norris's idea.

Leila nodded as she read it, agreeing that if you're not well, you aren't as precise as you are when you're well, understanding Norris' train of thought.

The torrential rain hammered onto the gravestones and surrounding grounds, "eliminating some marks of dirt on them due to not being attended to by anyone since Norris died," Lilly factually joked.

Leila frowned at her, displaying her annoyance, lowering her eyebrows with a stare that could kill.

"What else happened, Norris?" Leila encouraged him to continue, aware that the story hadn't finished yet.

"Every day, I'd come here, open the gate, get the tools out of the building and maintain the grounds. Clean the gravestones, remove any dead plants or weeds, cut the hedges and trees where they were overgrown and causing a hindrance. But one day, something caught my attention and the best way to say it is, from then, it all went rather strange." Finishing the sliding of the planchette, Norris indicated that this was the end of that message for the moment, so they could read over what they'd written from copying down each letter he had slid it to.

Leila changed her standard bic pen to her new favourite purple barrelled pen, because it had just run out, but thankfully just as she'd finished copying down the letters. She scribbled at the top of the page to ensure the pen worked before carrying on, as being unable to copy down the letters and prevent them from understanding a message because the pen didn't work was something she didn't want to happen. She made another little black squiggle at the top of the page—to double check the pen was indeed working!

The early hours progressed. The darkness outside

somehow felt a lot more intense than before. The moon had disappeared and been fully overtaken by rain clouds, leaving the girls with only the light from their torch, and the flickering dim light in the building that would flicker several times before staying bright, then flicker again.

"It's weird, don't you think, we didn't hear Harmond come up the stairs. He just appeared behind me, but we heard his footsteps when he left the building?" Lilly mumbled in fascination, bringing it to Leila's attention.

Leila reluctantly responded with minimal interest, still strongly annoyed with her sister, "Hmm. I guess."

"And you'd think we would have heard him coming up the stairs rather than on the path when he left the building because with the stairway, every noise echoes making it so much louder," Lilly continued, trying to prise her way back into Leila's good books. "I don't know why it happened, Lil. He probably thought he would frighten us if we heard him coming up the stairs."

A dainty tap was made on the board as Norris informed them that he was ready to carry on when they were. Leila grabbed her pen and had it poised at the ready, eager to find out the next part.

"During the daytime, everything was seemingly normal, until evening, and darkness fell early on those cold, dark, long winter nights, and then later in the evening on a summer's night.

"At first, it seemed as though it were all in my mind. I'd come and shut the gate behind me whenever I went to lock the building, just to make sure that when I'd gone to lock the building up, someone might have thought the premises were still open, and I could have accidentally locked them in.

"To begin with, it worked a treat. I'd be able to lock the building every night and when I came back the next morning, I'd be sure to be at ease never finding anyone there waiting for me so they could give me a piece of their mind and accuse me of keeping them there locked up all night. It's not exactly the most joyous place to spend a night, but you certainly wouldn't feel alone, not with all the graves for company.

"It happened for years before I passed away myself. It started in the November, the November of 1899, just a few months after taking the caretaker role upon myself," Norris slowly revealed, ensuring he spent enough time on each letter to spell the words correctly; instead of rushing through.

"I began to really struggle with the experience I was encountering on a regular basis. I continued throughout the daytime as normal, ensuring I'd lock the gate before going to lock the building to provide myself with confidence that I'd not locked anyone in the burial grounds for the night.

"On the first occasion, I had locked the gate in order to go and lock up the building for the night. However, once I'd gone back to the gate, I stumbled across an unpleasant bout of confusion—the gate was open."

The girls looked at each other instantly, believing that he had locked the gate beforehand, just like their first visit when they'd pushed it to; yet once returning to the gate to exit the premises, it had come open.

As well as that encounter, they'd witnessed it again that evening as the gate opened on its own before their very own emerald green and sky-blue eyes, leaving them both extremely puzzled as to how, and why, it happened. They recalled hearing it open earlier on that night whilst Harmond was out patrolling the grounds in the blurring fog and mist.

"I was ever so shocked and quite nervy, feeling a sense of panic and haziness as I was certain I had locked the gate, but had I? I questioned myself over and over, fearing I'd somehow forgotten, or it had slipped my mind, despite doing it every day since I became caretaker. I shakily felt around in my pocket, grabbing the key. Despite strongly believing that I had locked the gate before this occurrence, I was unwilling to go home before searching the graveyard to put myself at ease in case someone had entered the graveyard, believing it was still open due to the open gate," Norris continued, giving the girls more information.

Leila emotionally felt a sense of sorrow and uneasiness that Norris had experienced this alone. Whilst they were in the building now, which offered a windbreak from the whistling wind outside, and being in the company of her sister, she felt sorry that Norris had been alone, out in the cold, and had questioned himself and his daily routine.

Due to their little adventure tonight, she could understand to some degree how frightful it would have been for him, as with so many headstones and graves of all shapes and sizes, some could be quite deceiving in how they looked, such as a person standing there, or even cause a hazard if plant holders or ornaments had blown over and were in the way of your step making you trip in the dark.

She thought about when Lilly had that awful moment of shock seeing Harmond staring down at her through the window, and Leila was on her own. Then afterwards whilst Lilly was there with her, but she had been unable to have any say or act if danger approached, as her nerve-induced trance took away all her opportunity to move, or speak, until it had passed.

Also, there was not to mention the number of different sounds and cries from nature's nocturnal animals treading on twigs, rustling branches and bushes, and appearing from all directions. "Oh dear, it must have been so scary for Norris to have been on his own whilst being in this situation. At least we had and do still have each other, Lil. Just imagine if we were on our own, and looking through the whole grounds alone, at night, in the winter, when it's absolutely freezing cold."

"Yeah, it must have been spooky. We were both jittery when it happened in front of us tonight. I can't imagine if it had happened to me on my own, I'd either run until I had a stitch from running and running and running, or I'd completely freeze and go into cardiac arrest," Lilly also sympathised. "I wonder why it happened, well, happens. How does no one know or come here anymore? It makes me wonder because we haven't heard anything about this place, and when people continually ask us about the house, they never say why. What is it? Why is it? It's confusing but also annoying because they want to know all these things about us and Mom and the house but are reluctant to tell us why."

Leila nodded along, agreeing with everything Lilly was saying. A wailing duet from a nearby fox and an owl increased the eeriness of the dark cloak of night. Rustling of the leaves on the ground as they were being blown around the fields surrounding the building accompanied the chilling, compelling composition performed by the owl and the fox. "What a noise. It sounds atrocious. Like a painful cry."

"As if they are mourning, isn't it?" Lilly added, smiling a bit as both the animals were in the right place if they were feeling mournful.

"That's not funny," Leila snapped, "but, yeah, they are actually." She gave a little smile too.

Norris revealed some more of the story once the girls were ready as he signified his desire to pursue.

"I made my way around the fields, having locked the gate for a second time now. I understood that if someone had been locked in whilst I was looking around to see if anyone was still on the property, they'd be at the gate waiting, as they'd be unable to get out. I looked everywhere, often being fooled by the sounds of twigs snapping or falling, or quick, sudden movements when animals ran into or out of bushes, carrying on with their day. A few times I'd almost slipped, with no light on me once I'd locked the building, and leaving the candle inside as I always did, for me to use the next morning and evening when walking down the steps. I had to rely entirely on the shine from the moon. It made it hard for me to be able to clearly see where I was going. I approached the final field; the one where my grave is now, only of course, it wasn't there at the time. And appreciated the fact that there were no memorials at all, so no one would be using that field or even be on that field, as there was nothing to see or visit.

"After searching the graveyard, I made my way back to the gate. The stiff, stern great load of metal had remained closed. I couldn't believe it. Had I really forgotten to close the gate before? I must have done. Have I just looked around and wasted another half an hour searching when I didn't lock it in the first place and if I had, I could have gone home and have been in bed by now? I felt so mortified and cross with myself. I opened the gate and locked it again behind me as I left.

"On the walk home, I continually feared that I had left it open, or if I had indeed locked it, how the heck did it open again? I'd followed that same routine since taking up the caretaker job role and this was the first time this had happened.

"Once arriving home, I got into bed, hoping for a good night's sleep. My head started spinning with queries. I thought I might be more tired than I felt and that was perhaps the reason why I'd forgotten to lock the gate, but I so surely believed I did. Or perhaps I was coming down with something and had got a step ahead of myself, thinking I'd locked the gate and I hadn't. Nevertheless, I was certain that I had locked the gate before locking the building and then going back to open and lock the gate so I could go home. I just seemed to have remembered doing it out of habit, like I had done every day since becoming caretaker." He effortlessly demonstrated how strongly he believed he had locked the gate; it was clear for the girls to see just how much this strange episode had affected him.

Still, both the girls were convinced believing he had locked the gate, and it came open some other way. What way that was, the girls didn't know, but didn't doubt him for a second. "I believe you did lock the gate, Norris. I really believe you did," Leila assured him, feeling certain, just as he had felt.

"Me too, I believe you did too. Since moving to Wikkington, I've seen and heard things I would never have believed were true if someone had told me them or I'd seen them on TV. Wikkington has made me less sceptical, but because there was no proof of cause for a lot of it, I still feel somewhat sceptical, but not as much as before moving here," Lilly admitted. She allowed Norris to continue, intrigued and emotionally touched by Norris's fear of not closing the gate, having felt a bout of confusion herself when she had left the gate open, and gone back to find it tied shut.

"After this, on days I'd be working here I'd get told by visitors that they'd had the same experience, only by tying the gate shut with a rope, not fully locking it. They'd find the gate open yet hadn't witnessed anyone actually coming through the gate, although they wouldn't take much notice as they came to visit loved ones, not watch a gate. They believed that at first it was other people coming and going and not shutting the gate behind them with the rope, so that the wind could have been blowing it open and shut.

"I didn't think of that at first, I thought it was me being silly and forgetting to lock it. But, throughout the daytime when it started happening, I noticed that even with the rope tied after use, and no one having come or gone from the grounds, it would still open and close unaided. Other people joked, of course, putting it down to 'oh it's a graveyard, there's a ghost', which of course was another valid idea, for those who believe in that sort of thing. Myself, I didn't really think much about it. Yes, I believed they exist, but didn't think they would be able to open and close that gate. I had a fight with it myself sometimes when it's stiff to push; it's so hard to close if you're tired or haven't the strength to push it. Sometimes it opened fine in the wind but other times it is so stiff and heavy it's hard to make it budge open, or closed. It's always been the case, but I've no idea why it changed so drastically from being able to blow open and closed in the wind to somehow taking all my strength and breath to open or close it. Sometimes the wind can blow it open but on many occasions it took all my strength to open and close it. Whist I thought it was an idea, I didn't at all believe that a ghost would be the case, so therefore put it down to the wind." Further elaborating, Norris took a long pause to enable the girls to read what he had said, understanding with such long passages they'd need enough time to write and read and then respond.

"It is heavy to shut. It's no wonder the rope frayed when we came the first time. The poor rope was trying to hold it shut all those years when somehow it would open and close with no cause, other than the wind, which often wouldn't be strong enough to blow it open. If we struggle to open it, the wind would have to be blowing a gale, a blooming powerful one." Leila laughed. "A gale!" she repeated, finding that phrase highly amusing.

Lilly thought about it logically, seeking some sort of idea as to how and why it could be happening. Although Norris hadn't yet told the full story, so maybe she could have the idea completely wrong, but even at this time when Norris went over it himself, he also had no idea as to how it became such a regularity.

"It really would. It is a hefty weight. To open and close it enough to get through isn't too bad or too heavy, but if it had been opened all the way, it would be incredibly tough to do single-handedly. Maybe that's why it is only ever slightly open, and not all the way. It would be just enough for people to get through, and the wind can't blow it all the way open either, so it could be the wind that's doing it. It doesn't need to be that strong a wind to blow it open a jar or so," Lilly explained her belief of what was going on.

"It wasn't until around six months or so later of it first happening and being witnessed by visitors, that I actually witnessed the gate open and shut purely without force or cause from a visible source. Summer days were confusing when there wouldn't be a breeze at all. The mighty anti-trespassing device would open and close every day any time without fail, morning, noon, evening or night. With the nights drawing in when winter was approaching, and all through the winter too, when there were longer periods of darkness; nonetheless, it had no impact on the gate whatsoever. It still continued to open and close each day. I thought it may have reduced it happening so often due to it getting darker earlier, and less people out and about. But still, with no proven cause, I couldn't act upon it to prevent it happening.

"That was the start of all this mysteriousness. Each day it would be the same. Occasionally it was happening just minutes after I'd shut the gate behind me. It got to the point where I'd often leave it open and then return to shut it after a while. It was quite annoying having to shut it only for it to then be open moments later. Especially when it went on all day long! This continued regularly for the best part of ten months, and then things got even weirder," he concluded, allowing them a short amount of time to write down and read this latest message, before giving a definitive, strong, singular tap, informing them he was ready to carry on when they were.

"Weirder?" Leila hesitated, wondering what else could have possibly happened, eager for him to carry on.

Lilly agreed, shown by the short "hmm" mumble she gave, before allowing Norris to continue. She felt more comfortable chatting with Norris now but still remained cynical with some things he said, as they just sounded so strange and impossible.

"It wasn't only the gate giving trouble now. Once I'd settled down and taken the gate episodes in my stride, the light started playing up.

"After finishing a shift here, one long, cold, wet winter day, I was so tired, and of course, cold. I'd completed my usual daily duties, swept the paths free of as many leaves and twigs as I could. I tidied up some gravestones that had been disturbed and dirtied in the downpour from the night before. I removed as much mud from the memorials as I could, got rid of the dead plants and leaves that covered them, and picked up and put back the many memory markers and ornaments that had been blown around the fields. I took away any nocturnal animal waste and dog and cat waste I found, also spread around by the previous day's wind and rain. I just wanted to get home by 6 pm and have a bath, and go to bed, do anything to keep warm.

"So then, I went to put the rake back in the building as I'd eliminated all the things I'd spent raking up that day, as well as the broom I cleared the paths with, and the watering can from washing off the gravestones. Lastly, I turned the light off and locked up. Once I had locked the building, I made my way back to the gate, which I had just heard squeak open, once again.

"After tripping up on a brick that I'd clearly missed when clearing the path off, I turned around to see where it was, and then I noticed. I went into, yet again, another state of panic, questioning myself and my routine, 'Did I turn the light off?' 'I'm sure I turned it off, I always do before locking up.' My mind was like a carousel, spinning and spinning with questions and huge bouts of self-doubt. It was all happening again," Norris explained.

Leila gave a pitiful tut and sigh after she had finished reading his message, "Not again! What was happening?! I bet you thought you were going mad. This is just totally…" She shook her head with her mouth wide open, searching her mind for an appropriate word to describe the situation she was hearing about, "I don't know—bizarre!"

"It just doesn't make any sense, any of this, does it? Now do you see what I mean, Lei? Sometimes hearing this kind of story is just something you wouldn't believe unless you'd experienced it yourself. It seems impossible—first the gate with a mind of its own, now the light can't make up its mind if it's on or off," Lilly projected her belief, pointing out to Leila that sometimes people are so sceptical because in a lot of situations where a ghost is believed to be present, it just seems fully impossible.

"I ventured back to the building, this time taking extra care in an attempt to stop myself tripping up or potentially injuring myself; I knew I had turned it off, as when I got to the building, the door was locked. Exactly what I thought! I knew I had turned it off after all. I always turn the light off and carry a candle downstairs with me so I can see the steps. I unlocked the door anyway, and on the bottom step was my candle. I always placed it there for when I arrived in the morning and lit it so I could see my way up the stairs." Norris made it known that he did, well, in fact turn the light off despite his sudden haze of doubt, sounding a little more positive now that both girls believed him and were also baffled by what the heck was happening.

"After unlocking the door, I steadily made my way to the

top of the stairs, an uneasy feeling that maybe someone was in there and had turned it on, maybe someone had broken in once they saw me leaving the premises, but how could anyone when the door was locked?

"I turned it off again, and did the same as before, locked the door, and then the gate, and made my way back home. I felt a little vulnerable, wearily taking small steps to avoid tripping over, and keeping as quiet as possible, afraid I was being watched or tricked. The thought of getting home was the only thing on my mind, like a desire I never thought I'd want as badly as I did that night. Looking over my shoulder several times, increasing paranoia thinking someone was following me, ready to pull the next prank. I got to my house, checking I couldn't see anyone, which might give away my address."

"How frightening! It really must have been quite an alarming situation. After already experiencing a similar ordeal with the gate, then for that to become regular, and now something else happening that you're certain you did, I mean, it would have affected your feelings and made you question yourself in terms of your own memory. I bet it was as if you were becoming forgetful, not to mention the sickly, shuddering feeling of being followed or spied upon," Lilly addressed, sympathising with Norris as recently they had both, and Susan, often found themselves second guessing their own actions when items within their household had been moved or misplaced, into places they'd not even begin to imagine or consider.

"When Mom's keys went missing, we were all in two minds about their whereabouts. After searching high and low, beginning to lose hope, we found them in the empty bathtub.

Okay, it's not the same as turning the light off to then find it on again, but it's the idea of how did they get there? And did one of us really do that because there was no one else in the house nor any other suggestion as to how it happened.

"Whilst logically you knew you turned the light off because it was part of the same routine you carried out each night, we also knew and understood that in no way did car keys need to be in a bathtub. So we were full of confusion and puzzlement as to how they could have possibly got up the stairs and then across the landing, then into the bathroom, ending up in the bathtub on their own? They physically can't." Lilly repeated one of their experiences, understanding to a degree how Norris would have felt.

Leila recalled the time they'd had similar feelings to Norris following another experience they'd encountered. "And when the television came on, all on its own, remember, Lil? It was so loud it woke us up, and probably half the street as Mom said jokingly. None of us are deaf so wouldn't need it to be on full volume, and plus none of us even liked the programme that was on. Things have minds of their own or seem to walk to ridiculous locations despite not having any legs."

Leila mimed walking with her index and middle finger strolling around the outside of the board, onto Lilly's knee and up her arm. "Things walk these days." She fell about laughing.

"They don't just walk; they seem to jump up and fly around and plummet down onto whatever surface is beneath them," Lilly added, making Leila laugh even more until little puddles formed in her eyes from giggling too much.

Norris continued once Leila placed her hand back on the

planchette, when Lilly told her to calm down.

"This happened not too often, but enough for it to, in the same way as the gate, become a regular thing. Some days, I'd turn the light off three or four times before I was able to go home because it'd keep coming on. I thought about removing the light. However, if I only used one candle light to light the room up during the winter days I was there, I wouldn't be able to see very well at all, so I had to keep the light to enable me to be able to see all of the room and what I was doing whilst in there.

"I remember one nasty, awful, winter evening, when it had drizzled all day, and was perishing all day long. I think it was minus two, but I still had to go to work. It was coming up to Christmas, and of course people came to visit their loved ones' memorials, and bring flowers, ornaments, wreaths too. Not many visitors came that day. I can't really blame them. It was probably the coldest, longest, most undesirable shift I'd had so far, and still, to this day, is a day I still consider my worst. Being on my feet all day, unable to get warm, the only heat from the candle I had by me, and the gas light we have in here now. I continued my daily jobs, all part of my care-taking role; only, I felt I hadn't completed them to my best ability, as it was just too cold and miserable to be out there for so long.

"Once 6 pm came, I felt as though I'd been waiting for this time to come forever! I turned the light off, and locked the building, but another three times I had to return to open, turn off, and lock the building before I could make it to the gate and vacate the grounds. I promised myself that if it came on again, I'd have to leave it and go home. I couldn't stand being outside in it much longer, I was beginning to feel hypothermic, my fingers tinting purple.

"It didn't come on again after being turned off for the fourth time, enabling me to venture home along the dark, muddy path, through the kissing gate, the ice cold wind blowing sharply, slicing across my face and ears, and blowing the leaves at my side along the same route I was taking." He described everything so well, grasping the girls' attention and portraying the story exactly as it happened. Giving assertive singular taps after finishing each snippet of information to the girls.

It was clear to them how much it meant to him, for whatever the truth he was yet to reveal, was given with such time and detail in each message he portrayed.

"Minus two, that is so cold! I can't believe he actually came to work when it was that cold, I wouldn't have even got out of bed." Lilly laughed, as she spent most of her time in bed anyway.

"You're always in bed! Or at least if you're not *in* bed, you're lying on the bed. The planchette is leaving marks across the board, look, it's left an indented trail."

Lilly smiled at Leila's comment, 'always in bed'. "It's okay, it doesn't matter. When it moves, we push down firmly on it to keep our hands there so when Norris moves it, we indent it by pushing it down so hard to keep it steady on the board. It does make your arm ache though, doesn't it? Our fingers will be tinted purple soon when the circulation in our arm cuts off."

"It hurts too when you write all the letters down. It's like a game of hangman." Leila laughed, encouraged by Lilly's smile to laugh a little more. "Oh yes! Purple. The best colour ever," she added, unsure of what could actually happen if her circulation did happen to cut off.

"Shhh, okay. Norris, carry on," Lilly quickly rushed. Both girls were engaged with every word Norris spelt out, raising their eyebrows and their facial expressions altering, revealing their emotions to coincide with Norris's snippets of information.

"Wait," Susan paused; a sudden realisation filled her mind. "How did you know my surname? And my first name? My name in general? How do you know my girls are safe?" She stared right into Mildred's brown eyes, before closing her own and raising her left hand to hold her scrunched-up face, pushing out many tears. "Oh, no. You? Where are my kids? What have you done with them? Why are you here? How did you find me? Who are you? If you have hur…"

"Excuse me! I am in my nineties, dear, and I'd never dream of committing such action, nor do I wish to be accused of it. You are upset, far worse than upset, and I completely understand. I can assure you that your children are fine. I cannot tell you just yet of any information regarding their disappearance, nor how I am aware of your name and address. When all is done, I shall, until then, we wait," Mildred quickly interrupted, disallowing Susan to pin such blame on her, yet withholding any information regarding the awful situation.

Norris continued on, reciting the next passage of information. "Whilst I was getting ready for bed, following a quick bath, heated by the fire in my lounge, I went to my bedroom window to shut the curtains as most people do. It was only 9 pm but darker than in a coal mine. I felt afraid, uneasy, I thought it was because I wasn't feeling well—being out in the cold, and wet all day, with a minimal source of heat. That's enough to make you feel as though you're not your usual self.

"Peering through the curtains, as I pulled them both to, I felt haunted, shocked, and discouraged at what was before my tired eyes. Just as I'd had a bath too, and felt nice, relaxed and clean. I felt the sweat trickle down my face, and my heart about to pop out of my chest. I suddenly felt sick, more ill than I could explain, and I had to catch my breath, but to breathe I was in so much pain. I could see through the trees, the trees in my back garden, and the light was coming from the building, it was on! On again!

"I didn't feel well enough to go back and sort it out. After all, it may have come on again if I'd gone back to turn it off, and I didn't want to be going back and forth all night long. I didn't know how to explain what was happening, well, I didn't know what was causing it, so how could I possibly explain it to myself? I managed to calm down, overcame the state of panic, and looked out of the window again, only this time, the light was off. I just couldn't understand it, one minute it was on and then it wasn't shining through the trees at all; it was off! At that point, I decided to go to bed, making sure to check again during the night if I woke up to use the toilet or get a drink." This particular passage of news interrupted the relaxed feeling both Leila and Lilly had been experiencing once knowing they weren't at any risk by being inside the building.

Lilly gave an involuntary shiver, cuddling into her thick coat for warmth, covering the goose bumps prickling her now covered, thin arms. She snuggled into the faux fur lining on her coat hood, pulling it over her head and moulding it round her, only displaying her face.

"I just can't get my head around all of this," Leila grumbled as if she were reading the instructions of a new product which in fact wasn't even the game the instructions were explaining about. She fantasised about being in her own bed now, huddled under her duvet, fast asleep, Hooter perched on her shoulder or lying at the side of her, clutched by her hand, and not here in this old building.

But Norris was ready again. "Thankfully, I slept the night through, and felt a lot better the following morning. I drew back the curtains, letting the daylight in, and was ever so thrilled to see that the light was still turned off," Norris narrated how his night had been following his traumatic experience rather like a game of playing table tennis to and fro with the indecisive on and off light.

Lilly looked across at Leila, who was still processing the message. "Oh, my word. Don't you remember!" her mouth fell wide open. She repeated "oh, my word" six times, shaking her head as her baffled mind brought up a memory from not too long ago.

"What? What?" in confusion, Leila replied, after just reading the fully composed message. "I don't know what you're on about."

"YOUR BEDROOM!" Lilly yelled, flapping her hands with her eyes wide open, as if she was trying to find a pen to write something down, only writing would take too long.

"What about my bedroom?"

"Remember!! Remember when there was knocking going on at our house and Mom had gone to work and Mom said if we heard any knocks, we had to go to her bedroom window and look who was there because her bedroom is on the front? Well, remember you woke me up, and there was no one there, and I said for you to go back to your bedroom and if there was another knock we would look? And then you called me, and I came to your room so quick, and we saw the light on, the light in the building, this building, remember now?" Lilly desperately related, hoping Leila would remember.

Leila quickly recalled that moment, reliving the memory they'd experienced not too long ago. She shuddered, the hairs on her arms standing tall; little goose bumps covered her pale skin. "Oh yeahhh, I remember. Wait… that means… his bedroom, is my bedroom now! His bedroom was my room! And he could see the light… just as we saw it."

Leila looked around the room, before staring back at Lilly, and stared around the room again, as if she were following a fly. She shook her head. "I can't believe this. What a mess! Why are we noticing it all? What did we do wrong to end up in this position?" She sighed, trying not to burst into tears.

"It's okay. Remember, Norris told you, well, us actually; he wanted us to come here so he could tell us what happened. So far, just as you said, throughout the whole time we have been experiencing these odd happenings, not once have we been harmed. He said us doing this will help free him and bring an end to all this. I don't know if I believe it or not, but the least we can do is respect the fact if Norris is real and is being honest. He hasn't hurt us, and to me that's the most comforting thing I'm getting out of all this right now.

"We have both been in the same room as a ghost—Harmond. He saw us, could hear us, and he also didn't harm us, apart from when he accidentally nudged your shoulder. I believe that somehow, this is something we needed to do, and with other people speculating and asking questions about our home address and querying any experiences we have had, if Norris said we can bring an end to it all, I'm sure it'll be worth it. Mom can't sleep properly, eat properly, we can't keep hiding this from her. We need to do this, and if it doesn't work? We can't say we didn't try. We go home and tell Mom everything, and we find a new way of coping with it—an exorcist? Priest? Anything or anyone who can help us bring all this to an end, but I think we should give Norris the chance to try and sort this his way, because right now, we haven't any idea how we can stop this," Lilly supported her sister, and involved Norris in the explanation even after she was still partly sceptical. Providing him with a chance to tell them everything and sort this all out, she felt it would be worth it if it worked, yet if it didn't, they'd reveal all to Susan, and go from there with what they could do next.

Norris tapped the board, diverting the girls' attention back to the board as he was eagerly ready to deliver the next part of his story. The girls nodded to each other each time he tapped, showing each other that they were ready too.

"I got used to the light situation, often getting fed up having to keep turning it off before leaving, but if I ever got home and the light was on in the building, I'd refrain from going all the way back to turn it off. I made all the visitors aware of the situation that, like the gate, the light now had started to do things without any physical cause or action to explain how. They were glad of being made aware, especially as they'd often see it as well, and were fearful it was someone who'd broken in or was messing around in there during the night.

"The individuals who came to visit their loved ones' memorials had also started to feel a little uneasy with all of these baffling incidents becoming far more regular but felt a lot more comfortable now they'd heard it from myself and felt a little more settled that I was aware that it happens, as were other people who came to visit too.

"With a gate that opened and shut all day and all night, and an accompanying light, it was beginning to be the talk of the place both in and out of Wikkington. Some people would come from different areas to see if they could witness any of it happening. However, when people came to catch a glimpse, it would often upset and interrupt people paying respect to their late friends and relatives. Therefore, I had to intervene as they were being pestered by these people, and had consulted me about their dissatisfaction. It was disturbing their visits to their loved ones' graves. The reason for visiting the graveyard for some, was to be the first to capture any sighting of the unusual events. I'm afraid however, things got even more weird, and it just kept on proceeding that way," he concluded, finishing his piece on the mind-of-its-own light.

"People would come all this way to Wikkington just to see that? Those poor people who actually used the place for what it was intended, to wind down and be around their loved ones. Whilst it would attract attention, it wouldn't be as pleasant a visit for those who came to the graveyard to use it for its purpose of admiring their loved ones' memorial," Leila sympathised.

"You only came here to look, in the first place though, Lei."

"Yeah, to look and see all the graves and people's names, their ages and the date when they passed. I love graveyards and seeing how people are loved. I didn't want to come here to see mysterious gates and lights. We didn't even know about the place and all these things when we moved here, so I didn't come here for that. If I did know, I may have wanted to come and see if I could witness it, but I wouldn't come and interrupt people paying their respects," she pointed out, truthfully. "That's just really rude."

Lilly agreed with everything Leila said. "It is rude. It's quite disheartening really. If you wanted to come and see it, that's fair enough, but for them to be disrupting people paying their respects like talking to them or paying more attention to the gate and the light than the person or family who were heartbroken over their late associates, that's just wrong. I'd have liked to have come to witness it too, well we have now, but if I was born back then, I'd have liked to have come and seen it but I'd have asked the caretaker about it, not just consider myself to be more important than a deceased relative or friend and interrupt the grieving person as they attended to their loved one's headstone."

After their short discussion, they took to the board and planchette, nervous as to what the next revelation was as Norris had described things as getting 'weirder'.

"I can't see how things can get even weirder, well, I kind of can because of the past two items with their unprovoked abilities, but if there's any other instances of items doing things as they please, I shall lose my mind completely," Lilly grumbled, yet was fascinated too.

"I noticed that there were more things starting to happen and with no sort of apparent cause. It seemed for me, and for

169

you both now I guess, that different objects around the graveyard had somehow come to life. Perhaps that's not the best description in view of the location, the graveyard, but it very well seemed that way. Strangely enough, this next ordeal took longer to show itself than the distance in time it had taken for the light to play up after discovering and witnessing the gate opening and closing.

"For a few years after those incidents, at least, and it had never once happened before throughout all the years of me being caretaker there up to that current period, so when there were no disruptions for a good few years after the gate and light had started self-operating, it came to me as quite a shock!"

Lilly shuffled, quickly glancing at Leila before returning her eyes to the board.

"I was once in the field of graves on the front, where the entrance is and, of course, people would walk by quite often. I was going about my daily jobs as usual, chatting with the mourners who were coming and going to their loved ones' headstones, paying their respects to the individuals lying below them; I was greeting members of the public passing by on their journey to wherever it was they were going, when suddenly, out of nowhere, the bells began to ring." Norris cut that message abruptly, leaving the girls confused for several seconds expecting him to continue.

"What's strange about that? It's a graveyard, churchyard? Anyway, that's what bells do?" Leila giggled.

The hard, concrete floor caused Lilly to shuffle as she was so uncomfortable and her bottom slowly going numb. She crawled onto all fours and rocked back and forth to help the ache in her back from hunching over the board. "Bells?"

she queried, sighing uncomfortably as her bottom still remained numb despite the short period of relief.

"I myself, just as you say, took no notice as that is exactly what bells do. And it wasn't until a regular visitor collared me whilst I was sweeping the damp, slippery path, and said, 'I thought the bell ringers were on holiday this week!' that it dawned on me. Yes! They were on holiday!"

Lilly closed her eyes and sighed, at this new discovery. "I feel sick now from rocking, but even sicker after knowing that," she added, shaking her head and gulping as if about to heave.

Leila dropped her eyebrows mid-thought, suggesting a possibly more realistic scenario with regard to the likely cause as to why the bells had started ringing with no known or proven cause.

"It was probably just someone sneaking into the building, taking advantage and playing them—like kids. Maybe they were watching you and when you were out in the front field they crept in and started playing them. I guess it's better than them stealing something or vandalising the place and the graves." She repositioned herself so she was lying flat on her stomach on top of her coat, one hand on the planchette and her other holding the pen.

Lilly grasped the torch, jolting it dizzily as she struggled to get in a more comfortable position.

"That was the first thought I came across when discovering the bell ringers were in fact on holiday—kids. At that moment of realisation, and my confusion had subsided a little, I discontinued sweeping the path and went to investigate. I was happy with the condition in which I had left the path before attending to the bells. There were less than a quarter of the leaves left on there than there was that morning when I had first started, so for me, knowing it was less likely someone would slip over on the leaves as they navigated around the burial grounds, I felt contented and sure to be able to go and see what was happening with the bells." Norris always allowed the girls time to write and read what he had spelt out, and also a few moments where the girls could talk or converse about what he had said, before continuing to his next message.

Leila again lowered her eyebrows with a look of confusion as to Norris's use of the term "investigate". "I just can't seem to follow what on earth is going on. It's like once one item starts working on its own accord and becomes a regular thing, another piece of equipment decides to join in." She shook her head repetitively, squinting her eyes at the message as if she had read it wrongly.

"Norris, I don't mean to interrupt but I am really starting to grow anxious as to Harmond's whereabouts. He is not here, and we can't see him. Because you said, 'in his absence' you will tell us all this information. But why can't he be present whilst you're doing so? And if he comes back, will this revelation have to be conducted at a different day and time like if he comes back, what happens then if we haven't finished?" Nervously looking around the chilly room, Lilly made Norris aware of how long Harmond had been gone, displaying concern about what happens if he came back before Norris had finished the revelation.

Norris helped to put Lilly at ease. "I will explain. I am getting there slowly, don't worry. He is fine, he is walking the grounds and will be gone a long while, he keeps himself busy."

Lilly nibbled her lip, warily glancing up at the room door, hesitant lest Harmond would somehow, without sound or indication, enter and start patrolling the room, as he had done previously. The nervous flutter in her stomach mirrored that of a roller coaster, dipping and diving, plummeting at such a high speed. "What if he comes back and we don't hear him, and suddenly we turn around and he is standing in the room and has already heard some of it? What then?" she queried, unable to see how Leila and Norris could remain calm knowing this was a potential scenario.

"Carry on…" Leila instructed Norris, "Shut up, Lil, Norris has already said, he keeps himself busy. I'm sure Norris, more than anyone, knows what Harmond gets up to and what he does. Just trust him."

Lilly sighed deeply, "Okay, okay. Sorry for asking, jeeez."

"No one. No one. Nothing. The door to the room, this room you are in now, was locked, and I was the only one who had the key. It hadn't been opened that day due to the bell ringers not being present, and as for my tools, not needing any but the broom for the majority of the day, I had locked it that morning when I'd come down and hadn't been up there since 9 am. I'd left my lunch-box in a carrier bag at the bottom of the stairs for easy access. I never locked the main door due to me going in and out, but always locked the door to this room. As I say, I'm sometimes out of view of the door to this building but I know if anyone does get in, they're unable to get into this upstairs room and pinch the tools. The two bell ringers had a key each, but as they were on holiday, there was no evidence of anyone being in the building at all, let alone the room.

"This, after this first episode of it happening, the gate and the lights, continued for a few years. Once again—this mysterious act soon became normal. I was starting to forget what normal was before all of this had first begun.

"It continued in the daytime for many years, but it was when it started happening at night, that it became a big problem. Not only did it annoy people, waking them up and ringing at all hours, sometimes for an hour at a time, it was frightening for all of the residents in Wikkington. With no logical or proven cause to blame it on, people were afraid, and upset by the noise. Although it was a blissful tune, as many of those who lived in Wikkington agreed, it was not very much appreciated when it was disrupting their sleep and frightening them and their family and friends. So they, the bells, were eventually taken down."

"What the…"

Lilly stared at Leila, sharing the same thought but ensuring Leila didn't revert to bad language.

"Fu-dge," Leila exhaled, utterly taken aback.

"This is just getting worse and worse now. I want to go home now, like right now." It added more stress onto Lilly; suddenly she jumped. "OH!" she screamed as one of the tools fell from where it was leaning against the decaying brick wall. She placed her shaky hand upon her racing heart, breathing rapidly from the very sudden scare. A magpie landed on the open window-like sill, as if the wind had stopped him from flying, allowing him to catch his breath before continuing his journey.

Leila's torch light had now become so dim she was unable to see her hand when she held it out in front of her face. The poor lighting gave no visibility of her near or far surroundings. With no spare batteries that worked, having failed to charge when Lilly didn't turn the plug on at the wall after unplugging her laptop charger, they used the last and final torch they had left. "We will have to only use your torch, Lil. I haven't got anything to provide light. You'll have to come and sit here for us to be able to see the board properly," she explained. The room light was also an almost useless source of lighting too, flickering like the flame of a candle.

Lilly shuffled round by the board, all hunched up in her coat. Her rosy red cold nose poked out from her coat hood slightly revealing her eyes. She brought her knees up, resting her chin on them. "You write again, and I'll hold the torch. I am so cold I can't move my fingers."

"Okay," Leila agreed, sitting poised with her pen.

"We'll have bloody pneumonia tomorrow. And you will actually be ill then, Lei, you won't have to pretend," Lilly muttered, dissatisfied.

"I actually don't feel well. I feel sick, terribly. Norris, please carry on, tell us as quick as you can. It is reallyyyy cold in here now and we aren't feeling well."

"For a long time after the bells had been taken out, the only issues present then were the gate and the light. It is more frightening and a lot more confusing to those living in Wikkington, because of course, no one visits here anymore. The whole graveyard was abandoned and with no caretaker to take over my role after my passing. It has entered a state that both Harmond and myself would forbid happening if we were able to. Like you both and your mother, some people aren't aware the bells were removed due to it being so long ago and people no longer talking of it or being made aware of the story behind it all. Your mom heard the bells ringing this morning yet had no idea that the bells aren't any longer on the premises.

"When I was caretaker, even for a decade and longer, until I passed actually, and following the time the bells had been taken down, new neighbours who came to live in the area would attend the graveyard. But, when walking past it they would alter the route they were taking if only to see if there was a couple getting married, or to pass a compliment on the harmonic chorus echoing across the small Wikkington area." He gained more and more of the girls' attention with every marvellous revelation he enlightened them with.

"I've just thought," Lilly devised a potential suggestion which could contradict the story, "If less people know about what happened regarding the bells, or whatever this story is leading up to, why then, if less people know about it, is this place not used, visited, or attended to anymore?"

"Oh yeah, I never thought of that." Leila nodded, agreeing with her sister's somewhat sensible and interesting query and initial thought.

"I bet, though, actually, thinking about it, people could have known nothing of it and just came here to search for their loved ones' graves, you know those who are interested in the family tree and visiting archives and memorial grounds to hopefully find graves of their ancestors, or old friends? Or like when neighbours did walk past to hear the bells and see the happy couple or generally walked by without taking any specific detour or route to purposely see the graveyard, as not everyone would be so interested in coming to see it, if they witnessed the gate opening and closing and the light coming on and off at all hours, it could have really scared them. This therefore could have been preventing them from coming close by or using the graveyard due to fear. If these people told any friends or relatives about it, or they seek the information from other people with regard to the unexplainable actions they'd witnessed, less people are likely to visit—they'd be scared witless.

"If some people heard that a graveyard was totally unoccupied but at all hours during the day and night different elements of the place would come on or open and close or ring with no apparent cause, it'd be pretty distressing and most likely intimidate them, therefore leading them to avoid going to, or near the graveyard altogether.

"I guess an office or a shop or somewhere unrelated with the dead would be less frightening, but with it being the place most associated with the dead, it's got to have frightened many people. If someone tells someone else about it or mentions their friends or relatives have experienced it, it's going to have put many people off even wanting to go to visit, or go anywhere near the graveyard in the first place," Leila explained.

"Hmm, that's true. It's weird, though, because people were asking if we'd experienced anything in our house. That's not the graveyard, it's our house, what's our house got to do with this graveyard?" Lilly recalled.

Leila reminded her sister that their house was Norris's home, therefore as he was the caretaker at Wikkington Graveyard, and no one had been there or knew what happened exactly, there must be more to the story. "Maybe, I know we didn't tell anyone, nor did Mom, about the happenings at home, but maybe someone lived there before us and had similar experiences to us. If they did, they're bound to have told neighbours, family members, friends, different authorities about it, and then it spreads to even more people."

"And, I bet the estate agent knew but didn't mention it to Mom when she was considering purchasing the house, as it'd put her off. Of course, that's IF a previous family had experienced any unusual happenings while living here," Lilly added, slowly understanding now and adding her own thoughts and suggestions to help steadily consolidate their individual interpretations and ideology referring to the abandoned, unused and once well-loved graveyard.

"But some people, like myself, if I'd heard from someone that the local graveyard, or of any graveyard really, had been experiencing such a varied, or any, type of unfathomable episodes of phenomenon, I'd want to go and see the place and visit, so that I could see it for myself and maybe witness something," Leila discussed, having a completely different view and sense of adventure, where as Lilly's was the total opposite.

She understood, acknowledging that other individuals would desire to see it happen, as Leila would, well did, and has. "You're right, other people would love to witness it too, especially those maybe who disbelieve in that sort of thing. But this could actually be the reason why less and less people, and now no one, visits here anymore. Most likely because they might have come here and witnessed it themselves, thinking they wouldn't be afraid and most likely think it wouldn't faze them, but when they were here and having been present and witnessed something unexplainable, it could have really scared them, and put them off coming again.

"As well as that, those who have witnessed those situations the same as Norris had, and us, and other members of the public, if they had told someone, it could deter those people from coming also. Almost like a whole wall or barricade of fear turning everyone away from the one thing, or place, they had felt quite comfortable in. Visiting their loved ones and having moments beside their memorial to remember them, is suddenly turned into a place full of horror and distress, the total opposite of a peaceful, beautiful setting to spend visits on special days and deliver flowers and comforting messages to their family and friends. Talking to someone whilst you're at their graveside can be so comforting and makes people feel as if their loved one is there and listening and taking in what you're saying, and they know that you're there.

"For this to have been taken away from them due to the most peculiar, mysterious, obscure events with no justifiable source, I imagine would be more upsetting rather than scary to a lot of families as they'd be terrified to go and visit but even more upset that they can't go to visit their gravestones anymore because of the irrational fear they'd feel the whole time they were here. I bet a lot of people thought if they went there, they'd never get out, or start having things happen in their own home, they'd probably fear a ghost or entity would follow them home. I imagine it got to the point where people would be absolutely petrified and frantic just to walk past this place, being unsure as to what on earth they'd end up witnessing next. Imagine someone walking by and suddenly their deceased friend or family member was walking around the grounds, it'd frighten the life out of them, excuse the pun.

"I didn't believe in any of this ever, I wouldn't have even

given the thought of ghosts and spirits and all things sinister the time of day. I believed ghosts were bad, and only come back to torment people, and the fact people gave up coming here in the end suggests that they shared the same belief as me. Yet, from this situation we are in now, Norris never came to hurt us, but to only attempt and fulfil his desire to deliver and reveal the truth, whatever that truth is."

Leila agreed with her sister, taking off her hood as she had begun to warm up again. She felt a warm feeling close to her heart, joyful with pride that Lilly had yet again made known how her belief had changed towards spirits. After her constant grumbling and being so ratty, Lilly had finally managed to reverse her belief altogether.

The magpie still sat peacefully on the open windowsill ledge, spreading out the feathers of its tail like a fan, along with fluffing up his body plumage, to keep him warm whilst he rested. Both Leila and Lilly watched, admiring the authentic imitation of a paper fan, adhering to their only suspicion, saluting as they made eye contact knowing exactly what each other meant. "One for sorrow."

The gas light, poorly emitting a minimal glow flickered as the flame began to dance. "We'd better let Norris carry on, before this light, and the torch gives up and we can't see anything." Leila laughed, imagining the pair of them having to feel across the walls to get to the door, and to try to make it down the stairs without tumbling. She took a deep breath from laughing and placed one of her lovely warm hands on the planchette next to Lilly's not so warm one, and she clasped her pen and paper ready to scribble down the next message.

Norris continued, "When people would come by and

show interest in bells playing, praising the bell ringers and hoping to catch sight of the married couple, but of course as there's no church here, there wouldn't be any marriages nor funeral services taking place, only cremations and burials. It was hard to explain all of this to those passing by. Marriage and funeral services took place at a church elsewhere, not located here in Wikkington itself. As for its whereabouts, I can't be entirely sure which one that would be, but the family and friends would come here to have and watch the burials. Or they'd come here following weddings, to sometimes have pictures taken; especially as when Harmond was caretaker here the graveyard had such positive and well-known reports, it was often referred to as one of the best-kept and most beautiful graveyards in the country, so coming here for some nice photos on their wedding day was a popular thing back then.

"Of course, since Harmond had passed, and I took over, I never really felt I would ever be able to live up to the standard which he'd single-handedly delivered and maintained throughout his career here, but I certainly did my hardest to ensure the place did not slip too low in standard to the point where it grew a bad name and reputation, erasing all Harmond's hard work and the exceptional, outstanding reviews and scenery he had achieved for this place.

"Sometimes we would ring the bells here to celebrate loved ones' lives and memories as they were laid to rest, showing signs of respect and helping bring the family closure and sentiment. Being a graveyard that could play bells at funerals, well, cremations and burials, it shocked a lot of people who walked by presuming to see a wedding taking place, and the happily married couple, so when explaining it was only a burial, it seemed rather odd to them. I was shocked myself actually. So of course, I took it upon myself to continue in the footsteps of Harmond and carry on ringing the bells when people were just married and came by for photos, or when a cremation or burial was taking place. Although, what was even odder, was having to explain to the passers-by that the bells had in fact been removed. The bells were heard still, despite not even being here. Only then the ceremonies were a little quieter, and not so frequent, maybe perhaps four times a year which wasn't so disrupting, but as you can imagine, still terrifying for many people," he elaborated.

Leila and Lilly discussed how different it must have been back then to have bells rung at someone's burial or cremation, and how the tradition nowadays is only with weddings. Marvelled, Lilly exclaimed how lovely and precious it must have been for the mourners to receive a bit of closure, and how each time they heard the bells, it would act as a reminder of their loved one's memory.

Leila commented on how pleasant Wikkington Graveyard must have been for married couples to decide to have several photos there and visit such a place on the happiest day of their lives. "I know some people get married at church and then have pictures where some graves pop into the shot, but there isn't even a church here, so they'd have to be really, pleasantly made up with this place for them to have chosen to hold their wedding photos here!" She dreamily envisioned how beautiful the graveyard and grounds would have had to look for herself to choose to have such special photos taken here.

"With one freakish happening after another, it seemed

that nothing was impossible any more, that literally anything could happen and it had somehow, in time, become to be accepted, " Norris had explained the third issue he'd experienced during his time as Wikkington Graveyard's caretaker; firstly, it had been the gate, then the light, and now, the bells.

Leila added to her previous memo, "I think the ringing of the bells at a funeral, well burial or cremation, is a nice idea. You're celebrating the life and memory of somebody and even though it's a sad time, the tune is beautiful and adds a bit of happiness to a not so happy situation. I think it's lovely." Leila proudly showed her support for such an unexpected, non-familiar action or situation she'd not thought of before or even imagined happening.

"Lei… Did you not see what he said?" Lilly interrupted Leila's loving praise. The information from Norris suddenly hit Lilly like a ton of bricks.

A great big huff came from Leila, directed at her sister for interrupting and cutting her off as she was talking. She bit her tongue the best she could whilst the raging anger inside her filled her with heat and she scowled in annoyance. "Why do you ALWAYS cut me off or discourage my ideas? Yes, I can read what he said. I'm the one who wrote down what he said. Do you want me to read it to you? Did you not manage to see what he said??" she sarcastically snapped in aggravation, shaking her head with fury.

Lilly rolled her ocean blue eyes at her sister's drama, "You just can't help yourself, can you? I am trying to point something out to you—I thought you had finished what you were saying. Yes, I think it is a lovely idea too, but my attention drifted from that once I remembered something from this morning, but hey, it doesn't matter, does it? Forget it."

"What?" Leila asked, shrugging her shoulders with a sour look on her angelic face.

"What? What?" Lilly queried, mistaking Leila's "what" as if she was somewhat actually interested in what Lilly was going to say, before previously biting her head off.

"Go on."

"Go on, what? I don't know what you're talking about." Lilly looked at her sister, puzzled yet feeling the need to smirk as she knew she had got her sister's attention one way or another.

"Arghhh, just say what you were going to say," Leila snarled, grunting and sighing in agitation as Lilly was beginning to wind her up.

"No, it doesn't matter," Lilly coaxed her along, "Finish your complimentary appraisal—tell him how I also agree it's a lovely thing he did by being caretaker off his own back, and ringing the bells in people's memory, and for a big congratulations as the couple's married life was just beginning. I think it's really special, wonderful."

"Tell him yourself," Leila entered a sullen mood, crossing her arms as Lilly had managed to get on every single one of her nerves—yet again.

Lilly refused to argue any longer, snatching the planchette out of Leila's hand and placing it down on the board in front of her. "I know you probably cannot stand me right now, Norris. After all, I've not been the kindest, and this would have all been sorted sooner if I'd have believed in you. I am so sorry you have had to suffer so long due to my sceptical self. I am sorry for all I have done to hinder you from obtaining peace and freedom. I'm sorry I labelled you as bad, assuming you were only here to torment and terrorise us. It's making more sense now, and I am asking you this, Norris, forgive me for asking, but where were the bells?" Lilly pleaded, now realising her entire perception of him had been wrong and that she couldn't have been any more wrong. She gulped, fixed her eyes on the board, refusing to blink.

"It's okay. Nearly there now and then this is all over," he replied rather more hurriedly than he had done with any messages in the past, as though he was very grateful and accepting of her help and apology. "Above your head, either side of the light."

"So, my mom said she heard them this morning, only they aren't actually here. If they were above us, that means the bell-ringing sound would have come from here, this building, this room. But if the noise happens without the bells even here, how will it ever stop?" Lilly, seemingly desperate to get to the end of all this and return to normality, queried, conversing with Norris by herself whilst Leila sulked and whined at the back of the room.

"Sometimes," he began, preparing to inform Lilly with news she'd not heard nor expected before, and probably didn't even in the long run actually want to know, leaving her covered in goose bumps and experiencing palpitations.

"When people pass away, they only remember places as they were when the person themselves was actually alive and on Earth, not how the places have been refurbished or altered since their passing. When Harmond was alive, on Earth, and was the caretaker here, the bells were always here, his entire career here, they were always here throughout his duration. Now, to us, the bells aren't here; we can't see them and that is because they were taken down many years ago. I cannot see them, and that is because when I passed away, the bells weren't here. It works from the time you passed, rather than the start of your life, it's from the end. Yes, they were here in my lifetime as I started here in November 1899, and they were removed in 1906, yet I can't see them because at the time of my passing, they were no longer here.

"Harmond can see them clearly, and whilst every day he comes here, in his mind he is ringing those bells. But you don't hear it and neither did I after a while, apart from a handful of times a year when they'd ring, that seemed a little odd. The only way it can be heard by humans is by the amount of energy and power and strength put into it by Harmond himself.

"As each day passes, the amount of time he has been deceased increases; therefore, he's requiring more and more strength each day and it is likely it will get to the point where he may well lose the power to play them altogether. Of course, if the bells were here, the amount of effort needed for him to play them would be lower than it is currently, but as they aren't even here for him to play, the strength which he needs in order to make that bell-ringing sound is increasing daily.

"I'm unsure if Harmond will ever be able to notice that the building has in fact changed, minus the bells, as well as the glass window that used to be there when I was caretaker, and Harmond also. I don't recall exactly how it smashed, but it was extremely near my death date, but visiting the place with the window no longer there, I can remember it did once have one. "

Lilly's hand ached from holding on to the planchette

which had felt as if it had been circulating the board for the past hour just on that one message. "I'll be getting very strong muscles when all this is over," she joked to herself, as both hands were equally active, one writing, and the other moving around the board.

As Leila was still in an off mood, Lilly had to improvise and rest the torch on the part where her legs were crossed, so she could have both the board and the notepad in view together. "What… Oh my life. That's so mesmerising. That explains why things have happened both when you were caretaker, Norris, and with Leila and I noticing it all! It all makes more sense! WOW!" She shuddered in amazement. Her blue eyes shone brighter than the Caribbean Sea, with surprise. She continually shook her head, entirely baffled each time she had to take a few moments to allow it to sink in.

"Norris, if this is being rude, then I am very sorry; however, you are providing us with all of this information with regard to your personal experiences as caretaker here, but how is this relevant to Leila and I being able to help you to rest and change the beliefs of others by enlightening them to the truth? If we, well, don't know what the story is that we are supposed to be proving was incorrect, how can we alter what it is you want us to do?" she contemplated, trying to absorb all the information and feeling an uneasy amount of insecurity and fear of letting Norris down. She allowed Norris time to portray his significant, strong, stern tap on the board showing he was ready to carry on. She reached out onto the planchette and placed her hand on it.

As the rain hammered down, creating a misty fog and unclear shadows lingering in the graveyard grounds, Leila turned immediately from the window, jumping aback and startling Lilly, causing her to jump too.

"Frigging hell, Lei, what the hell are you doing? You scared me to bloody death!" Lilly snapped sharply, feeling as though a tight belt had hurriedly been tied around her chest. "God, I feel like my trachea is being squeezed and my heart is about to leap out of my chest," she whispered in a startled, gasping manner.

"I... I... think that I... might knowww," Leila slowly dragged out each word, allowing "knowww" triple the length of any other word as she examined the thoughts in her head and what she may or may not know in reference to this whole situation.

She suddenly remembered a specific night, and how she believed there was a possible link. Without knowing the story, or if what she'd even considered is actually a fact of anything at all to do with it, she flinched and took several steps forward as the dynamic, compelling iron gate slammed shut, as though she were standing right next to it.

Moments later she moved across to the building's window to be met by the sound of graceful, delicate footsteps, seemingly a lot heavier and defiant as they approached the building, closing in the distance between both the individual whose steps they were, and the building and the girls themselves. The nearer the footsteps came, their increase in volume and intensity grew, and an angry atmospheric feeling came about.

"But?" she halted, displaying that her self-claimed "insane, probably a load of rubbish idea" quickly felt ridiculed and idiotic. "Never mind." She discontinued, walking away from the window having just caught sight of

Harmond strolling past the building and into another part of the graveyard.

Lilly followed Leila with her eyes, unwilling to ask any questions, but focused all her attention on her until she came and sat down beside her. "Ready?"

"Go ahead," Leila certified, placing her hand on the planchette.

Norris took a short moment before beginning his next message. This giving Leila an uneasy feeling, sprouting an impression in her mind that he was feeling a little anxious about what Leila may have thought and if her thought was in fact valid, and how she would react.

"After a constant battle several times a night, I was finally used to part three of the unexpected rituals. Whilst throughout the day and during summer nights, or at late evening, when the daylight allowed you to see, all three weren't as worrying or nerve wrenching. Whereas, during the winter nights and evenings, when darkness approached and set in, it started to take its toll.

"The bell ringing was what was terrifying the people the most, especially those living close to the graveyard. I know Wikkington isn't a very big village, but to be living so close to the graveyard, even closer to it than I used to and where you live now, ringing so suddenly and at all hours of the night, it would be very worrying. People had reported to me on numerous occasions that they would more often than enough, wake up jumping from being startled and feeling as though they were resting their ear right next to or even onto the bell as it sounded so loud. Of course, it goes without saying, this disturbed their sleep, not to mention left a lot of folks afraid to go to sleep as they'd awaken in all of a frantic state if the bells rang.

"It seemed the gate slamming and light coming on and off whenever it pleased had a minimal effect on the neighbourhood in comparison with the bells. It was also known to cause a lot of night terrors or leave people fearful suspecting it was a sign of a ghost, or even a demonic entity or poltergeist. They imagined it being inhuman and without any logical explanation as to what was causing it, and not able to pinpoint what it was. It made it extremely difficult to prove that the cause was in fact in no way associated with anything of that sort.

"Of course, we couldn't prove it, and therefore that meant people couldn't rest or find any relief from the idea of it being something along those lines. With no reassurance in being able to sleep and put an end to such disturbances and fears because there was no justifiable cause apparent, we couldn't deter their mind from this belief. This also meant there was no way of actually being able to stop it either," Norris delivered the message.

The girls read in puzzlement, feeling tense and unable to fathom a way out of the problem; it seemed each new snippet of information was growing more and more bizarre, and convinced Lilly that at one point in the near future a message would seemingly reveal a solution.

"This whole story, or tale, or whatever it is, it just seems to be getting weirder and weirder like totally out of control. It's like some really strange sort of long joke, only it's getting funnier, but not in a laughable type of way like a standard, normal joke. It's more like what the hell is going to happen next?" Because to the girls, the whole what's going to happen next concept, was so surreal they literally couldn't guess what the next revelation would be. "You just can't guess what's going to happen next, because whatever it is, you just can't guess it; it's madness." Lilly shook her head, confused and feeling unable to process this whole load of information.

"Like a weirder, stranger type of funny. Like a funny feeling in your stomach, only I feel it in my head instead. I feel as if my head can't hold the information any more and it's all spilling out of my ears and I'm trying to catch up with it, but it's gushing even faster and I can't sort it into order or understand exactly what's going on." Leila mimed with her hands as if things were pouring from her ears and onto her little shoulders, right down to the floor.

Lilly flicked viciously through the previous pages of all their notes from tonight, then raced through them back to the most recent. "Look, there's a lot of things happening in this entire story. Only, it's all to do with here, this place, Wikkington Graveyard. Yet there's not a single sighting or proof of any cause for any of the different series of events that have happened here. No one knows why the light comes on, no one knows how the gate swings open and shut without any physical or any sort of human interaction with it, and the bells ring without there even being any bells here. I just can't understand it."

Leila sighed, looking around the rim of the ceiling as though all the information was printed up there. She cast her eyes lower onto the various tools scattered around the old abandoned room, wondering how on earth they'd been here this long and not been stolen or tampered with by anyone due to the graveyard being discarded for such a duration of time. "How on earth had no one been there or tried to break in, surely anyone would have done if they knew it was empty?

Wouldn't they look around or come here to shelter? Maybe they were scared due to everything happening here?" she queried over and over in her mind.

Lilly flipped the pages over again and again, deep in concentration. She sat quiet for two minutes, staring at some of the tools lying on the floor and some leaning against the wall for support. She rested her left elbow on her left knee and cradled her head in her left hand. "I just don't get how we didn't know, or haven't been told about any of this prior to now. Of all the people here in Wikkington, and all those people who kept questioning us about any mystifying and odd situations and occurrences, not one of them told us why. They hadn't told us a single thing, and I think that is something that would never have happened where we lived before. The community here doesn't seem to be as welcoming as we imagined it would be. We have had some people on our doorstep asking us about the peculiar behaviours in our home, yet didn't even provide a reason why, they just left it." She ranted in annoyance and upset.

Leila on the spur of the moment piped up, "Wait!!" She flapped her arms with her mouth open. "Where is Mrs Berkshire from?"

Lilly thought hard for a moment or two, scrunching her forehead up and lowering her eyebrows as if that allowed her to retrieve information, or at least look as if she was actually thinking. "Ermm, I don't know really. I mean... I would have thought she would live nearer to Wikkington as it takes her less time to get to 10 Wikkington Way than our old house. It takes her ten minutes now, it used to take her around twenty minutes. I'm not entirely sure of her whereabouts, but I'd certainly say much nearer to Wikkington, maybe the outskirts? Or maybe she lives a few streets away from us and just does two miles an hour which takes her the length of ten minutes." Lilly laughed jokingly.

Leila smiled and rolled her eyes. "Well, it takes Mom longer to get to work now than it did when we lived at our old house, remember," she contributed.

Lilly sat deep in thought, nodding at Leila's reminder. "Yeah. My back is starting to ache again, I think the cold is beginning to make all my bones ache. I'll be frozen here soon in this position and turn into ice and be stuck here forever."

"Don't be silly. I don't think it's that cold now. I'm getting used to it. Mind, we have been here hours now. I bet Mom is worried sick. Oh Lil, what if she has woken up and has found us missing? She could telephone the police or be out wandering herself and then she might go missing because she gets lost. What will we do? What are we going to do? What—?"

Lilly put her right index finger to her lips. "Shhh! We will soon be home. Let's carry on chatting with Norris. We must be nearing the end of his story. I'm not exactly sure how much weirder it can get. Mind, I wouldn't put it past it, the way it's gone so far anything could happen. We'll find the ghost of Elvis next and find out he lived in our house too." Lilly laughed, although a little apprehensive because she could literally be told some other uncanny thing in a matter of seconds.

"You fool." Leila laughed. Leila flitted her eyes from the board, to the notebook, from the board, to the notebook, hesitating before her signal to Norris to carry on.

"Wait, before we do, Lil, text Mrs Berkshire, see where she lives."

"NO! It's the middle of the night, first of all. She's not going to tell us where she lives, she's our tutor. She will think we are going to rob her or spy on her or she'll report us for harassment. You can't contact people in the middle of the night requesting their home address. She will want to know why we want to know, and what we were doing up at that time. Not to mention would most likely contact Mom and pass on her worries as to why we are so desperate to obtain her residence address so urgently that we have to contact her in the middle of the night."

"Just ask her the name of the village that she lives in. You don't have to ask her for her address, the full number and street name and all the rest of it, just the village."

Lilly shook her head, quickly refusing the idea, and declining the second choice of just asking for the name of Mrs Berkshire's village. "Can't," she muttered, "see, no signal or connection. Even if I wanted to text Mrs Berkshire, I couldn't. She wouldn't receive it until signal or connection came back in range, and that'll be when we are home anyway. Plus if I did text her, we wouldn't be able to receive her messages, or anyone's messages and calls, for that matter so zip it."

Leila felt hurt by Lilly's harsh tone. "I only said it so we could ask her and find out if she lives in Wikkington, then she could tell us about all this information and happenings and everything else we have encountered. If she knows, she would tell us. But fine. Don't ask her then."

"Lei I just told you, even if I wanted to text her she wouldn't receive it anyway and neither would we get her reply." Lilly repeated.

"What if Dad wanted to contact us? How does he ever

know if we have connection or not? He isn't with us. Or what if we were in an emergency and needed to contact the police or emergency services? Then what?" Leila queried.

"Just forget about it we aren't in an emergency, but we will be if we don't let Norris carry on and we get chilblains and turn hypothermic. Come on now quiet. And why would Dad contact us? He works away on a cruise ship it could be any time wherever he is. He knows what time it is here in the UK and when's best to call. Anyway, he isn't going to just randomly pick out from thin air that his two kids are sat in a graveyard canting to the dead." Lilly laughed.

A loud, thorough tap drew both girls' attention back to the board, cutting the Mrs Berkshire argument short and drawing it to a close, along with the Dad talk too.

Leila waved her hands and tapped Lilly repeatedly in case she hadn't heard Norris's assertive tap, which couldn't have actually been much louder.

"Yes, yes, I know, I heard!" Lilly tutted, mimicking Leila's wavy hands and wriggled around into a better position, as her bones were beginning to ache a lot more.

"As the time went on, the number of bell ringing occurrences during the night was increasing and I'd received a number of complaints about it frightening children, and some adults, to a point where they feared not only going to sleep, but afraid that there were spirits in their home or rooms. Of course, this led to a lot of children and adults experiencing nightmares and night terrors due to the anxiety and disturbed sleep routine."

Staring at the notes that Norris had just given, Leila felt a little absent herself. Her initial thought about the story Norris was telling made a little more sense.

"Nightmares, anxiety, night terrors," those three terms circulated her mind. She understood how they must have felt; those three terms were far too familiar, and she'd gained increased knowledge of each one of them. She displayed no signs of this discovery, revealing no suggestions to the information given in support of her original idea.

"Lei!"

She jumped, as if Lilly had just hit her with a shovel around her back.

"What are you doing? I shouted you three times and you didn't answer? HELLO? Lei!"

Realising her mind had wandered off drowning out all sound other than her own thoughts and voices within her own head, she turned to face Lilly. "Sorry, I…" She rubbed her eyes with her little clenched fists,

"Youuu?"

"I'm tired. I must have been a bit dazed, sorry." She rubbed at her eyes again, as if it somehow proved she was tired despite her actually not being as tired as she should be, when the realisation and thoughts in her own head were preventing her from concentrating on anything else. She was alarmingly awake, far from able to settle. "What anyway? What do you want?"

"Oh," Lilly said, "Oh, nothing, just are you ready? Put your hand on the planchette so Norris can carry on."

She placed her little hand on the planchette next to Lilly's, nibbling the inside of her lip whilst she felt uncomfortable about what those three words were defined as and what the people had experienced for them to be labelled as night terrors, anxiety, and nightmares. "No, wait," she interrupted before Norris could even begin.

Lilly sighed triumphantly, blowing a raspberry at the end and rolling her eyes. "URRGHHH!" she growled. She watched as Leila took what felt like an hour, staring down at the notebook, in utter fixation at the most recent message Norris had given them. Lilly rubbed her eyes and the bridge of her nose; she was desperate to just get all of this over with and go home. She was brimming on the edge of utter annoyance, as well as nervousness towards how Susan would be feeling, and behaving with regard to her discovery of both her children missing, presuming that she must have woken by now.

Inhaling deeply, Leila brought herself to question Norris about the nightmares, night terrors and anxiety, asking him to give an explanation or definition as to which he recognises these to be, and also some examples of these phrases and the emotions he had been told about during his time as caretaker.

"He's already said, Lei. Anxiety, thinking spirits are in their house or room and not sleeping very well. Dreaming about it or being woken up by the bells with no one actually responsible for playing them, therefore causing nightmares and night terrors. I imagine they felt how Mom would feel if she knew that the bells which she heard ringing this morning didn't actually any longer exist. You know, scared. The only difference is, whilst the bells were physically still there until they were removed, then how could they specifically ring automatically. Well, without any proven or specific cause.

"And as if that wasn't frightening enough, on top of that the gate was opening and closing at all hours making that terrible screeching sound, then a bang as it closed shut, or flung open and hit off the fence, and not forgetting that light turning on and off of its own accord throughout the night. I think we would be flaming terrified too! So it wasn't just the bells that would have caused the nightmares, night terrors, anxiety, the other elements of the graveyard played a pretty big part in it too," Lilly explained, defending the residents' perfectly normal and expected thoughts and reactions to such strange events.

Leila agreed with Lilly, perfectly understanding the effects it would have had on Wikkington locals at the time. She nodded in agreement but put across her reasoning for quizzing him.. "Yeah, I get that. I completely get that. But what I was *actually* aiming towards was how he himself defined those terms like: anxiety; nightmares; night terrors. And, what those people who had said to have experienced those terms or watched someone else experience those terms, how they personally felt," she explained. She cuddled up into her coat as tight as she could. Feeling vulnerable, she looked out into the deep darkness of the night, as if a thousand stalking eyes were watching through the building window, staring right in at the girls like they were prey.

She gave a very quick glance over at Lilly, instantly diverting her eyes back into the mysterious black sea, the moonlight rippling over the heavy grey clouds. "Don't forget, in the late 1800s and early 1900s illnesses weren't as well understood nor spoken about too often, let alone diagnosed and having treatment provided. Mental health illnesses even now, in this day and age, aren't totally understood by everyone."

She felt her own anxiety levels increasing, coming to boiling point as if her ears were about to release steam like a train engine. She sat gawping out at the haunting darkness, feeling as if it was closing in on them and would soon burst into the room through the window, the front door and room door, and make her and Lilly disappear forever.

"Hey, calm down. Don't look so worried, Lei, we are here, and look how long we have been dealing with all this. It's been months, and we haven't got hurt. I don't think Norris would actually allow anything to happen to us. I know I was sceptical before, and I didn't exactly make this easy for him to have us on board. But you are the reason we are here tonight and bringing it all to a close. You persuaded me, you helped me push through the fear of coming here. And, you're helping Norris. Without you we wouldn't be here now and dealing with the final stage of all this array of brain-boggling happenings. He wouldn't let anyone hurt us, Lei, you should know that. You're the one who told me that, after all."

Leila hung onto her sister's every word, nodding as she repeated what she'd just heard over and over in her head and letting it sink in. "Yeah. I was just a little, well, anxious I guess, at what Norris will reveal next."

Placing one of each of their hands on the planchette, the girls awaited Norris's response. Intrigued, but uncertain at what his reply would be they devoted all their attention to the board, forgetting the darkness and awful crippling wind swirling around them like a tornado.

"Anxiety is what I'd define as nervousness. An intense feeling of nervousness regarding a situation or thought. For example, it caused some individuals to encounter a very unnerving feeling when they thought things were in their room, or when they were suddenly woken by a rather beautiful ringing of the bells, only it was far less beautiful after finding out no one was actually there playing them in the first place. Nightmares—a nasty, unpleasant dream which frightens the person having the dream. Night terrors occur when someone is asleep, and they're totally unaware they're having them."

Leila swallowed, looking warily at Lilly, who didn't take any notice, staying fixated on the board.

"Night terrors can cause someone to scream or shout or thrash about in their sleep. In terms of the anxiety, many parents had informed me that their children would experience great difficulty in being able to settle of a night time—this in case of the bells waking them up, fearful it was a spirit or ghost causing it to happen or there being a spirit in their room alongside them whilst they were sleeping.

"This then led them to nightmares, highly likely because they were so focused on the horrid torment they may face or wake up to during the night, it'd be on their mind and play a huge part in their dreams—well, nightmares. The poor young souls would wake up crying and shaking, desperate for reassurance from their parents or guardians. They'd tell the adults about their dream and what happened, yet plentiful adults had told me that they'd mirrored the same dream, or one similar to it. Some residents who didn't even have children, or hadn't lived in Wikkington very long, had all involuntarily lived in those profoundly comparable unpleasant dreams. A lot of residents in this village had also on a number of occasions woken up and heard the bells as if they were right next to their ear. However, they weren't always sure if it were in reality, or in a dream," he explained, providing Leila with his personal definition of the phrases, and accompanying them with several different examples.

"One family in particular had many prolific, terribly disturbed nights' sleep and would often wake up once or twice during the night, after a prolonged fight to try and settle and nod off to sleep. Assuming the bells had woken them, they'd go to the bedroom window and look outside and listen hard. Upon discovery, they were certain the bells weren't always to blame for waking them, despite them hearing them as plain as can be when awake. Whenever they looked out of the bedroom window, they'd always see a tall, smartly dressed man walking along the end of their driveway, as if passing to walk up the street. Every night that they looked out, this man, which they described to me, would be passing their house.

"Many others have mentioned seeing this person over the years, always patrolling the streets at silly hours during the night," Norris disclosed.

"Gosh, my arm aches from all this writing. My eyes have gone funny and the cold makes them feel as if they're burning. Read it aloud, Lil, please. My eyes hurt, they are blurry, please read it aloud." Leila rubbed at her eyes and scrunched her face up tight.

Lilly cleared her throat, reading what Norris had said. "Wow!" she managed to vocalise after a long pause.

"Who is this person?" Leila thought, "Who wanders about at night at all hours?"

Lilly gave a great laugh, chuckling as if she'd just heard a brilliant joke ten minutes ago and she still couldn't get over it. "You're so funny, Leila, you really are. US! WE are doing exactly that right now. We wandered the streets and now we're sitting in a graveyard building in the early hours of the morning, doing stuff on an Ouija board when we're one hundred percent NOT meant to be using one, and having a good old chinwag with some ghost."

Leila shook her head, giggling. She soon realised it was right and laughed some more. "Oh yeah." She chuckled. "What are we like?" She took a few moments to stop laughing, yet it was hard. "But… ALL night, EVERY night? This story is getting past believable now. I bet we won't be Leila and Lilly after all this is over. We will be something from back in time, ages ago with old-fashioned names like Maude and Mary-Anne. There's that many new identities I can't keep up with it, I'm slowly beginning to forget who I am." She giggled some more.

"It's time," Mildred announced, after gawping at the clock, frequently analysing the time in between conversing with a very upset, worried, and ill feeling Susan who was lying on the two-seater sofa, rubbing her bloodshot eyes with her shaky knuckles. She lay still, her head so painful and throbbing. Her stomach in a terrible tangle like that of multiple necklaces all jumbled up together. Her fingers twiddling the fringes on the blanket Mildred had found out and covered her with whilst sitting and providing her with company.

Mildred repeated, "It's time."

Susan turned her head slightly to look at Mildred. She glanced at the clock; her blurred vision made it impossible to be able to accurately read the time. Time didn't matter to her, nothing mattered right now apart from her two girls. "For what?" she quizzed Mildred.

"We must go now. I'm developing a nervous quiver in my stomach. This is how I know it's time. We must go now. Quick."

Susan didn't move an inch. She stayed just as she was,

as if she'd not heard a single word Mildred had said. Or at least if she had, she was providing the impression she'd not processed, nor understood it.

"Susan! Come on! Honestly, chop, chop, your girls need you! Now… more than ever." Mildred enthusiastically shuffled around the lounge, thrusting Susan's coat at her and dropping her shoes at her feet.

"I can't. I need to be here in case they come back. I'm sorry to have kept you. I'm a terrible mom. I'm so sorry, Mrs Bluethorn, for disturbing your night," she muttered apologetically, her mood lower than a snake's stomach.

"No, you must come with me, at once. They need you now; we must get there as soon as possible. Before it," she gulped, "I know where the girls are, we must go now." She continued persuading Susan. "Gather the neighbours, shout, scream, knock on their doors and windows. We need as many people as we can find. The girls need you; I need you; Wikkington needs you. Before… before it's another year too late," she blurted out, the words pouring from her mouth in a torrent making Susan finally get moving.

Susan cried frantically with relief that this stranger had suddenly informed her she knew of her daughters' whereabouts. "Oh, oh, quick!" She slipped her shoes on and hurtled after Mildred who'd already gone through the front door, and was striding up the road.

Norris hurried to hastily regain the girls' attention, performing one of his determined heavy taps on the board to alert them, desperately trying to push on with the story.

The unexpected great tap startled Lilly, flinching as if someone had just held a giant rock and dropped it onto the board.

The torch light did a short dance as Lilly's hand jolted, shooting up and back down so fast erratically casting a golden globe onto the board like a glorious bold sun rising and setting in all of a second.

A little gardening trowel gave a rhythmic rattle as it rocked from side to side. "S'truth!" Lilly yelled in shock, "My bloody heart nearly stopped!"

Whilst Lilly was crawling over to the trowel to discontinue the quickly-already-annoying rattling it made, Leila placed the planchette back onto the board. Lilly had knocked it off accidentally in a sudden panic-stricken jump when Norris made his last dramatic tap. Laying her hand on the trowel, Lilly made it quiet again.

A ferocious loud heart-stopping slam followed the aggravating trowel only seconds after the irritating rattle had ceased. Lilly flopped onto her stomach mimicking an attitude as though she had just been shot. Leila clutched at her chest staring at the building room door, believing that someone had just sprinted up the stairs and forcefully pushed the door open, slamming it off the building room wall. She held her breath after the gigantic slam, fearing the building was about to fall down when the door hit the wall with such tremendous violence.

It was as if someone has pressed pause on that specific moment, making everything stop completely. No sound, movement, nothing.

Lilly lay panting. Five minutes passed before she or Leila made any communication with one another.

"What the heck was that?" Lilly lifted her head, assuming all was clear following the undisturbed silence.

"What the heck was that?" she repeated, looking around as if the cause was somewhere in or around the room.

"I don't know, but it was so frightening. I thought the building was about to crumble and fall down. I really, really need a wee now."

"I honestly thought we had been shot, I really honestly did. I'm trembling. Come on, let's get this sorted out and over and done with. I want to go home. I want to see Mom and tell her everything and put an end to all this. I fell right onto my stomach. Literally, I thought we had just been shot. My heart is thump, thump, thumping!"

"Me too. I love you, and Mom, so much," Leila whispered, still holding her hand on her chest as the rapid thudding in her chest and her ears hadn't fully settled.

Leila and Lilly huddled close together, each with one hand on the planchette. "Norris, please tell us all of it now, and as quickly as possible," they pleaded. The nervous tremor of them both made it harder to fully grasp the planchette to prevent it slipping. With Lilly's hand on top of Leila's for steadiness Norris began.

"That horrendous slam-bang is what your mom heard this morning. It happens rarely now, very, very rarely. The terrific clang is the noise the cremator here used to make once it'd finished, you know, cremating." Norris revealed. This time with no long-winded story, almost as if he had told them already a thousand times about the cremator, when indeed the girls had no such clue.

"What? Cremated here? A machine? Where?" A Million questions fizzled their minds.

"The machine was taken out in 1900. It was my first year of being caretaker here and it used to make that awful sound when it'd finished. I hadn't arranged to have it removed; it was something that Harmond had arranged prior to his death. He'd said it was too noisy and no longer wished to have the machine as it was also in this room. Of course, it took up so much room and wasn't the most pleasant thing to be around when bell ringing, or moving the different tools. It made me jump on most occasions, even though I knew it was going to happen and expected it. It was still a sudden surprise."

Norris gave a short pause.

The girls looked at each other, still gasping. Lilly chuckled. "I thought I'd been shot! That machine itself is enough to cause someone a death by the hair-raising slam it suddenly impounds on you, especially when you least expect it."

Leila exhaled deeply, her body slowly returning to normality. She held her head as all functions returned, the gushing of the blood to her head eventually decreasing to calm, and eliminating the violent pounding.

"The row is very rare to hear these days. Sometimes the noise happens randomly. I believe it's something to do with the light. The gas emitted from the cremator fuelled the light above you as it is a gas light, the one here now.

"I am glad it was removed, especially as cleaning it out and hauling the bodies up those stairs was heavy work. I think when I finish explaining all those happenings I experienced for so long and are still happening now; I think they will stop altogether. I don't know about the light, though. It's had no gas supply since 1900 when the cremator was removed, but it still works and comes on, I don't know how. I used to use a candle to light it that is how I would turn it on but as you know, it just automatically comes on its own accord.

"I've been the one behind all the things you and your mom have experienced, but Harmond was responsible for it all when I was alive. As I previously mentioned, the events that have happened can be due to Harmond, but like I said, the prolonged time since his death date, the more the energy is needed by him to be able to fulfil these tasks.

"I have been responsible for what you have witnessed at home. As you live in my old house, it seemed contacting you would be the easiest way to get things sorted." Norris provided a reason as to why contacting them would be his best chance at being able to set the story straight.

"So the incredible bang Mom heard was the cremator! But how? If it's not there anymore, and you didn't make it happen, how did it?" Leila queried, a discombobulated look on her face.

Lilly scanned the room imagining and pinpointing where she thought it would have been. "It'd take up a lot of room! And to be here around it whilst bell ringing or fetching tools and all that, it just seems so weird, and... well, eerie," she said observingly.

Norris replied right away, revealing some more information, to say that even he couldn't shed a light on it as he clearly had no idea either.

"Sometimes it just happens. I think maybe over time it won't be heard any more. I think all the events will end once the truth is out. I can't confirm, but I really do think so. I don't know how it does it, I'm sure. Maybe it used to do it when Harmond was caretaker and that's why he'd arranged to have it taken out and completely removed from the premises. Or it could be him managing to create the noise, just as he did with the bells and the light and gate. I know he was responsible for all of those, but the cremator noise I can't be sure. After all, I don't know. I can't explain it as I just don't know."

Leila rested her head on her hand, supporting the left side of her face. She sat still, as if re-reading that same message over and over.

"A lot of stuff has happened in this one graveyard. Like, I don't get how, though, or why? Like if you didn't see or know Harmond, how do you know it was him doing it when you were caretaker? Why him of all people? His grave isn't visible here," Lilly said, looking down at the board as if it was a computer screen and she was on a video chat service with Norris.

After an apparent muteness, Lilly shuffled her hands in her pocket. The pause spilled into minutes. Several. Norris was moments away from delivering the news he'd been waiting to impart for all these years to finally help bring all his worrying to an end. The emphasised silence made Lilly's heart pound, as if it were about to break out of her ribcage.

Leila fiddled with the zip on her coat and nibbled the inside of her bottom lip. The noise resembled the gentle sound of a caravan awning being zipped open early in the morning and zipped closed again in an evening on holiday. It bought the stretch of silence to a close.

Norris gave four consecutive taps on the board, sending forth a sudden vibration and disturbing the still planchette, causing it to slide off the board. He was ready…

Susan and Mildred rapidly departed 10 Wikkington Way,

shouting and screaming as loudly as possible, and hammering on several houses' front doors along the way, in an attempt to awaken the occupants.

"HELLPPPPP!" Mildred yelled, a strong firm voice for an elderly person, somehow louder than Susan's beckon. However, she had been shouting and calling and crying and vomiting all night, irritating her throat.

"Why are we doing this? Where are the girls? Mildred, we need to find them. Please, if you know their whereabouts, HELP THEM! HELP ME! I feel so unwell I feel like passing out. I can't take much more... I well and truly can't." She lagged behind slower, weaving along the pavement as if she were rocking side to side on a skateboard, gripping at walls and nearby lampposts for steadiness.

"It was a nasty wet night. Well, evening. But it felt like night having been dark since around 4 pm. The dark always seemed to make it feel hours later than it actually was," Norris broke into the tale of that night, the story which he had been waiting years to reveal, to eliminate the lies and rumours circulating his passing.

"I was feeling very cold and tired. We'd had terribly awful winds the night before and leading into the early hours of that morning. Therefore, I had plenty of different ornaments and flowers to attend to and a great carpet of leaves to get rid of and sweep up off the pathway and throughout the grounds.

"I'd spent a good hour returning all the ornaments, teddies, and flowers, all the escapees from the wind, returning them to the right graves and headstones they'd been blown away from. I stood up any ornaments or flowers that had tumbled down or been tossed around by the horrendous gale. That was tiring. Very tiring. And that was only the one field! It took another hour and a half to accomplish fixing and putting back together all three fields, well two really, as the third was empty, and return the wandering property back to its original place.

"I had to have a little sit down and a drink, recuperate.

"After the recuperation period, I started working on doing something to the leaf-covered path. It lay before me—a great red carpet, featuring patches of orange and yellow against the gorgeous red majority. The path was alight, with all the reds, oranges and yellows. I stood back, admiring the flame-like leaves dance in a little breeze. I had to do something, though, an autumn picture would soon be a terrible Christmas present if a visitor were to slip and fall on the slippery mounds covering the damp cobbles.

"I got the rake and began clamping down on the leaves like the mighty claw grabber in an arcade amusement game and scraped them a foot or two either side of the path. Well, that one section anyway.

"The cleared cobbles peeped out soon, growing in number until there were more cobbles showing than were hiding. With all the raking and cleaning of the path and me treading over the path a lot, the lovely bright yellow leaves had become a very murky, dirty shade of yellow. The fiery orange leaves now closely resembled a dull brown, mixed with the mud. The red still bright but losing its shimmering shine." Norris happily recited the story, each moment getting closer to the truth.

"Two hours passed again. The dull ache in my right hand, wrist, and higher and lower arm from raking reflected the weather: dull, painfully cold and tired, was how I was feeling. The mountains of leaves looked at least neat and were freeing the damp path. Despite only resembling the height of a molehill, raking them felt like the piles were of equal height to Mount Everest."

This comparison made both the girls chortle, similarly to their comparison of the building stairs feeling as steep as the Empire State Building.

"I made my way back up the now fully cleared cobbled path, following its twists and turns, collapsing onto the second step of the mountain steep stairway up to the room. I dropped the rake and it landed with a sharp clang, and I landed with a deep thud, sitting still to regain my breath. The cold seemed to have taken my breath too, along with my energy.

"I felt giddy with hunger, lightheaded. I crawled up onto the next step. Twisting myself around I slowly guided myself to stand up, placing one hand either side of me and clutching the wall for much-needed support. The steps seemed to be proving more of a challenge than ever. The cold misty day had been one of the worst we had ever experienced, with the wind the night before and into the early morning, I am shocked it didn't blow a tree over! It was such a strange day. The energy was just being extracted from me."

Leila interrupted Norris's flow. "All this writing is extracting energy from me too!" She smiled, and then sniggered louder when Lilly gave a smile too.

"Here, swap, you hold the torch. Stay sitting there, though. I'm right-handed and will keep knocking your knee if you sit to the right of me. Pass me the notebook, and you can take control of the torch. Okay? Good."

Leila held the torch proudly, her aching arm grateful for the rest. Her other hand ready on the planchette, ready for Norris's continuation.

"I made it up the stairs and sat down in the room, this room, to have my sandwiches. It was warmer up here, still cold, but warmer, but more certainly not at all comfortable. I was a bit shocked, really, as I hadn't seen anyone come to visit the graveyard so far that day but had heard the gate squeaking and groaning as if it was being open and shut. 'Probably got a mind of its own again,' I said to myself, no longer fazed by it as it was accepted as normal.

"I checked the time and it was just nearing 3 pm. It'd start getting dark soon, although there wasn't much daylight outside anyway, just dull miserable graphite grey. I still had to bring the rake upstairs, and even though it only took a matter of seconds, hoisting it up the steps single-handedly made it feel like it took hours.

"After a short fight, I'd got it up the steps and back into its place in the room, leaning nicely against the wall. A couple of leaves clung onto the rake end, impaled. They soon became loose though when the rake head was lying on the floor, freeing the little flames of not so nice red orange and yellow now, and littering the room's concrete floor.

"I decided to stay in the building and try to make it a bit tidier. Although only I used the building, I did like to make it clean and tidy the best I could, especially as there were plenty of tools around and it'd look too cluttered if they weren't all visible and standing with a significant gap between them. However, you can't really do much tidying and cleaning with concrete flooring and bricks. I had a quick scan round either side of the steps to see if any leaves or mud or moss were lurking there, then planned to focus on the upstairs.

"Only, I didn't find any leaves or moss or mud, even right in the corner where the circular concrete flooring met the vertical wall and created a tiny degree of an angle. Right in the acute angle was a picture frame, a picture, looking as if it had been gently placed there for hiding. It was a newspaper article, about Wikkington Graveyard, the previous caretaker, Harmond."

The girls gasped, mouths wide open as they quickly turned to each other.

Lilly shook her head and gulped, saliva dampening her dry throat caused by suspense.

"Why are you shaking your head?" Leila's confused expression was back on her little rosy face.

"Because that doesn't mean it was Harmond doing the different happenings when Norris was caretaker. It's not proof."

Leila still looked thrown, her eyebrows twitching. "What? He didn't say it did. He only said he found a picture of the newspaper article."

"Yes, but it doesn't mean Harmond did all those noises and ferreted about with the gate and the bells and was playing with the light."

"He didn't say it did prove he was or that he knew. He said he found the picture frame with the picture of the article in it. Let him carry on telling us, Lil, don't be so quick to make up or twist the story."

Norris carried on. "I gently made my way back up the steps, my left hand gripping the wall, the picture frame in my right hand. I lowered myself down slowly, desperate to not drop the picture frame or throw myself down, my back leaning against the sharp knobbly bricks and small cushions of moss scattered around the wall. I focused hard on the picture of him, and the lovely article that assisted the equally pleasant photo.

"'The building holds burial equipment inside, and other garden tools to keep the grounds tidy, and certify everything is done to an incredible, unforgettable standard. The caretaker who won best organisation and ground keeping standards every year since 1854 has passed away. An exceptional worker who enjoyed his job so much and wanted to keep the graveyard looking lovely, and a place for visitors to come and visit and respect their late friends and family members' memory. As he spent the majority of his living years working here it seems any caretaker to follow will have to have high expectations and standards to match, or better. After explaining how much time and effort he dedicated to ensuring Wikkington Graveyard was a lovely, tidy, quiet, scenic place for mourners to visit their loved ones, and those resting, he has been awarded this due to his dedication and determination to fulfil mourners' lives with a splendid peace of mind that their family members and friends are able to rest and be visited in a well-respected and taken-care-of area, and how truly well looked after and tended to the gravestones are after regular cleaning and profound groundwork in the mourners' and deceased's best interests to make visiting their family members' and friends' graves a positive experience and show they are cared for even if they have passed on. A well-deserved and earned award, and so sad to be awarded it days before his passing.'

"I felt shocked, bewildered. I just didn't understand how

I hadn't come across it sooner, or even knew about it. I just didn't understand how I hadn't found it earlier. All those years I'd worked there and not once had I seen it. I focused hard on the picture of him, standing proud as he accepted his award for his super talent, time and dedication. I racked my brain stressfully, trying to recall if I had ever seen this man in my life, I didn't recognise him. Not at all. His big hazel eyes and his black short hair and the spectacularly neat shirt, no, I didn't recall seeing this man at any time."

Leila smiled, feeling more comfortable knowing that Norris had no recollection or any specific details as to how the picture had made its way downstairs and tucked itself up in the tiny little angled corner by the steps.

Lilly gave an extremely loud sigh of relief and clasped at her pyjama top by her heart, full of comfort and ease that Norris had also not found the article and frame despite finding it extremely hard to believe he hadn't seen it or even come across it before.

"That's what I felt like when I saw it! I just didn't understand how we had missed it and not come across it before. It was buried deep in the grass and unless you were looking for it, well even if you were looking for it, I doubt you'd look here, well, maybe if you knew it existed and had fallen. But unless you were purposely seeking it out, you would probably never find it. I had no idea it was there until I trod on it. If we knew it existed, we could have looked there because it would make sense for it to have fallen out of the window. But we don't know how long it has been there; surely someone would have found it. Or at least the wildlife would have trodden on it or been able to move it or have hurt themselves on it because it is sharp. It just seemed to have popped up from nowhere," Lilly explained, still confused but happy that Norris had also had a similar strange experience with it, especially as it was tucked right in the corner. The picture falling out of the window would make more sense than it magically appearing in a small corner by the steps, all tucked away. "What a discovery! It's just weird how things disappear and then reappear with no explanation or knowledge of them even existing."

Leila nodded efficiently, repeating "mhm" when in agreement with Lilly's comments.

"I sat for ages, smiling at how lovely he was to dedicate his time to ensuring the graveyard was of exceptional standard. I felt a fraud compared to him. I could never match up to the brilliant standards he'd achieved but I had done my best and took it upon myself to help keep the place to a substantial quality and expectation.

"I put the picture in the window, facing out so that he could admire the place he'd devoted so much of his time to for so long. I used a sharp edge of a knife and scraped all the fluffy clouds of moss off the walls and windowsill. The bubbles of moss littered the flooring as they fell after being cut away from the old yet strong damp bricks. I swept up all the little balls of moss and collected them up in a bag to tip out amongst the trees and bushes at the back of the graveyard's field, out of the way.

"By this time, I felt really unwell, like I was spinning but my head was spinning twice as fast. I sat at the old wooden chair that we used to have, but I avoided using it as much as I could as the legs used to squeak as it gently rocked on the hard, slightly uneven concrete floor, often giving me a short scare when it rocked with me on it. I was afraid I was going to fall off. I preferred sitting on the floor. I couldn't fall then, or the chair wouldn't give way. I had a good ten minutes of sitting and restoring my balance and back to normality for myself. The chair was right by the window, so I gently eased myself up and lightly plonked myself on it. I rested my elbows on the ledge, cupping my chin and head; the lovely refreshing cool breeze hit me right in the face, discarding the sudden sensation of vertigo.

"I watched the area of the grounds which were visible from the current location I was at and in, admiring the wonderful surroundings. The blades of grass created an optical illusion as if each tuft contributed to a quick performance like ripples on a wave in the sea. The falling setting sun left an assortment of reds, oranges and yellows as it peacefully brought the daylight to an end and the evening and night to begin. Each gravestone and memorial stone stood proud, tall and bold, the navy blue to black night sky highlighted each one beautifully, looking just like a city skyline behind bungalows, houses, blocks of flats and offices as the stones varied in size and shape. The stunning setting of the sun and the rising moon created a gorgeous masterpiece of a scene fit for a card. It was hard to believe how heavenly the graveyard and sky perfectly complemented each other, being one of the most unlikely suggestions and places you'd expect for such a wonderful scene. It was heavenly, gorgeous, beautiful."

Both girls thought of the delightful image Norris had described, smiling at his words, portraying an immaculate sight in their imagination. Outside right now for Lilly and Leila there was nothing quite so lovely, just darkness. Pure darkness.

"Just black… black, black, black, like a black blackboard," Leila mumbled.

Lilly gave a shallow sigh, almost as if she was expecting it to be mid-morning and light and be anywhere but the graveyard. She stared out at the depth of blackness that had swallowed up all the surroundings outside of the building, shaking her head.

Leila gave a loud yawn, tired and holding her head due to the onset of a harsh, sharp headache.

Lilly curled up and pulled her coat over her like a blanket, huddled up as if she were settling down into bed. Only this bed was rock solid, and she wasn't in bed; far from it. "I'm so cold now and tired too. I think we should head home now and come back later tonight to finish the rest off, after we have had some sleep. If Mom finds us missing at this time of night, she will be going spare. She could be out looking for us and be anywhere, absolutely anywhere. She might be miles away back at our old area, she could be calling the police or crying or have a shock and go into cardiac arrest. She could be up at the hospital to see if we are up there." She trembled, her eyes filling with tears and her voice shaky.

Leila cuddled up to her, cradling Lilly's head on her bony shoulder, wrapping her arm around Lilly's back. "Don't cry, Lil, it's okay. I just know it's all going to be okay. We have to stay, we have to, for all this to be over and bring it all to an end. Trust me, okay. I trust Norris, and you need to trust me. Then we will go home to Mom and explain everything and get on with our lives. By doing this for Norris, it will help him, and it will help us, it'll all be back to normal and we can get on with whatever we want to do." Comforting,

Leila reassured Lilly that things would be okay, and the importance of how it won't only get better for them, but for Norris, and everyone in Wikkington, and especially Susan, who was most terrified of all the strange happenings, more so than Lilly, and a heck of a lot more than Leila. She twiddled and twisted a lock of her hair around and around her finger.

Lilly both looked and felt very unsure. Her shaky voice now accompanied with shaky hands and her teeth chattering, knocking off each other, nearly biting her tongue. She gave an ever so timid nod despite her stomach churning.

"Norris, carry on," Leila said assertively.

Mildred walked ahead, banging on more and more doors. People raced to their doors in seconds of Mildred targeting them, gathering in their pyjamas and dressing gowns, slippers, socks, some barefoot.

"What's all the commotion?"

"What's the problem?"

"Do you know it's the middle of the night?"

"What the hell is happening?"

So many individuals with so many questions, vacating their houses and astounded by Mildred's lack of communication.

Men, women, children too, all grouping and following as Susan lagged behind Mildred, but still ahead of them all. They shouted, chorusing their many questions that hadn't yet received answers. The neighbours arranged themselves, breaking off into smaller clusters according to their friends, families, good neighbours, huddling but keeping up their pace, feeling too concerned to hang too far behind, yet totally clueless as to where they were going. They awaited an explanation whilst trudging along, bawling for any sort of clue as to why they were out strolling the streets at between 3 and 4 a.m.

"I had patiently waited all day for that evening to come so I could go home."

Lilly rolled her eyes with a sarcastically surprised coincidental grunt, "That's exactly what we are doing right now!"

"I was ever so cold, perished, and not to mention exhausted from all that raking at the twisty path."

Lilly gave another coincidental sarcastic grunt. "Oh, and so are we! Tired and cold too," she mumbled, being dug in the ribs by Leila who sharply told her to shush.

"And of course, from being awake half the night too because of that terrible wailing, whistling wind that disturbed my sleep. And most of Wikkington's residents too, for that matter. When home time came, I was utterly glad, bursting with joy at the fact I could go home and get warmed up and have an early night. After a nice warm bath that would be, to ease my aches and pains and get warmer still.

"I left the tools all nice and tidy, arranging them so they were all present and pleasing to the eye and not lying around on top of each other or thrown any old how like how the wind had arranged and left them that morning. The building was lovely and rid of the infestation of all the moss balls, and the many leaves brought into the room by the rake were all discarded, leaving the room mess free.

"As I was nearing the door to leave the building room, I lit up a candle, as I always did, and turned the building room light off. With the candle in one hand, I stepped out of the room, and began fumbling inside my coat pocket for the key to lock the building room door. After locking it, I made my way extremely slowly and carefully down the steep stairway, the flame on the candle merrily dancing, highlighting the route down the steps and out of the building.

"Having made my way out, I closed the building door behind me and took out the key to lock the main door from my other pocket. Having looked up as I always did to ensure the light was off, I noticed that the room light was on!"

Lilly sat looking but didn't mutter a word, almost as if she couldn't read nor understand what he was saying, refusing to be scared even more.

Leila kept her arm round her sister, gently rubbing her back amid writing down Norris's messages.

"Crossly, I unlocked the door, marched up the mountain-like steps and opened the building room door. I relit the candle and turned the light off again, one hundred per cent certain it was off. Once more when I had gone to the bottom of the steps and closed the main door behind me, lo and behold, the light was on AGAIN!"

Leila whispered, "What the heck?" as her facial colour faded from rosy cheeks to chalk white; the only colours to brighten her face were her emerald green eyes and her red lips.

A chorus of many voices then filled the vacuum-like silence from outside the building. Men, women, children too.

"Oh, my God. Oh, my God," Lilly eventually verbalised after mouthing it several times but projecting nothing but air when she exhaled. "Do you hear it too? No way... it's from outside? But there's no one there, there hasn't been anyone outside or in the grounds all night! Only Harmond! Unless...

221

wait, Lei, do you hear it? Lei?" she whispered to her sister in a deep panic.

Leila suddenly shut her eyes, screwing her face up as much as possible as well as shaking her head as if it were in a dream and it would awaken her. She opened her eyes slowly, desperate for the revelation of her lovely bedroom: her being in her bed with her fluffy purple dressing gown and matching purple duvet and Hooter cuddled up on her shoulder. She repeated the same act, then again for a third and final time before opening them and staring blankly at the building wall. Her eyes skimmed across the walls, as if the damp moss were scuttling around the wall.

The voices outside grew louder and seemed to have increased in variation and range to those of a sizable group.

Lilly's eyes had closed whilst Leila was in a trance staring at the wall. Eventually, Leila somehow recalled her whereabouts and thumped her knee with her fist—it wasn't a dream—not even a bad nightmare—all totally real.

"I know what you were gonna say, Lil. Lil? You were gonna say..."

"Are they the voices of all the people who are buried here...?" Lilly turned her head causing it to jolt.

Leila's eyes widened. Her eyebrows rose and curled like an arch above both eyes and she shuffled backwards away from Lilly. "LIL, THAT'S NOT YOUR VOICE, WAKE UP WAKE UP!" she bawled, screaming as loud as she possibly could in utter shock and anxiety. WAKE UP, WAKE UP!" she chanted vigorously, shaking her sister by the shoulders.

She remembered what she knew about sleepwalkers... "Never wake a sleepwalker", but her panic-stricken behaviour went totally against that statement. She shook her sister, shaking her shoulders, her head, and arms as if she were made of fabric, her limbs lolling about; all floppy.

"FOR BLOODY HELL'S SAKE, LILLY, WAKE UP! WAKE UP!" she repeated constantly, fighting the hard cement-like ball in the centre of her throat, as if she was choking.

From standing up beside Lilly, she could clearly see through the window that no one was outside—this resulting in her believing they were in fact the voices of the many individuals resting within the graveyard.

"PLEASE, LIL, WAKE UP," she pleaded once more, losing hope, her bravery, and her voice. She threw her head in her hands as she dropped to her knees. Her wet cheeks from sobbing dripped onto the floor, some tears landing on her pyjama trousers. She crawled over to the door of the room and sat with her back resting against it. Like a barricade.

"It is me, Lei. I'm back. My voice went funny because I was desperate to cough. It's so cold my throat was sore, but I didn't want to cough out loud in case those voices were the people buried here and they came up here! I don't remember anything after that, though. What happened?" Lilly asked, her head lolling to the left as she lay on her back, staring up at the ceiling where the bells once were. "Why am I lying down?"

Leila let out an almighty sigh of relief, dashing across the floor as fast as she could to get to her sister. "You didn't answer me. I shook and shook you, and then suddenly you just fell backwards after saying what you said in that horrific tone. I thought you were dead. I thought you were possessed. I thought you wouldn't ever wake up again. I thought you were never going to come around. I thought you were dead," she narrated, her eyes filling with tears.

"I called and called, and you didn't answer. You did nothing, you were gone completely. I was so scared, I was terrified, Lilly. I love you so much I never want you to go anywhere. I want you to stay with me forever, Lil." She threw her arms around Lilly, unable to stop the little river from her eyes dripping down her sister's back. She hugged Lilly so tight, fearful to let go.

"I love you so much too. I'm so sorry. It's these episodes I keep having. It wasn't any of the dead people here, Lei, I promise you. You should know, eh? You're the one who's always telling me I've had a sleepwalking episode."

Leila rapidly commented, "But you weren't walking! You were sitting!! Then lay down," she explained in a hurry, feeling terribly shy and embarrassed that she'd tried to wake her, and hadn't realised it was one of her slipping in and out of vacancy episodes.

"I probably couldn't get up if you were shaking me so hard. How could I have gotten up if you were pulling and pushing me as if you're trying to manoeuvre a large heavy object up a tremendously steep hill? Like poor Norris when he had to heave that blasted wheelbarrow up these stairs at the end of his working day. Maybe it was only a short version I had. When some people sleepwalk they make their way back to bed and fall asleep, maybe I was in an episode but it passed before I could even get up and when I lay back I was going back to sleep?? I don't know, but I do know these episodes are so scary and I wish they would stop."

Leila nodded. "I did the worst thing too—tried to wake you up—you should never do that with a sleepwalker." She looked at the concrete floor, biting the side of her right thumbnail. "What was I thinking?"

"It doesn't matter. I'd have done the same, I guess. Especially if I was scared."

"I was scared you were dead. If you were walking, then I'd know you were sleepwalking and I wouldn't be scared but you weren't moving at all. I feel like my whole body is empty. I feel like every single organ in my body just failed and nothing in me works. I'm exhausted and tired and hungry and..."

Leila paused, watching her sister cautiously. She was still lying down. Her blonde hair sprawled out on the floor around her. The rake not far from her head, leaning against the wall. The rake end on the floor, just centimetres from her head like a giant comb. Her lovely ocean blue eyes glistened in the mixed glow of the gas light and dimming torch light. She looked up at her sister, Leila's eyes on her the entire time, relaying an emerald twinkle back at her.

"What's wrong?" Leila whispered, her voice quivering as the thudding bass of her irrational heartbeat pulsated in her cold ears. The thumping mirrored that of a deep heavy bass note at a disco, vibrating downwards into her feet and legs, quickly making its way through her entire body, causing her voice to shake.

Lilly looked at her and smiled. "You."

"Me? What about me?"

"You were scared. You're so sweet. I'm sorry that I didn't cooperate, and we could have done this all a lot sooner. For us, Mom, and Norris. It's draining me, and these sleepwalking episodes make me so worried about going to sleep. You know what I'm like; I'm always tired and asleep

225

or lying on the bed, but for a while now going to sleep is a terrorising thought for me. It feels lovely to be lying here, even if it is a concrete floor, and my back aches like my spine is about to crumble, but I wish you could be in my bedroom when I'm sleeping so I know you're there; it takes the pressure away. I feel, I don't know, relaxed. Like you won't let anything happen to me," Lilly softly said, rubbing her eyes and yawning.

"I won't ever let anything happen to you. I know what to do when you sleepwalk, remember, I'm not scared. When this is all over, hopefully the stress of everything will disappear. It's almost time now for Norris to tell us the final part. Then we can go home."

"How do we explain everything to Mom? She will be going out of her mind with worry. I feel so bad that we have done this behind her back."

"I guess we were protecting her; after all, she is the one who is most scared about it all," Leila assured her. "She probably wouldn't be able to rest properly if she knew everything we knew, and it's not like we haven't been afraid as well with these happenings from time to time. Mom would be too worried and wouldn't leave us in the house alone or maybe she wouldn't even go in the house; she might have moved us out right away. It's been hard to keep this a secret, but this way when it is all sorted—we can tell her EVERYTHING, and make it seem less scary by admitting it's all over now."

Lilly performed a chorus of groans and sighs, diverting Leila's attention directly to her. Lilly sat up harshly with her sky-blue eyes wider than ever, failing to blink. Her face full of colour, her cheeks having stolen the delightful red from

Leila's chubby cheeks. Lilly's hair swayed as she completed two 180 degree turns of her head from left to the right and back again, sharply coming to a halt and being unable to take her focus away from the building room door.

Leila swallowed, and again, and again, trying to wet her dry clear throat which felt clogged with food, which was scratching like sandpaper edges and scraping the skin from her oesophagus. A stitch attacked in her right side, accompanying a terrible fierce pain like all of her ribs piercing her heart and lungs. Her lungs went into overdrive as she so desperately tried to breathe deeply and slowly in a failed attempt to calm down.

The bright moon shone proudly in the daunting murky darkness as it surfaced from behind a fierce slate grey cloud. It shone like a giant spotlight, directly highlighting Lilly. She clambered onto her knees, effortlessly.

Leila nervously whispered, "No, Lilly. No! No, you can't be, not now!!"

Leila nervously hissed, "Lil Lil!!" She bellowed at her fully aware her sister wouldn't wake up but sure not to lose any hope. She moved to the furthest space of the circular cold room, away from the room door. Lilly swayed towards her in an ill-timed trance. Leila watched as Lilly continued her way to the room door, unaware that Leila had been there, and unaware she had moved.

Lilly scrambled around on her bony knees heading closer and closer to the door, like a bull at a gate. Her hair bounced up and down, on and off her shoulders as she scurried closer and closer. Leila, without thinking, got up and ran as fast as she could, desperate to protect her sister and disable any access she had to subconsciously open the door and trip down the stairs. "Never wake a sleepwalker," she chanted, feeling she was moving in slow motion and Lilly on fast forward. Leila dived towards the door cowered into a ball, huddled up at the bottom of the door, preventing Lilly from being able to open the door at all and afraid of her rolling down into a heap at the bottom of the steps.

Norris tapped the board heavily.

"Shhh!" Leila hissed, afraid that Norris would wake Lilly.

He tapped again, louder, again and again until Leila turned around in annoyance. She curled up even more, scrunched up tight, fearing Lilly had heard the tap and been woken up, and this would start her behaving distressingly after being involuntarily disturbed mid-sleepwalk. "Never wake a sleepwalker, Norris. Never wake a sleepwalker!" she whispered.

Lilly continued strolling past the board, not once slipping or tripping, a perfect walk of someone fully awake, not someone completely asleep and in a trance-like state.

Leila dashed forward and quickly clasped the board and planchette in one hand, notebook and pen in the other. She worriedly placed her hand on the planchette, ready for Norris to continue.

"It's time," he announced, "It's coming to an end."

Leila immediately jumped up. Both panic-stricken but delightfully comforted by the sound of crowds with different tones and volumes of voices. They became louder, and more voices became apparent as the distance between the building and Leila and the crowd reduced.

"I'm sorry, Lilly. I'll be back. I promise." Leila ran out of the room and fiercely slammed the room door behind her, ensuring it would take a lot more energy for Lilly to be able to open the door mid-sleepwalking episode. She sprinted down the steps and out into the crowd.

The enormous crowd froze, some startled, some confused. A loud gasp followed a merciful sigh of relief and a high-pitched cry from one individual in the front of the crowd.

"LEI! OH LEI!" Susan frantically fell to her knees, throwing her arms around little Leila in her purple pyjamas, her dressing gown belt tangled around her arms and waist and one arm hanging out of her dressing gown. Mildred stood back, a proud smile on her semi-pale face, lightly brightened up by bright blue eyes emphasised by tears of delight forming little spilling puddles in her eyes. Leila leant into her mom, able to feel both their synchronised heart rates, incredibly fast.

A survey of questions circulated among the uncertain crowd as they looked on at the moment Susan had longed for all night, although they weren't entirely sure what had happened.

Susan stood up, scooping Leila up, looking around and skimming the crowd, thinking Lilly had secretly emerged from the building when she wasn't looking.

She panted stressfully, realising Lilly hadn't secretly appeared from anywhere. "Where's Lilly? Lilly! Lilly?" she bawled but little sound projecting from her hoarse throat. She lowered Leila to the floor whilst gently continuing to call Lilly's name, at the same time holding a hand up to her sore throat.

"Inside, Mom, inside. I can't explain it all now; it's a long story, really long! I will tell you when it's over but right now you need to come inside. Lilly is upstairs. We need to go inside!" she blurted, spurting each word with a small break between to regain her breath, showing the importance of the dreadful hurry as she led the way.

The swarm of Wikkington residents followed Mildred and Susan into the building, still not entirely sure of what was happening or going on but felt they couldn't backtrack now. Susan took a deep breath before entering. Some members of the crowd patted her on the back, whilst some gave a little smile or a half-hearted nod of encouragement.

The group spilled into the building, some having to stand in the doorway as the floor wasn't able to accommodate the full crowd. Some very tired children were picked up and placed on their mother's or father's shoulders or being given a piggy-back, freeing up a little more space, allowing the group to just about all squeeze in.

Too busy huddling together and freeing up space, feeling cold and tired, and any other thing they were worried about, they didn't put much focus on what was in front of them, until they'd all squashed up like sardines.

"At least it will help us keep warm." A woman sleepily laughed. Multiple murmurs and quiet giggles were made among the crowd.

They all settled down, ceasing the whispers and talk amongst themselves.

"Oh?" "Oh my…?" "Who is that? How and where did he get here and come from?" Thousands of questions and surprised noises accompanied Susan's "Oh my goodness," as she saw what stood in front of her.

More questions flooded up from the building floor, like water filling and filling up Susan's body, getting to be too much as if she were on the verge of drowning. "LEILA! LEI! OH MY GOSH, WHERE ARE YOU? LILLY! LILLY, LEILA, I'M COMING," Susan screamed, wailing, thrusting her body forward in an attempt to make her way up the steep stairway.

Mildred struck her arm out in front of Susan, creating a barrier preventing her from making her way to the top of the stairs. Mildred gave a joyous happy smile—a sight she had longed to see for such a long time.

"Who is he?"

"Where did the girl go?"

"He's going upstairs?"

More and more questions span out into the crowd, the room dizzy with unanswered questions.

The questions kept on coming, but no answers seemed to follow.

"Who are you? Where are my girls?" Susan screamed, again trying to push past Mildred to get up the stairs. "Let me go up there, Mildred! LET ME GO!" She fought Mildred, not strong enough to push past. She fell to the floor in a heap, tears rolling down her face like miniature streams, falling from her chin like a waterfall.

A large number of the Wikkington residents comforted Susan. Some knelt beside her, others begging Mildred to allow her to pass. A few members had eyes full of tears, watching despairingly as Susan fell apart in the search for her daughters.

A tall, medium-built elderly gentleman stood on the second step of the grand steep stairs, providing neither comments nor actual acknowledgement of the great audience he had. His wispy white hair enhanced his big blue eyes, and his bushy white eyebrows were raised as he looked around before climbing onto the next step.

The stunned arrangement of men, women and children watched in total awe as he looked directly at them, but clearly couldn't see them. They jumped slightly as he made his move, slowly making his way onto the next step, then the next, then the next.

The man in his blue patterned shirt and navy jumper placed each hand on the wall either side, after adjusting his glasses in need of support with his balance as the stairway increased in steepness. His deeper blue trouser bottoms made him look especially smart with his black laced shoes and the navy tie at his neck. His shirt covered his slightly plump stomach very well, and his brown strapped watch fitted nicely around his wrist.

The crowd adjusted their own positions, increasing their view of what was happening and remained perfectly silent as he passed by.

The man carefully paced up the stairs as if he were climbing a mountain, struggling with the steepness but plodding along desperate to reach the top. He stumbled at the head of the stairs and the audience gasped, conversing abruptly in shock. He was now holding a candle.

Mildred hushed the group when they queried why and how a candle had just appeared and what in the world was going on. As the man finally reached the topmost step, he bent his head down and fidgeted in his coat pocket for the key to unlock the door. Whilst he searched around in his pockets the surprised, inquiring group remained completely silenced, with only a little shuffle of tenseness and uneasiness.

A tall gentleman with short black hair, and big hazel eyes, a black blazer covering his white shirt—collar and sleeves folded back, appeared unexplainably in the doorway when the white haired man dressed in different shades of blue managed to unlock the door to the building room and open the door.

Taking no notice at all of the black haired man, and having just unlocked the door and given it a quick nudge so it slowly creaked open, he slipped the key back into his coat pocket. As he did so, he came to a start after noticing a pair of black shoes right in front of him, and then some legs. He nervously looked up, scanning the person in front of him, until they met face to face.

He drew a deep breath and stepped back a touch as the man had so unexpectedly appeared without any warning or logical explanation or reasoning. He stepped back, only a little *too* far, missing the top step completely. He reached out his arms, attempting to grasp hold of the wall with his aging fingers in a trial to gain some control. His lighted candle fell and blew out, rolling and rolling down the steps bouncing every so often where it caught on the corner of the step, almost breaking it in half. Clank, clank, clank, clank, clank.

A harmonic "Ooh!" and heavy gasps performed by the bewildered crowd accompanied the rhythmic clanking from the candle on its journey down, right from the top.

All parties moved back to let it pass, some being shoved a little out of the main doorway by those who had stepped back in shock, hands over their mouths in distinctive distress as the elderly gentleman came hurtling down the steps just like the candle, bouncing off several steps along the way, landing right beside the candle, flat on his back and his head ending the awful sight just witnessed, with a terrible bang on the concrete flooring.

A small number of them ran forward instinctively several seconds after the dreadful incident, desperate to try to help the poor man lying there as still as a statue and likely to have suffered several injuries from having plummeted down the steps with such momentum having missed the top step completely.

Other stunned bystanders forcefully pushed through the transfixed people in the crowd, out of the building door, in order to gain some fresh air and recover from such a shock.

Susan stared in a numbed trance at the bottom of the steps, and the floor, just centimetres from her feet, replaying the poor man's head smacking off the floor over and over in her own head.

Several men and women, and children too, caused a stir by murmuring desperate to grab Susan's attention. Shaking and patting her and bellowing her name.

A smaller circle of individuals in the group chatted amongst themselves, oblivious as to how the circumstances had just suddenly changed, in recognition of who it actually was. Their troubled and querying minds making them dizzy as questions bounced from wall to wall and shock smacked them right in the face. It had all changed.

"Susan!"

"Oh Susan, my goodness!"

"Oh my, I don't believe it. Susan, Susan, it's…"

"Susan!"

An army of parrots repeated those phrases over and over, and over, and over. They shuffled and nudged and gave comforting pats on her shoulders and rubs on her back.

Her pale face somehow became paler, white as a sheet. She came around wearily from her terror-induced trance, wriggling her shoulders as the pats tickled her spine, and shuddered as they rubbed down her back.

"W-What?" she stuttered, staring around at those chanting her name, addressing all the pitiful looks on worried, concerned neighbours' faces as they woefully glanced at her.

"It's Leila… Leila? Your daughter… Leila!" a gentleman was calmly pointing to a still, peaceful Leila lying on the concrete floor in exactly the same place and position as the gentleman they'd just witnessed tumbling down the stairwell.

A variety of looks and expressions were written and displayed on the faces of those who formed the crowd. Some with their hand to their mouth, some with their hand on their chest, some with both hands on their head at the distressing moment they were now living in and witnessing.

Some mopped at their face with their pyjamas and night clothes as they dried the tears spurting from their tired eyes. Some were squealing and squeaking at the scene which was before them. Some shook their head in amazement and confusion at how they'd just seen a man strolling up the stairs and then suffering a terrible fall, but now he was no longer present; it was Leila lying still at the bottom of the steps.

Susan frowned, light-headedly clasping at those around her. Two men held her steady at either side as she regained full consciousness and looked down before her, as the blur at her feet became a lot clearer.

"LEILA! NOOOO, MY LEILA!" she bawled, screaming and crying, tears stinging her sore eyes. She reached and grabbed Leila's hand, rocking back and forth on her knees, frantically but determinedly stroking Leila's cheek.

The heart-wrenching scene bought many tears to a lot of the neighbours who were still watching in sympathy. Puddles in many eyes and tears like a river dripping from their cheeks and running off their jawbone. Mothers, and fathers, shook their heads, wincing at the awful thoughts racing through their minds; not even beginning to imagine the thoughts running through Susan's. The thought of it being their own child sent them into a saddened embrace and they grabbed at their own children's hands, keeping them close and hugging them tight. Smaller children asked to be picked up and cuddled, not totally aware of what had happened or what was playing on the group's minds.

"S-S-Someone call an ambulance... Now!" The message began with a stutter and echoed down the stairway over and over like a record sticking until it faded into silence.

Susan looked up carefully, struggling to regain her breath. Her salty tears dribbled over Leila's dressing gown, soaking the purple fluff from when she'd huddled up to her closely. She opened her mouth, desperately holding her throat and chest, choking on her own saliva. She coughed aggressively, aggravating her already dreadfully sore throat.

"No! No! No ambulance!" Mildred quickly intervened, causing a stir of confusion and disagreement amongst the bystanders.

"Lilly!" Susan eventually forced out, astonished.

A loud mutter and mumble followed Susan's identification of the individual standing mournfully at the top of the stairs.

"Lilly?"

"But it was a man?"

"Did you see him too?"

"Where is h…"

Lilly interrupted the whispers and comments abruptly. "Why no ambulance? She's my sister! We need to call an ambulance! Someone call 999! Why are you all standing there not doing anything? What happened?" She queried but received no response; the crowd gave Mildred a sorrowful look.

She gave them a look in return, *the* look, the kind no one argues with. No one spoke. Lilly neither.

The awful silence hung on the night air, and turned many people to lower their heads, all grunting and growling in a nervous churning chorus.

"You… p… p… pushed her. You… Lilly, you pu…"

"NO! No, she didn't. Susan, she honestly didn't."

"No, she didn't at all!"

"Of course, she didn't. It was a MAN at the top of the stairs, and even he didn't push the man who fell down!"

"Lilly DID NOT push her, Susan, she did not!"

The group immediately intervened and ensured Susan knew the truth.

Susan looked up at Mildred, who gave a little nod assuring her this was correct. She looked at each individual in the group, all following Mildred's action of a little nod. Then she looked up at Lilly. Her face grey, her body exhausted, her stomach churning, and heart thumping aggressively in her ribcage, but she managed to sympathetically give a little smile to Lilly.

Lilly loosened up, grateful for the crowd and Mildred

237

supporting her.

"She really didn't, Susan. Honestly, she didn't at all," one of the witnesses piped up bravely, contributing. She beckoned Lilly down the stairs, "Come on, sweetheart, we all know it wasn't you. Come and sit down with your mom and sister, there you are, darling."

"Oh, I am sorry, Lilly. I am so, so, so, so, sorry. I know you really wouldn't do such a thing. My head has been all over the place tonight. I've been going berserk, out of my mind. I didn't know where you and Leila had got to or what to do and I just… Sorry, Lilly. When I saw you standing up there at the top of the steps it's all I could think of. I just didn't know what was happening or had happened. But I believe you and all these lovely people who have been such a great comfort to me and have given me their support and stayed by my side throughout tonight. I am so sorry, darling, I really am, I know you wouldn't do such a thing. Come on, have a hug." Susan cried and cried, hugging Lilly. Her hair tickled Lilly's cheek but she didn't mind; all that mattered was she had been reunited with her mom and sister. They wrapped their arms around each other tightly, both holding one hand of Leila's.

"Yeah, we are all in the same boat in that regard, what did happen? We have been in this boat long enough, any longer and it'll be the Titanic we're in if tonight's episode is anything to go by." A young man ruffled Lilly's hair, smiling and joking, but still willing to know what had happened.

"Yeah that is a good question. What did happen?" Leila giggled, sitting up perfectly, overwhelmed by the scene she'd just found herself in.

Susan cradled Leila's head on her knee, but suddenly

jumping herself when Leila sprang up without warning. "Oh, Lei! You're awake! You're alive!" Susan grabbed her appreciatively, flinging her arms around her and kissing her cheek.

Lilly jumped too, flinging her arms around both Leila and Susan. "Lei! Mom!"

Whooping and smiling and with tears of joy coming from the marvelled crowd, who were still watching religiously. They hugged each other and gave warm touches on each other's shoulders. Those with children swooped them up in the air and tossed them from one parent to the other so they could both join in on the loving moment; they were all reunited and exchanging love.

"I'm a paramedic, off duty of course, but I would just like to check you over, just to be sure. Head injuries can be very dangerous," a kind middle-aged man announced, pushing through the swarm of happy neighbours and kneeling down opposite Susan, and next to Lilly who towered over Leila, who was by now lying comfortably with her head resting on Susan's knee.

"Lie still for me, sweetheart, it won't take too long. If when I am checking you over you feel pain anywhere, you must let me know, and if you are experiencing anything you don't normally experience especially when we move onto your head," the paramedic said as he checked Leila over, wincing when he conducted each test, seeming puzzled.

This worried Susan, and Lilly. All the neighbours held their breath, displaying deep concern and exchanging looks, not knowing if the wincing from the paramedic was good news or bad. Some whispered to Susan so as not to disturb the paramedic carrying out the examination, that if they were to need anything at all they would be willing to help, and she could rely on them. They chatted quietly and agreed, and Susan thanked them with a smile and apologised for what a night, and what an experience they'd ended up in tonight.

The examination came to a close after about five to ten minutes, and the paramedic revealed his conclusion based upon his findings.

Everyone stared at him in awe, desperate to hear and know how Leila was and what he would conclude with.

"What I have found, well, maybe I should say what I haven't found. It seems there are no evidential signs and symptoms present to describe or suggest you had fallen with a great tumble, and amazingly, your head seems all normal with no bleeding or injury whatsoever. You have no other signs such as cuts, grazes, or broken bones!"

Susan gasped in shock but smiled gladly, thanking the paramedic over and over, especially as he wasn't even at work.

Leila smiled happily, not actually aware she was supposed to have fallen down the stairs, bouncing and thumping down and down until she had smacked her head harshly on the concrete floor, landing right on her back.

Lilly gave a sigh of happy relief, although she wasn't totally aware of the whole situation or accident either.

The onlooking staggered crowd stood with open mouths in disbelief. The plentiful faces all showing different expressions; baffled, puzzled, stumped, thrown, shocked, or dazed.

"But, sir," one lady spoke, "there was a lot of blood when the man fell, and she is in the exact same position that he landed in!"

Those around her agreed, nodding, and muttering to one another.

"I know. I just don't get it. None of it. All Leila's vitals and observations are within a perfectly normal range. There are no obvious or clear signs for me to conclude you've broken any bones. And most miraculously there's no blood or anything else present or standing out to suggest an injury to your head or skull. You have got away without a single scratch, and I don't know how this could ever be explained. I have never seen anything like this in my whole life and career. You must have a guardian angel looking after you, my dear," he explained, delivering his findings to the group and Susan and Lilly and to Leila too, of course.

"Lilly, I believe that is your name?" he continued.

Lilly nodded timidly, scanning the crowd as they all looked at her while they listened to the doctor when he addressed her now.

"Could I please take a look at you and ensure you're okay? I know you haven't fallen and didn't push your sister. However, there is something I would like to check and would like to ask you."

"Yes, if you feel it is best," she mumbled, Susan agreeing on her behalf.

"As we were watching, something happened which even we are unsure of, but don't be alarmed. We followed Leila in here through the main door, just a few moments afterwards, as she had said you were upstairs. However, when we came in, there was a gentleman standing on the steps which we believe Leila had passed to run up to find you.

"This man was making his way up the stairs. He had white wispy hair, bushy eyebrows, wearing a lot of blue. Do you recall seeing this man?"

Lilly looked around nervously, twitching her toes. Her lips were so dry, her throat too. "No," she croaked.

"Okay, and Leila, back to you. Do you recall seeing the man of the same description as I just gave to Lilly?"

"No, I didn't see anyone at all. Only all of you and then I ran back inside." She thought hard, getting frustrated with herself. "I'm really sorry, but no I can't."

"Then I call upon all the members of this group and in this building. Is there anyone here who did NOT see the man of that description?"

No one raised their hand, although there was a shuffle of feet and whispers and clearing of throats. This confirmed that everyone in the group had seen him.

"Now, Lilly, when you were upstairs, and before Leila started to come back up, do you recall seeing anyone at all, of any description, either enter or was already present in the room?"

Lilly shook her head, sighing, and sorry she couldn't be of any help.

He turned to Leila. "Leila, when you were outside of the building and hugging your mom, did you see or know of anyone who was upstairs with Lilly?"

"No, I didn't. I promise," she confirmed, feeling a little disheartened that she too couldn't be of any help.

The paramedic, Steve, continued, "Crowd, did you all see the gentleman who was there at the top of the steps? Can anyone describe him for me?"

The group members called out various different features of the figure they'd seen standing at the top of the stairs. Black hair, hazel eyes, white shirt, black blazer.

The paramedic, Steve he later said was his name, thought to himself for a couple of moments, evaluating all the information he'd found out. He rambled on to himself, eyes scanning the walls as if all the information was plastered there from brick to brick, surrounding and filling all the gaps in the bricks and the wall. He gave a definitive nod, assuring all there that he had come to some sort of conclusion.

"So, after analysing it all, I've got a question to ask Lilly. Well, I can ask Lilly, Leila and Susan, but it is associated with Lilly."

Lilly looked at him nervously.

"Lilly, are you aware of any unusual behaviours you have had during the night or of an evening?"

Leila sprung her arm up in the air as if she knew the answer to a question in class and was waiting for the teacher to pick her. "I know, I know! She sleepwalks! She does it a lot! She did it earli—"

The man stopped Leila immediately before she could continue. "As in, how long ago was this and how often has it happened?" he queried, suddenly seeming to have a glimmer of an idea of what it could be and at least give some clear explanation.

"When you all came here tonight, like seconds before I came running down, she had been sleepwalking for a couple of minutes. I had to slam and bang the door shut behind me when I came running down because I was worried Lilly might open the door and fall down the steps and hurt herself. I slammed it shut so, so tight and forcefully and heavily, desperate to make certain, sure it would take a lot of Lilly's strength to open it. I was hoping she wouldn't have the energy to be able to open it during her sleepwalking as she would if she was awake," Leila recounted.

"Ah! Perfect. This concludes that Lilly has had recurrent episodes of sleepwalking, which therefore means she wouldn't have known or seen anyone in the building. And the fact you mention you had closed the door so tightly and strongly also concludes that no one got into the building room whilst we were outside of the building, because we would have seen them. Both of you had no idea of these two men being in the building. I think this lies deeper than we think."

The crowd watched tiredly as the off-duty paramedic thought about what the deeper issue or cause could be. A lot of the crowd sat down, resting their legs and their arms from picking up the children and balancing them on their hip or their back or their neck.

Mildred Bluethorn felt herself burning up, heat overcoming her body, scarlet red as she felt more and more pressure and emotion; she couldn't withhold it any longer. She sighed loudly and deeply, above all the little conversations and chatter between all of the members of the group, causing them to jump. She gnawed anxiously at her right thumbnail, swallowing mouthfuls of air as she summoned up the courage to speak.

She took the crowd by surprise, reciting a story to occupy them all whilst Steve gathered his thoughts and queries.

"Going back many, many, many, years ago, way before all you little kiddies were a twinkle in your mother's eye, and probably before your parents were little twinkles in their mothers' eyes too, there was a little girl, only a little dot, whose father passed away before she was born. God rest his

244

soul. With no memories, photographs, or any idea of who he was or what he did or where he even came from, she hadn't much interest or hope in finding out much about him. She'd often shrug and hum and hah, until she actually came here to Wikkington searching for his grave, longing to lay flowers and find out all about his life and who he was as a person.

"She had visited other graveyards all over her county but had no such luck in finding anything out whatsoever. Along with all those graveyards she'd visited there were no records of her father's name. She decided if she couldn't find his gravestone in Wikkington, she would cease searching." She spoke slowly and steadily, emphasising every word to show that the story as a whole was highly important.

The crowd listened intrigued and engrossed, sparkling eyes and faces full of concentration.

"She'd visited Wikkington Graveyard and returned back to her house outside of Wikkington but still quite local. Within her home, she experienced random recurring noises. The doors creaking open and left slightly ajar, floorboards squeaking, little short knocks here and there. She'd often find things had relocated themselves too. She didn't think much of it, assuming the noises were just caused by the wind or as the house was rather old, she knew they'd often squeak or groan with general wear and tear. Or if the heating were on, she'd assume it was the pipes or the water. She mostly believed that it was her mind playing tricks on her. She loved peace and quiet, and of course that is when you notice noises and they become more emphasised.

"Anyway, these noises and relocating of objects continued frequently, so she decided to record and document the list of noises and things moving along with the date and time." Mildred paused for breath.

"Carry on," the audience urged, too excited and drawn into the story that they wanted it to carry on and on. The younger kids listened intently as if it were a bedtime story, willing Mildred to continue by chanting "more, more!"

"Okay. Okay. Right—well, she then decided to come back to Wikkington Graveyard again to talk with the caretaker to ask if he had any information regarding her father, but sadly found that the caretaker had passed away, so she wasn't able to ask him after all. Having no success in finding the caretaker on her last visit, she was as you would expect feeling a little disheartened, but this gave her more inspiration to continue to find out more about her late father.

"She chatted to several locals here, wanting to ask about the caretaker and who the new caretaker was, to find anything out, anything at all about her dad. She felt even more let down when all the residents of Wikkington she'd spoken to refrained from giving her any information and details about anything at all associated with the graveyard."

A downhearted sigh of sympathy, questioning why and how awful it must have been for her to be getting nowhere, was provided by the crowd.

"Sadly, many years later, she came back here to Wikkington to make funeral arrangements regarding her own funeral as she was elderly now and had heard such positive reviews about the graveyard and its award-winning scenery and care given to the memorial stones and their surroundings. She'd been there before on two occasions hoping to find a worker and find her father's grave but had received no such luck at all. She was still dealing with the noises and objects moving around her house, but she'd become used to it and now no longer fazed her. But this time, she checked each and every stone, each field, and found the field by the building she'd missed, thinking there were only two fields, not three. And there it was, her father's memorial stone. She smiled happily. 'Hello, Dad,' she gleefully said with tears in her eyes, so happy to have finally found it and be able to say that after so long."

A cheer and array of congratulations and happiness for her delight came from the group.

"Awww, how lovely!"

"Hurray!"

"Oh, that's so special!"

"How wonderful!"

"She soon found out that the reason for such noises and peculiar places where different objects would vacate to, was all down to her father! Since her first visit here to Wikkington, he'd been trying to contact her! She had heard terribly troubling thoughts and remarks in the past, some talking of him being murdered, and that was why no one would speak of him or pass any information on with regard to him. But it was all untrue.

"He'd been trying to tell her all of that time and was so desperate to inform all of Wikkington that it wasn't the case at all, it was entirely false. The girl, well woman now, elderly even, had tried plenty and an increasingly high number of times to get people to listen, once having communicated with her father, but they fobbed her off with comments saying they were sure she was lying and she hadn't even known or met her father, so how would she know, and how it was more comforting to her to believe it wasn't murder, even though it was. They assured her she was lying, mad, delusional, not giving her or her true side of the story a second thought.

"She just couldn't get it through to them in the end and became intensely fearful. She was getting older as the days passed by and knew her deteriorating health would soon prevent her from getting out of the house. So this time it was her last chance to try and reveal the exact story and what definitely happened." Mildred finished.

The paramedic glared at Mildred, pulling different facial expressions and talking to himself as if he were analysing her.

"The man, her father I mean, he was simply walking up the stairs and was taken aback by something he saw, causing him to sorrowfully fall. He was all alone lying there on the floor, banging and thrashing the keys to make a noise and try to attract attention, an expanding puddle of blood oozing onto an area of his fluffy white hair, and dying it red. The trauma to his head was so bad that he wasn't conscious for longer than a couple of minutes and sadly passed away.

"As there was no evidence of someone calling an ambulance or staying with him or coming forward or even having been there and fled the scene, his injuries so serious and severe he was declared to have been murdered upon investigation by the authorities. That wasn't the case, though; he fell and tumbled and rolled and scraped and landed with a terrible thud right onto his back, smacking his head on the floor."

The building fell silent with people in shock and despair, marvelled but saddened by the story Mildred had told them all.

The paramedic smiled softly, putting his arm around a tearful, snuffling Mildred. "The lady in your story…" he paused as his eyes filled with tears, "It's you, isn't it?"

Mildred cried heavily, dampening his shoulder. Lilly and Leila gasped, suddenly being able to make sense of and understand the story properly!

"NORRIS! NORRIS ERICSON! YOU'RE TALKING ABOUT HIM! HE'S YOUR DAD?!" Leila blurted out, excitedly and giving Mildred a big hug, comforting her gladly.

Mildred squeezed her so tight. "Yes, darling. What you and Lilly did tonight is what I've been waiting to do for a lifetime." She dabbed at her bead-like tears.

"Norris Ericson, as in caretaker Norris Ericson, as in the Norris we have been chatting with through an Ouija board for months?" Lilly piped up, stunning the crowd but most of all not even breaking the news softly to Susan that they'd even been using one.

Susan's face crumpled with confusion and she warily took a step back as Mildred threw her arms around Lilly too. Susan looked around whilst deep in thought. "Ouija board?" she muttered in her mind, "Where from?"

She took several seconds trying to recall where on earth the girls had got one from. Then it dawned on her. "The garage."

"Yes Lilly, that's him. Leila, he made sure that when you took the tumble and landed that you didn't get hurt at all. The apparition of my father overshadowed you, so all of us in the crowd saw my father falling rather than you, until he faded quickly, and you were the one lying at the bottom of the steps.

"Lilly, he's been making you sleepwalk, just to build you up to that time, tonight, where you would appear as

Harmond. Harmond is the man who appeared at the top of the stairs," she explained to the crowd. "He is the man who startled my dad causing him to fall. You all saw his apparition but when he faded, Lilly was in his place, stood at the top. His apparition overshadowed Lilly. That's what happened that night my father passed; he looked up and was startled by the apparition of Harmond standing in front of him and he took a bigger step backwards. It wasn't murder, not at all; you all said yourselves earlier that even Lilly or the man at the top of the stairs didn't push the man or Leila. My father was not murdered, so this tale must end now. Allow people to come and visit their loved ones again and celebrate their friends' and relatives' memory. The murder tale is exactly that, a tale. It has been upsetting Wikkington's residents ever since my dad's passing. It has been weighing on my dad's mind too, preventing him from being able to rest because of the dreadful lie and the tales, scaring people, inhibiting them from coming to see or attend to their loved ones' memorials." Mildred rambled, delivering another side to the story, gaining more and more interest from each party in the group, as they shook their heads in amazement, and gave a little smile at poor Mildred.

Lilly and Leila gazed at each other, so proud of themselves that they were able to take on this challenge, accept the opportunity to make it work and happen, for Norris, Mildred, Susan, themselves, and of course, all the others in Wikkington too.

"We did it, Lil. We did it!" Leila cheerfully whispered, reaching out and holding her sister's hand.

"We sure did, Lei. We really, really, did." She whispered back and turned to Mildred, who was being bombarded by light taps and gentle hugs.

"Harmond was the caretaker before my father, and sometimes the light would come on with no cause or the gate would open and shut or another strange event would happen, and that day was the first time he'd seen Harmond as a figure, his apparition, which caused Norris to step back in shock, but fell just as we witnessed earlier. That was a replay of what exactly happened that night. Not murder at all, just a shock. He'd been planning it for some time and was waiting for the chance to be heard and listened to in order to make it happen and portray exactly what had occurred. I can't thank you enough, girls." Mildred turned to them both, taking hold of a hand of each one of them and spurting words of utmost gratitude.

The crowd gasped and mumbled amongst themselves. Their comments of amazement, disbelief of what they'd genuinely just witnessed, and comforting words to Mildred making her beam proudly. They'd all been so supportive and truly praised both Leila and Lilly for their efforts and bravery for helping Mildred, the residents of Wikkington and Norris himself to be able to rest in peace and be no longer tormented by the rumours associated with his death.

"The sleepwalking will end now, and it was never harmful to you and you'd never have been hurt; my dad took great care of you, Lilly. You got a little anxious about it I know, because it was a new thing. It was just to prepare you for what was to come, so that when it happened to Leila on the day, well this day, when it would all come out into the open, she understood what you were doing and it ensured she didn't allow you to get hurt. He made sure when Leila left the building, running down to us crowd, she had shut the door firmly for Lilly not to get out and trip and fall. He also made sure that when Leila tugged at Lilly whilst she was in a vacant episode, she didn't lash out or harm you or herself, as you must never ever wake a sleepwalker. He made sure Leila knew what to do, and to keep you safe, and most of all not be frightened of you Lilly at all when you were in a sleepwalking episode, for all this tonight to have worked and demonstrated to us all what really happened." Mildred revealed the reason for the sleepwalking, which Lilly had never encountered before moving to 10 Wikkington Way.

"So that explains it, Lei, it was Harmond! Norris saw him right after the light came on! He was the one fiddling with it! And the gate and everything else that happened whilst Norris was caretaker, it was Harmond!" Lilly jumped up and down, with her hands, on Leila's shoulders.

"Yeah! And when Norris died, he started doing things to connect with Mildred, and because we live in his old house and had been here to the graveyard, he targeted us to help reveal the story, and was responsible for everything we heard and witnessed! Now it will all end, Lil, we did it!" She gave her sister a high five and gripped her tightly in a long, long, hug. "I'm so proud of you Lil, we did it!"

"I'm so proud of you too, Lei. It's done. We actually did it!" Lilly exclaimed.

The group all smiled and grinned and chuckled lovingly, as if they'd been in on it all along.

One mother, with her young daughter perched on her hip, asked for more information about Harmond.

Mildred smiled at the girls and let them explain a little more about him. "They're little experts on him and Norris now," she joked, smiling gleefully at Leila and Lilly.

"Oh, he's called Harmond Hordenton. He was the previous caretaker here but passed away before Norris took over. It was the first time we saw him tonight too, before all of you guys did, I mean. It's scary when you least expect it because we thought it was just another human like us in there. He didn't harm us at all; in fact, I don't think he could harm anyone if he wanted to.

His apparition just walks around at night, and day, all the time really, patrolling the grounds," the girls configured between them.

Mildred happily caught all their attention, even Lilly and Leila's. "Here's something you don't know about Harmond, girls." At this, everyone fell silent as they all listened intently, the room so silent it felt empty.

"He always opens and closes the gate. Whenever the gate moves without human force, it is Harmond. He can see us humans, and he can also see spirits and apparitions too. He opens the gate for us, and for the many buried here who stroll the grounds. He's unable to tell the difference between us humans and the spirits of those buried here, so he opens the gates thinking that all the people here are humans. That's why it used to happen when my dad was caretaker, because Harmond can't tell the difference between spirits and humans, he opens it for everyone, so sometimes it will open randomly, and that's just Harmond's kind courtesy. Even now he will open and close the gate when he sees someone, human or spirit approaching, but he is harmless."

"WOW!" the group exclaimed as one. Sudden surprised gasps, whoops, sighs, squeals of amazement and laughter, some shudders all from the group as they took in the information. Leila and Lilly too, at that piece of information, which they didn't know about either.

"So ghosts are real?" a little girl asked quietly but enough to indicate she wanted an answer. She sat tightly in her mother's arms.

"Yes, sweetheart, if you believe, you will see."

The little girl pointed to the stairs; everyone turned suddenly expecting to see another apparition of someone magically appear from nowhere. "Were they really ghosts, those two men on the stairs? The one fell but the other one just stood still. They are okay now, though, aren't they?" she caringly squealed, elaborating, referring to that particular part of the story to show she was listening and had seen the whole thing. She was encouraged by the neighbours congratulating her on a very good question showing she was so kind and caring.

"Yes, darling, they were," Mildred answered. "You are a clever girl remembering it all, aren't you? Yes, they are okay now. The man who stood still was Harmond, and the man who fell was my poor dad Norris. They are fine now, don't you worry. Thank you very much to Leila and Lilly, for you two have made my dad's eternal wish come true. You have shown all of us here, the many residents of Wikkington, what happened that night and confirmed it wasn't murder. My dad can now rest in peace and be free. He can forget about having to ensure the secret is finally told, as it is now out there and has been witnessed by so many. He can rest easy and be free and let go of the worry he had associated with the human side of life. Thank you, girls, for my father has worried over this since the night he passed. And I've carried this story for so long, slowly losing hope that I'd ever be able to make Dad's wish come true. You two amazing girls made it happen and to you from both my dad and I we are eternally grateful." Mildred filled up with tears of happiness and tears of pride.

"Susan, I told you they'd be unharmed, and would be returned to you safe and well and here they are. True little heroes. Please treasure them, you should be so proud at the comfort and delight they have brought to myself and my father. Because of these two girls the taunting stress and lies about what happened that night can now be scrapped and the truth known by all here tonight. Please pass it on and inform all other Wikkington residents of what truthfully happened that night. For we have all witnessed it. God bless you all. Lilly, and Leila, thank you, from the bottom of my heart."

Susan beamed with pride and happiness, holding both girls by the shoulder and kissing them gently on the head. She was standing proud and lovingly, but still felt left in the dark about the whole thing.

"I won't go to the press as they'll say I'm going mad. And you two girls can get rid of your Ouija board now too, for it is all over at last," Mildred chattered.

"Don't you worry, Mrs Bluethorn, I am a paramedic and I saw both of those men with my own eyes. For now, let's go home, it's been one heck of a strange night. Congratulations, Leila and Lilly, for your tremendous courage and kindness. You really are little heroes. The truth is out there. Norris can rest and find peace, and Mildred can live the rest of her days now knowing her dad's eternal wish has been granted. Well done." The paramedic proudly helped to escort them out of the building.

The crowd gave congratulatory taps, hugs and comments, all still in an awful lot of shock and frazzled at the night they'd had.

"Well done, girls, my brilliant daughters. I love you so much and am so proud of you.

The pair of you must be exhausted. I know I am. Let's go home now and get some sleep and you can tell me all about it tomorrow."